**St. Martin's Paperbacks Titles
by Julianne MacLean**

Captured by the Highlander

Claimed by the Highlander

Seduced by the Highlander

Seduced
by the
Highlander

JULIANNE MACLEAN

St. Martin's Paperbacks

This is a work of fiction. All of the characters, organizations, and events portrayed in this novel are either products of the author's imagination or are used fictitiously.

SEDUCED BY THE HIGHLANDER

Copyright © 2011 by Julianne MacLean.

For information address St. Martin's Press, 175 Fifth Avenue, New York, NY 10010.

ISBN: 978-0-312-36533-2

Printed in the United States of America

St. Martin's Paperbacks edition / October 2011

St. Martin's Paperbacks are published by St. Martin's Press, 175 Fifth Avenue, New York, NY 10010.

10 9 8 7 6 5 4 3 2 1

He has a way of making you feel like the most beautiful woman alive. When he corners you up against a wall and kisses you senseless, it's a thrill like no other, but sadly, the thrill does not last. He will soon back away, leaving you breathless and brokenhearted, and for the rest of your days, you will lie awake at night, wondering what you did wrong.

So if you know what's good for you, do not be seduced. Find yourself a different sort of man— the kind who'll want to marry you, and give you lots of babies.

On Lachlan MacDonald,
Laird of War at Kinloch Castle
Speaker unknown

Seduced
by the
Highlander

Prologue

Desire. Lust. Sex.

In the dream, he was drowning in it, sinking deeper and deeper into a sea of desperate, tempestuous need. Soft, searching hands teased and stroked his chest and shoulders while warm, wet mouths licked at his stomach.

He was Lachlan MacDonald, Kinloch Castle's Laird of War, battle-seasoned warrior, and Scotland's most infamous seducer of women. Yet he loved only one, who was nothing but a vague, shifting memory in his mind.

Where was she in this dream? Was she even here? And was it truly a dream? It felt more like death. But if that were the case, he would be with her again, would he not?

The current began to churn faster around him. No, she was not here. Not in this place. He did not know any of these women. They were all strangers. Suddenly he found he couldn't breathe.

Lachlan woke with a start, sucking cold air into his lungs. He tried to sit up but couldn't. His arms were stretched over his head, each wrist bound by a rope. His legs were spread wide, his ankles tethered. He was outdoors in some sort of pit, staring up at the clear night sky.

A throbbing agony exploded in his skull. It was worse than death, and he shouted with rage, his muscles straining as he tugged and jerked at the bonds. But it was pointless to struggle. They were secure and his body was weak. Nausea burned in his gut. He went still and looked around through the gloom. Vertical walls of stone surrounded him. He was lying on a bed of cold gravel.

This was no pit. It was an open grave. An ancient burial cist.

Lachlan balled his hands into fists and shouted with fury, but that only caused the grave to spin in dizzying circles.

Had he been drugged? If so, by whom? And how in God's name did he get here?

Groping through a dense haze of incomprehension, he strove to remember his last steps. He had traveled alone to Kilmartin Glen on an errand for his cousin and chief, Angus MacDonald, Laird of Kinloch Castle. He had stopped for a midday meal at the alehouse. . . .

His labored breaths came faster, puffing rapid clouds of steam into the cold night air.

Images slowly came back to him. There was a woman. He had gone with her to the haystacks in the field. She'd giggled and laughed when he slid his hands up her skirts and blew into her ear. But nothing existed for him after that. It was as if he had simply fallen into the dream.

Footsteps approached; then a figure appeared overhead, at the foot of the grave. A woman. He watched her move like a shadow in front of the moon. She bent forward to retrieve something on the ground—a wooden pail with a rope handle—then straightened and fixed her eyes on him.

He was disoriented, but by God, he recognized that silhouette. It was Raonaid, the oracle. One month ago, she had vowed to make him rue the day he banished her from Kinloch Castle.

"Raonaid . . ."

Lachlan had never feared death before, but this woman stirred a hellish dread inside him. She worked with ancient powers from beyond, and from the first moment, he had sensed her venom. It was why he had encouraged Angus to cast her out of Kinloch.

She stepped forward and dumped a bucketful of bones on top of him, and he winced with disgust as they clattered onto his kilt.

"What are these?" he asked. "The bones of all your ex-lovers?"

Raonaid gathered her skirts in her fists and hopped down into the grave. Straddling her legs around him, she sat down and wiggled her skirted bottom over his hips.

"If you're hoping to ride me," he growled through gritted teeth, "you're going to be disappointed when I don't rise to the occasion."

She was a beautiful woman—one of the most desirable in Scotland—with thick red hair and a buxom figure, huge, lavish breasts, and a face like an angel, but he despised her.

"I don't want *you*," she said, her eyes on fire with antagonism and loathing. "I never did. But I wanted

Angus, and he was my lover for more than a year—until *you* came and took him away."

It was a struggle for Lachlan to think straight through the pounding agony in his brain.

"Angus was not put on this earth to be your bed partner," he replied thickly. "He was born to lead the MacDonalds, to be Chief and Laird of Kinloch Castle, and I helped him reclaim that right. If you truly cared for him, you would never have denied him his destiny. You would have let him go."

She leaned forward and whispered maliciously in Lachlan's ear, "But Angus was forced to wed his enemy's daughter. Nay, Lachlan—*you* are the one who dragged him back to a world and a life he had forsaken, and you poisoned his mind against me."

Raonaid sat back and withdrew a small dirk from her boot. Slowly, tauntingly, she waved the blade back and forth in front of his eyes, then reached down and sliced a lock of his hair. "I'll need this for the curse," she said, "in order to keep it going." Then she nicked him fast across the cheek with the sharp point of the knife. "And this drop of blood."

In a fit of rage, Lachlan thrust his hips forward to buck her off, but she only laughed, as if it were a child's game.

Whatever substance she had given him was still infecting his brain, and the sudden movement caused his head to spin. Shadows clouded his vision, and nausea pooled in his gut. He shut his eyes and felt a trickle of blood flow down his cheek and slowly seep into his ear.

When at last the dizziness subsided, he glared up at

her. "Are you going to gut me like a fish?" he asked. "Will that satisfy your twisted need for vengeance?"

"Nay, that would be too easy. What I really want is for you to suffer. For many years to come."

She reached for one of the bones that had fallen onto the gravel beside him, picked it up, and whispered into his ear again. *"I know about your wife."* Using the edge of the bone, she scraped the blood off his cheek.

Lachlan's nerves turned to ice. He lay frozen beneath her with raging fury.

"I know that she died a painful death, giving birth to a son," Raonaid continued. "She screamed and cried and would have given anything for the child to survive, but alas, you lost them both. It was ten years ago to this day. Did you not realize that, when you took that tavern wench to the haystack?"

Of course he had realized it. It was why he had done it. He'd needed the distraction.

"Was she the one who poisoned me?" he asked. "Did you pay her?"

"Nay, she just made it easy for me to pour something into your wine while you flirted and teased her into thinking she was your one true love."

Lachlan's lips twitched. He squeezed his hands into fists. The ropes creaked as he slowly pulled with all his might.

"It's too late to break free now," Raonaid said. "You're already cursed. It was done before you woke."

"You put a curse on me?" He tugged again at the bonds and bucked angrily beneath her.

She stood up and climbed out of the pit, then looked

down at him from above. "You killed the woman you loved by planting your seed in her womb, yet you continue to seduce and bed every bonny lassie who crosses your path. You would have bedded *me*, Lachlan, if I had been willing the first time we met."

He jerked hard on the ropes. "That was before I knew what a spiteful witch you were."

She bent forward and picked up the empty pail. "I don't deny being spiteful, but if I had been easier prey, the deed would have been done before you had the slightest whiff of my malice. How many other spiteful witches have you bedded? Do you even know?"

He had no answer, for he rarely stayed with a woman long enough to discover her true character.

"I didn't think you would," Raonaid said, "which is why I have chosen a fitting curse." He waited in silence for her to explain her wicked conjuring, while a gentle breeze blew across her skirts. "From this day forward, any woman who spreads her legs for you will conceive— without fail—and die a painful death on the birthing bed. There is nothing you can do to prevent it. One night with Lachlan MacDonald will be a death sentence for any lassie foolish enough to fall for your charms, and will bring death to the child as well."

With that, Raonaid turned and walked away.

Lachlan shouted after her and struggled violently, but she did not return. Her footsteps faded into the night.

Hours later, his eyes fluttered open with the rising sun, and he was no longer bound by the ropes. There was frost in the air. He could see his breath. His cheeks and lips were numb from the cold.

His head still throbbed. The pain was so profound,

he rolled to the side and retched up the contents of his stomach.

Weak and shaky, shivering uncontrollably, Lachlan crawled out of the burial cist and looked around. He was standing on a stone cairn, at least forty feet in diameter, somewhere in Kilmartin Glen. He looked down. A small circle of tiny standing stones formed a ring around the grave, and farther out, a second larger circle of taller stones encompassed the entire cairn.

Lachlan blew into his hands to warm them, then touched the dried blood on his cheek.

Staggering across the loose bed of stones, he made his way to the edge, where the grass beyond was blanketed in a crusty layer of frost. He dropped to his knees and collapsed onto his back. Blinking up at the morning sky, he pondered the situation.

He was not a superstitious man, and he had never believed in Raonaid's gifts the way Angus had, but how could he live like this? What if there was truth in the curse?

Rolling over and rising up onto his hands and knees, he coughed and struggled awkwardly to his feet. As he made his way back to the village, he vowed that he would find Raonaid again. No matter how long it took or how far he had to travel, he would find her. One way or another, he would force her to lift the curse.

Maybe he'd threaten to kill her with it.

Aye . . . that would certainly inspire her. The notion gave him strength.

Chapter One

Drumloch Manor, Scottish Borders
October 1721

FROM THE PRIVATE JOURNAL OF
LADY CATHERINE MONTGOMERY

I have decided that today, since the weather is fine, I will write my first entry at the stone circle. I cannot explain it, but something about this place comforts me, and I am in dire need of comfort. It has been four months now since my return. Though return is not at all the proper word for my status here.

I still remember nothing of my life before, despite the doctor's many efforts and tireless attempts to experiment with my head. He is both perplexed and shamelessly enthused, and I am beginning to think he will be disappointed if he ever cures me of my malady. He frowns at me when I say this, but I feel as if my spirit is in the wrong place—as if I have taken possession of another woman's body and claimed all that she once had as my own. I feel like a charlatan, and sometimes I wonder if that is what I am—a wicked, scheming imposter—even though Grandmother and Cousin John assure me on a daily basis that I am she.

Lady Catherine Montgomery. Daughter of a Scottish earl. A woman who went missing five years ago.

They tell me my father was a great war hero, and that he died fighting for the Scots in the recent rebellion (on the side of the Jacobites, which I allegedly supported, and quite passionately so). I remember none of that. All I know of myself is what I have been told, and what I experienced since the spring, when I was discovered in a farmer's stable in Italy, huddled in an empty stall, hungry and shivering.

Nuns took me in, and I was, in a way, reborn in that convent abroad, nursed back to health, questioned relentlessly, and finally identified as the long-lost Drumloch heiress.

Am I truly she? I do not know. The portraits of Catherine Montgomery all show a rather plump and innocent-looking young girl. I am neither plump, nor am I quite so young any longer. I am six weeks shy of my twenty-fifth birthday, they tell me. And no longer innocent. The doctor at the convent confirmed it.

I am not sure how to feel about that. Sometimes it disturbs me, when I imagine what I do not remember. In my mind, I am still a virgin.

I am also very slim, which is why some of the

*servants did not recognize me. They all agreed
that I had the same hair as Catherine—which is a
rather unusual shade of red—but other than that,
some of them believed I looked nothing like she
did. They were promptly dismissed.*

*But what if they were right? Sometimes I feel
as if Grandmother is hiding something from me.
She says that is not so, but I am suspicious. Could
it be that some part of her simply needs to believe
that I am her grandchild, even when she knows I
am not? She has already lost her son, after all—
the great war hero who was my father. I am all
she has left of him.*

If I am, in fact, the heiress.

*Either way, heiress or not, I cannot seem to
keep from watching over my shoulder. I am always expecting the* real *Catherine Montgomery
(or her ghost) to appear at any moment and expose me as a fraud. . . .*

Catherine closed the leather-bound journal and tipped
her head back against the flat standing stone, wishing she
did not have to write about all this, but Dr. Williams
had encouraged her to record her thoughts and feelings, suggesting it might help unlock something in her
mind.

Another experiment. Would he insist on reading it?

Flipping the book open again, she glanced over what
she had written about her virginity and considered
scratching out the part about his shameless enthusiasm. . . .

No. She would leave it. It was honest, and if the point

of this exercise was to cure her strange illness and solve the mystery of her five lost years, she would need to open her mind completely and let everything spill out like a bag of pebbles onto the floor.

Feeling tired all of a sudden, she set the journal aside and stretched out on the grass in the tall, cool shade of the standing stone. For some reason she felt great comfort whenever she came here.

She crossed her legs at the ankles and folded her hands over her belly while staring up at the bright blue sky, dotted with fluffy clouds. They floated by at a leisurely pace, shifting and rolling. It helped to relax her mind. Perhaps today would be the day when the past would come out of its box.

Soon she was dreaming about autumn leaves blowing across an endless bed of lush green moss. She could hear the faint rustle of footsteps through the grass, a horse nickering on the breeze. . . .

In the dream, she saw herself in a looking glass and heard her own voice calling out from across the distance. She reached with a hand and tried to speak to the woman in the glass. *"Come and find me. I am here. I've been here all along."*

Suddenly the woman vanished in a rush of fear— like a ghost that did not want to be seen.

Stirring uneasily, Catherine felt a presence all around the stone circle, but it was not the spirit from the dream. Her body tingled with awareness, and she moaned softly into the breeze.

Someone was watching her, circling around the outside of her private sphere. She could feel his eyes on her, waking her with a strange power of will that aroused all her senses. It compelled her to sit up, but she could not move. She was still asleep, and her body seemed made of lead.

At last, her heavy eyelids fluttered open, and she blinked up at the sky. She sat up and looked around.

There, just outside the ring of stones, a wild-looking Highlander was seated high upon a massive black warhorse. The man observed her with an eerie silence that made her wonder if she was still dreaming—for he was a breathtaking, godlike image in a shimmering haze of sunlight.

His windswept black hair matched the shiny mane of his horse. It reached past the Highlander's broad shoulders and wafted lightly on a whispering hush of a breeze. He wore a dark tartan kilt with a tarnished silver brooch at his shoulder, a round shield strapped to his back. Upon his hip, he carried a claymore in a leather scabbard.

Everything about him oozed sexuality, and the shock of such an improper awareness took Catherine beyond her depth.

She wanted to call out to him, to ask who he was, what did he want?—but she could not seem to find her voice. It was as if she were still floating in the dream.

Or perhaps this was not a dream but a hallucination. She'd had a few of them lately, often seeing herself moving about, doing everyday things, and she never knew if they were memories of her life or the lazy inventions of a woman who simply had no past.

But there was nothing lazy about *this* man, she realized with a dizzying swirl of fascination as she rose to her knees. He was a warrior, clearly, who looked as if he'd spent days, maybe weeks, in the saddle. The evidence was all there to behold—in his weapons, his brawny strength, and the dark shadow of stubble on his finely sculpted face, the grim hue of his exhausted, angry eyes, and the grimy appearance of his shirt.

The horse snorted fiercely and tossed his huge head, and Catherine gasped at the sound. It was exactly what she needed—something temporal, something vociferous, to finally pull her out of her reverie.

She knew now that this Highlander was no hallucination. He was true flesh and blood. But why he was staring at her like that, with such angry, bold intensity?

Did he know her?

Slowly, she gathered her skirts in both fists and rose to her feet, prepared to confront this man from her past, whoever he was.

His gargantuan warhorse sensed her movement and spun in a skittish circle. The Highlander whipped his head around, never taking his eyes off her.

"Be still!" he commanded the great black beast, in a guttural voice that made all Catherine's nerve endings quiver.

She braced herself, steady on both legs. . . .

The animal instantly obeyed, and the Highlander swung out of the saddle, landing on the ground with a heavy thud.

He and Catherine faced each other squarely.

Her heart beat like a mallet in her chest.

She struggled to recognize him. Surely she knew him, if only she could remember. . . .

God! Why couldn't she? It was inconceivable that

she would ever forget a face like that. His black eyes were piercing. They blazed wickedly at her with a savage determination that almost knocked her backwards against the stone.

She should run. Her instincts were telling her that she was in grave danger, but her feet would not move.

The Highlander's eyes narrowed, and he began to stalk toward her, entering the ring of stones that had, until that moment, been her own private domain. This man's fortitude, however, seemed to conquer and invade the whole world.

His gaze never veered from hers as he strode across the grass, his muscular legs taking long, sweeping strides, his big hand wrapped around the brass hilt of his claymore. At any moment he would reach her, and what would he do?

Catherine backed up against the stone, crashing into it. She sucked in a breath.

Suddenly he was upon her.

"Surprised to see me?" he asked in a deep Scottish brogue, pushing his big kilted knee between hers and pinning her to the stone. Whether he wanted to ravish her or rip her to pieces, she had no idea. Perhaps he intended to do both. One right after the other.

The firm pressure of his body, so tight up against her own, sent a hot ripple of shock through her veins.

"Should I be?" She was determined not to show fear, even while her body quivered and her breaths came hard and fast. "Do we know each other?"

"Don't tell me you don't remember our last encounter."

Now that he was closer, she noticed a small scar across his left cheek—one small imperfection on an otherwise perfect canvas.

He placed his hands flat on the stone above each of her shoulders, keeping her trapped there while his infuriated gaze swept down the length of her body. He smelled woodsy, like leather and pine.

"I'm sorry," she answered shakily, her knees going weak, "but I remember nothing."

Had she been his lover once? Was he the one who had taken her virginity? It was entirely possible, for although she sensed danger in him, she found him brutally attractive.

"You remember nothing?" the Highlander said. "Nothing at all?" His eyes glimmered with challenge. "Well, do not fret, lass. I remember everything. I've been going over it in my mind for three years, and I never gave up my quest to find you. And to do *this* to ye."

He wrapped his big hand around the back of her neck and thrust his body closer.

Bewildered and breathless, she willed herself to remember. He had been searching for her. For three years.

But what exactly had they been to each other? Why was he so enraged? Perhaps she had jilted him.

God help her. . . . Everything about him—the way he smelled, the husky timbre of his voice, and the crude manner in which he held her up against this cold wall of stone—was causing a fever inside her brain.

His palm slid around to the small of her back, and he pulled her even closer with a rough grunt, crushing her breasts against the solid wall of his chest.

She tried to shove him away.

"That's it, lass," he whispered. "Fight me. I *want* you to. For old times' sake."

She knew she should tell him to stop, for she was not some lusty tavern wench. He had no right to treat her this way. She was, according to her grandmother and cousin, a lady of noble blood and superior breeding.

"I demand to know your name," she managed to say.

"Don't pretend you do not know it." He spoke with a low snarl of hostility.

Catherine regarded him steadily in the sunlight.

"This may be difficult for you to believe, sir—for clearly you know me—but I do not know you. I remember nothing. I wish I could, but I have no idea who you are. You must stop this."

There. She'd said it. Firmly and without hesitation.

He gazed at her for a heated moment, and Catherine's heart turned over in her chest. Something was very wrong.

"So this is how it's going to be?" he asked. "You're going to play innocent?"

She fought to recover her wits. "I honestly don't know what you—"

"Did you think you would get away with this?" He grabbed hold of her wrists and held her arms up over her head.

"What do you mean?" The words slashed out of her as she tried to struggle free. "Let go of me! And get away with *what*?"

Wake up, Catherine. Wake up!

"You cursed me, lass, and now you're preying on these innocent people, pretending to be something you're not. How long do you plan to stay here? Just long enough to steal the inheritance? You once told me you would die a wealthy woman. Is this how you're going to achieve that?"

She frantically shook her head while the likelihood that he was speaking the truth shuddered in the air between them.

"Or maybe you plan to assume Catherine Montgomery's identity for the rest of your life? Is that it?"

A terrible pang of dread pitched through her. "What do you know of me?"

He sneered. "I know that you're a vindictive she-devil and a lying thief. I ought to kill you right now and spare everyone a lot of trouble."

His loathing cut her to the quick, and she fought harder against his unbreakable hold.

"I am not stealing anything!" she shouted, even though she knew nothing about herself or her past. Half the servants believed she was an imposter. Now it seemed they were correct.

Nevertheless, she felt compelled to defend her honor, for she had not come to Drumloch to deceive anyone or take what did not belong to her. That much, at least, was true.

"I don't know what you speak of," she argued. "The dowager countess traveled to Italy to claim me as her granddaughter, and she insists that is who I am."

"With no help from *you*?" His fierce gaze swept over her whole face. "No spells or potions?"

Catherine winced at his words. "Explain what you mean, sir!"

He dipped low and thrust his hips between her legs.

"*This* ought to remind you. Surely you know what I can—and cannot—do with it."

His arousal was undeniable, his size and strength overwhelming. Her heart thudded against her breast. "No, it only tells me that you are a brute!"

He wrenched her closer, his grip punishing on her arms. "Aye. That's what I am, only because you made me so. But I shouldn't need to explain it to you. Do you not see *everything* in the stones?"

She didn't know what he was referring to, but she could not risk angering him further. "I will be honest," she said, swallowing tightly. "I have no idea if I am the real Catherine Montgomery or not, but I did not come here looking for any of this. I meant it when I said I don't remember meeting you, because I have no memory of anything. I do not know who you are."

His dark eyebrows pulled together in a frown.

"No one here knows where I have been for the past five years," she continued to explain, "but you seem to know something. If you could tell me why—"

Suddenly he covered her mouth with his big, callused hand. Her eyes grew wide with panic.

"I admire the effort, Raonaid, but you cannot fool *me*. I've been hunting you down for three years, and now that I've found you, you're going to do exactly as I say. Do you understand?"

A mixture of rage and desire burned in his eyes. As a result, she did not dare provoke him. She would do what she must to keep him calm. Catherine nodded her head.

Slowly, he withdrew his hand from her mouth, but used his body to keep her pinned against the stone.

Everything inside her—all her thoughts, senses, and emotions—screamed with alarm, but she had to keep her head. She had to explain herself logically. Make him understand.

"You called me Raonaid," she carefully said.

"Aye, that's your name." His voice lost some of its hostility in that moment. A quiet, more curious arousal seemed to take its place.

Catherine took in a shaky breath. All she wanted was to understand why he was here and to find out what he knew about her past. Perhaps if she heard something familiar, her memories might return. And if she understood what she had done to him, she might be able to appease him somehow.

"What is it that you want me to do?"

"I want you to fix it."

Her pulse throbbed. "Fix what?"

"The curse."

He had mentioned a curse before, but still no memories returned to her.

"Have you cursed so many men that you don't remember one from the other?" he asked as he pulled her snugly against him.

All her instincts roared at her to go along with this, at least until she understood what he wanted. He seemed to be growing more aroused. Perhaps if she could get him to let down his guard, she might be able to strike back at him and escape.

He reached down and gathered her skirts in his hand, and began to tug them upward. "You look different," he said, his voice husky with desire. "The clothes, the hair, the perfume. It's a wonder I even recognized you."

He slid his hand up her thigh.

"What are you doing?"

She squeezed her legs together and pushed his hands back down, but he was persistent.

"Lift the curse, Raonaid. You know what will happen if you don't."

"No, I assure you, I *don't* know." She punched at his arms and tried to shove him away. "Stop, or I will scream!"

"You want me to stop?" he scoffed. "And you expect me to honor your wishes? Thanks to you, it's been three years since I've had a woman, and suddenly, I'm as randy as a bull. I didn't expect it to be quite so stimulating—not with *you,* of all people—but I suppose I'm in a worse state than I imagined. Since it's your fault I'm this way, here is my proposal." He paused and brushed his lips across her cheek. "You're going to do one of two things for me today. Lift the curse, or relieve some of my pent-up frustrations. It's your choice."

He used his body to hold her captive against the stone while he pushed his kilt to the side and began to wrestle with her skirts. A blazing hot fireball of terror shot through her bloodstream.

"Tell me how to lift it, and I will!"

She squirmed against him and tried to escape, but he was too big, too strong—and all of a sudden he was brimming with sexual need.

"You can feign innocence all you like," he said, looking into her eyes, "but I'm not as easily swindled as your doting grandmother. I know who you really are, and I've been waiting a long time for this moment—for you to undo what you did to me three years ago. Lift the curse now, or you will soon fall victim to it."

Instantly Catherine gave up any hope of appeasing him. *"Let go of me!"*

She spit in his face and kneed him in the groin. He doubled over in pain.

Bolting toward the manor house, she shouted, *"Help! Someone help me!"*

She barely reached the other side of the stone circle before the sound of the Highlander's heavy footsteps pounded fast in pursuit. She glanced over her shoulder, and the slight twisting of her body caused her skirts to tangle around her legs. She flew toward the ground, scraped the heels of her hands on the grass, and split her lip open.

He came down on top of her, then flipped her onto her back.

"You're insane!" she cried, fighting to shove him away, glaring at him with fierce and vicious determination. She slapped him across the face, kicked at his legs, and scratched his neck.

"Lift the curse!" he demanded. *"Do it now, woman, or I swear, by all that is holy . . . !"*

"I cannot!" she insisted. *"I cannot remember anything! Let me go!"*

For a moment, the whole world went quiet, and the Highlander paused, suspending the attack. He stared down at her in a cloud of hazy shock; then his eyes focused on her bloody lip. It seemed almost as if he were seeing her for the first time.

Catherine lay motionless beneath him, afraid to move, lest he grow violent again. All she could do was stare up at him in bewilderment, waiting for him to do something, to say something. *Anything.* He squeezed his eyes shut and touched his forehead to hers, grimacing as if he was in terrible pain.

Catherine slid out from under him and scrambled backwards. He withdrew onto his haunches, gaping at her with dark, suffering, bloodshot eyes.

"Look what you've done to me," he growled, shaking his head. "I despise you, Raonaid."

"I'm sorry . . . ," she replied, even though she had no memory of what she had done. And it was ridiculous for her to be apologizing to *him,* under the circumstances.

He watched her with a strange mixture of shame and desperation, then spoke quietly, through gritted teeth. "I beg of you—just lift the curse, and I'll leave you be."

"I assure you, I would have done so already if I'd known what you were talking about, but I have no memories. I don't know who I am."

His eyes darkened. "You are Raonaid, the oracle. The witch who put a curse on me three years ago. You are not the Drumloch heiress."

All the blood in Catherine's body rushed to her head as she tried to comprehend what he was saying. Was it true? Was she some kind of mystic, and had she unknowingly been deceiving the Montgomerys all this time? Half the servants believed she was a fraud. But why would her grandmother lie? Or was the woman simply in denial, refusing to believe that her only granddaughter was still missing, or possibly dead?

Just then the resounding *crack* of a gunshot ripped through the air. Catherine jumped back while the Highlander fell to his side, cupping his upper arm.

"*Shit*," he groaned, utterly defeated as he rolled onto his back and grimaced up at the sky.

Catherine rose to her hands and knees, just as her cousin John came striding into the interior of the stone circle, reloading his pistol.

"I heard your screams," he explained as he dismounted. "My apologies, Catherine, for taking so long to arrive, but I needed a clear shot."

Lying flat on his back, moving his legs about in discomfort, the Highlander swore something in Gaelic. Catherine could not understand the words, but she recognized his tone of self-recrimination. Blood seeped through his linen shirt and dripped onto the grass.

John finished reloading his pistol, cocked it, and strode closer. He stood over the wounded Scot and pointed the gun at his face. "I am John Montgomery," he said. "Fifth Earl of Drumloch. This woman is my cousin, and I would be within my rights to shoot you dead, you vile savage."

Catherine rose quickly to her feet and laid a hand on John's arm. "It's all right," she told him. "He didn't hurt me, and look, he is wounded. You can lower your weapon now."

John refused to do so. "This dirty Highlander tried to disgrace you, Catherine."

"Indeed," she replied, "but he regained control of himself before doing so."

And she could not let him die, for he was the first

person she had met who seemed to know something about her whereabouts over the past five years.

"I cannot let him go free," John declared.

The Highlander's lips pressed together in a thin line while he glared up at her cousin with contempt. "She's not who you think she is."

John raised the pistol again. "And how would you know anything about it?"

"Because I know this crafty lass," the Highlander ground out, struggling awkwardly to sit up. "And she's a nasty, vengeful witch."

Catherine sucked in a breath at the cold insult to her honor just as her cousin swung back a heavy boot, kicked her attacker in the head, and knocked him out cold.

Chapter Two

Lachlan woke to the burning agony of a red-hot branding iron searing the flesh on his upper arm. Eyes flying open, he thrashed about with violence but could not strike back, for he was strapped down to a table. He bellowed a few vile profanities, but a balled-up rag had been stuffed into his mouth, so nothing resonated quite as he intended.

The sound of his skin sizzling like bacon inflamed his anger to dangerous levels, and he spit out the rag. He roared savagely while the smell of his smoldering flesh churned in his guts.

A second later, it was over. The hot iron came away. Lachlan lowered his head onto the table, panting with rage, while he brooded over the fact that he was still cursed and Raonaid had won. *Again.*

What the devil had happened back there at the stone circle? How could he have failed so miserably after all the months planning and conniving, imagining his freedom at last from this hellish torture?

Bloody hell, he knew the answer, and it lit his existing frustrations into an even bigger inferno of rancor.

After three years of celibacy, the mere act of touching a woman—*even Raonaid*—had provoked him to such a state of desire, he'd lost sight of his goal.

He could barely comprehend how quickly it had happened. How could he have so strongly desired the woman he despised? As soon as he put his hands on her body, a fire exploded in his veins and all he wanted to do was take her, without preliminaries, up against that rock. It was not what he'd expected.

And now here he was, tied down, yet again. . . .

Letting out a sharp breath of annoyance and needing to get a handle on his bearings, he lifted his head and glanced around. He was being held in a stable tack room, surrounded by leather bridles, harnesses, and whips, all hanging from the walls. A fire blazed in a hot forge, and when he turned his head to the side, he saw an anvil and a bucket of hammers, chisels, and tongs. All useful weapons, if he could get to them.

"Unfortunately it was just a surface wound," a voice said.

Lachlan flashed a threatening glare at the Earl of Drumloch, who stepped into view as he moved around the side of the table.

"Untie me," Lachlan snarled. *"Now."*

The earl was a large man, but not a handsome one. His cheeks were pockmarked, his eyes set too close together on a greasy face that was pudgy like the rest of him. He wore a long dark curly wig and an embroidered waistcoat over a white shirt with a full cravat. His riding jacket was tossed over a nearby chair.

"I'm afraid that's not possible," Drumloch replied.

"I cannot take the risk that you might strike out at me, or flee back to the Highlands. The magistrate is on his way, you should know. I sent a lad to report what you did to Lady Catherine."

Lachlan shut his eyes and spoke through tightly clenched teeth. "I told you before, she's not who you think she is."

The earl leaned over him. "And why should I believe you? You're nothing but a foul, rutting savage. If not for my cousin's delicate sensibilities, I would have shot you dead when I had the chance."

Rutting savage, indeed. He *still* wanted to rut her. Good and hard.

Raonaid stepped into the doorway just then. She wore the same rich green gown of plush velvet and silk, with a low neckline that showed off her opulent bosom and deep cleavage to fine advantage.

Her fiery red hair, swept into a curled pageant of elegance on top of her head, was tousled from their brawl in the stone circle, and the dishevelled look of it—along with the memory of how it got to be that way—quickened Lachlan's blood and stirred his loins to an irritating, unmanageable degree.

Again he kicked and thrashed against the bonds, wondering how the cold-blooded oracle he once knew had transformed herself into this. Though beautiful, Raonaid had always been impoverished, and coarse in behavior. Clearly she'd put some effort into improving her manners in order to pass herself off as the Drumloch heiress.

And pretending to have lost all her memories . . . That was pure genius.

But had this powerful Scottish family truly been duped? How could they not see that she was an imposter?

Raonaid moved forward and touched her cousin's arm, as she had done before, when he held the pistol. The earl met her eyes, glanced at the hot branding iron still clutched in his hand, then set it down, hissing and sputtering, into a tub of water.

"I must speak with this man," she said, "before the magistrate arrives. He claims to know me. Perhaps he can help us solve the mystery of my disappearance, and explain where I was and what I have been doing for the past five years."

"Untie me," Lachlan demanded again, "or I'll tell ye nothin'."

"You'll bloody well talk if I reach for that branding iron again, you disgusting, miserable piece of—"

Raonaid spoke firmly. "Please, John, that is quite enough. Perhaps we *should* untie him."

"He attacked you!" the earl reminded her. "I'll not let him get away with it. Lord knows what he might do next. He might return and slit all our throats while we sleep."

Lachlan pondered that for a moment, and decided that yes, he'd quite enjoy returning after dark. The first thing he'd do would be make up for how he had botched the attack at the standing stones. This time he would use a different approach. He'd seduce her and make her *want* it. Hell, he'd make her *beg* for it. Then she'd have no choice but to lift the curse.

He thrashed wildly again and struggled against the bonds. He had to get off this friggin' table.

Lifting his head, he spotted his sword and belt on a shelf on the other side of the tack room. He wondered what they had done with his horse. . . .

"Fine," Raonaid replied in response to her cousin's refusal to release him. "But can we at least give him a drink of brandy? Clearly he is in pain."

A drink would be good.

Unfortunately, the earl refused.

Raonaid gave him a pleading look, and to Lachlan's surprise, the man surrendered.

"Very well. I'll send a groom to the house." Drumloch turned and went searching.

At last . . . Here was the woman Lachlan had always known and reviled. She had an inexplicable, or perhaps mystical, power to manipulate.

She moved closer—close enough that he could smell her strawberry fragrance—and his thoughtless, brazen body responded instantly with another hot surge of lust.

God damn it, Lachlan. Get ahold of yourself. Ever since he touched her in the stone circle, everything about her seemed erotic, and he hated himself for responding that way.

Because he didn't want to feel that way about *her*.

"When we spoke before," she said, seeming oblivious to his teeming lust, "you told me that my name was Raonaid, and that I was an oracle. A witch."

"Aye."

She paused a moment. "You seem quite certain that I am her, and because I have no memory of my former life, I have no way of knowing whether or not your claims are true. But I can tell you this: I do not believe I am the vengeful person you describe. I am not . . . *like* that. So perhaps you are mistaken."

He chuckled bitterly. "Nay, lass. There's no mistake. You are the oracle, without a doubt. I know your face very well, and the particular cadence of your voice. I would know it anywhere. It has a way of grating on my nerves."

She slowly walked around the foot of the table.

The sway of her hips was seductive and alluring. Her eyes burned with resolve. *Hell!* He could still smell her juicy fragrance, and he wanted to leap off the table and slide his hands up under her skirts . . . wiggle his hips against hers . . . taste her sweet hot mouth with his lips and tongue and rip that heavy gown right off her.

He was getting hard again, and beginning to think she must have put another spell on him. She might have done it when he was still sitting in the saddle back at the stone circle. Maybe she had never been asleep while he was watching her. Maybe all those lustful moans and breathless sighs were some form of erotic sorcery.

Ah, Jesus . . .

"My family tells me I went missing five years ago," she said, still oblivious to what was going on under his kilt. "How long have you known this woman called Raonaid? Where did she live?"

"I met her—" He stopped abruptly and corrected himself. "I met *you* for the first time four years ago. You were living far from here, on the Outer Hebrides. With Angus."

"Who is Angus?"

He glared at her accusingly. "My cousin and chief. Angus the Lion. But do not try to pretend you don't know him. I know that you do. You were his lover for over a year."

Raonaid's eyes lifted, and all the color drained from her face.

"What's wrong?" he asked with mocking pity. "Does your family think you are an innocent virgin?"

She lifted her chin. "That is none of your concern, sir, and it is an appalling question to ask a lady."

He wanted to laugh at her virtuous airs—for the Raonaid he knew was no stranger to depravity. She once threw a tantrum and tore apart the kitchen at Kinloch Castle. The cooks fled like mice. That same day, she punched Lachlan in the face and nearly broke his jaw. On top of all that, she could hold her whisky better than any Highlander twice her size.

Lachlan tried to focus on those memories of her, hoping it would take care of his maddening erection, but nothing seemed to make a difference.

"Could it be possible," she asked, changing the subject, "that I somehow assumed another identity when I went missing, and that is how I ended up in the Hebrides? Perhaps I lost my memory then, too, and became this other person because I felt very confused and alone, as I do now."

There was something desperate in her eyes, and yet something deeply intelligent in her attempt to put the puzzle pieces together.

Not that any of it mattered. All he wanted to do was shag her witless and get back to his old life.

"I'm sorry to disappoint you, lass," he replied, working hard to ignore all the aching sensations down below, "but Raonaid has been living in the Hebrides all her life. When she—" Again, he had to stop and correct himself. "When *you* left your home to follow Angus back to Kinloch, it was the first time you had ever set foot on the Scottish mainland."

She frowned. "How do you know this? Is there proof of Raonaid's childhood on the islands?"

"Aye. You've always been known to the people of the Western Isles because of your strange gifts. Your reputation as an oracle was known throughout the Highlands as well, because you had visions of the future." He paused, taking note of the discontent in her eyes. "But why am I explaining all this to you, when you already know it? It is your own life, lass, and I don't believe for a single minute that you don't remember. You're a fraud. These people have been tricked. It's a case of mistaken identity, from which you clearly stand to profit. Aye, I know all about your inheritance. You're due to collect it soon, are you not? You must be almost five-and-twenty."

"You offend me, sir," she argued. "It is not my intention to mislead anyone, and if I am not Catherine Montgomery, I will not try to take an inheritance that does not belong to me. I only want to know the truth." She paused. "It's just that . . ."

"Just *what*?" he prodded, fighting any urge to feel sympathy or compassion, for he could not let himself fall under any more spells.

While she circled around the table again, he felt her inexplicable power and tugged fiercely at the bonds.

This was all too familiar—to be held hostage by her—and he certainly didn't want to listen to her tragic story. He just wanted to be rid of the curse, one way or another.

And to get off this damn table.

"I find it difficult to believe," she said, "that I could be the woman you describe. First of all, I cannot see the future, or even the past for that matter. I do not have that gift. Nor can I imagine putting curses on people, and my doctor assures me that a loss of memory does not change a person's character." She looked down at him. "And what kind of curse is it? You never explained."

Growing impatient with the conversation, he continued to tug at the leather straps. He tried to tear at them with his teeth. When that didn't work, he regarded her snidely. "You know very well what it is."

"If I did, would I be asking the question?"

He shook his head in utter disbelief. "Who knows why a witch does anything?"

"Stop calling me that. Tell me about the curse."

Lachlan scoffed. "You don't remember drugging me, and throwing me into a pit? The bones were a nice touch, the curse itself especially twisted. What better way to curb my sexual exploits than to promise that any woman I bedded would die in childbirth and take the innocent bairn with her."

Raonaid's lips parted, and she frowned.

"What's wrong, *Lady Catherine*? Does the idea offend you? Do you find it cruel?"

"Of course I do."

"But *you* are the one who concocted it."

She spoke with a rising pitch of anger. "How many times must I say it? I remember nothing."

"And I believe you are a liar." He stared up at the ceiling and lay still for a long moment as he contemplated his life since the curse.

"I once scoffed at such tales of magic," he quietly said. "But each time I wanted to bed a woman . . ." He glared at her. "I thought of *you,* and what you did to me, and I could not take the risk."

A flood of loathing moved through him as he suddenly recalled the death of his own wife and unborn child, and all the grief and guilt and inescapable regret that came with it.

"Where is my horse?" he demanded to know.

"He's in the stable. He has been fed and watered."

"Untie me. Let me go before the magistrate arrives. It's the least you can do."

"The least I can do?" she snapped back. "You tried to ravish me and make me a victim of that curse."

"But I *didn't* ravish you, did I?"

She regarded him with uncertainty.

Lachlan stopped struggling and worked the situation through in his mind. There had to be a way out of this.

"When you first kissed me in the stone circle," Raonaid said, "I thought we were old lovers."

He turned his head to look at her, and scoffed. "Hardly."

"Then why did you kiss me like that?"

He fumbled for an explanation when he didn't even understand it himself. "I was desperate. I would have done anything to make you lift the curse."

"And you thought that I would be so overcome by lust for you that I would simply swoon, and beg you to take me?"

He shrugged, for that was usually the effect he had on women. Or it used to be, at any rate.

"Aye."

"Well, you were off to a very good start, Highlander, until I asked your name."

Lachlan darted a surprised look at her, just as the earl returned to the tack room.

"Whisky's on the way," Drumloch said. "And the magistrate should be here at any moment."

"Wonderful." Lachlan winced at the pain in his shoulder, which he had forgotten about while the earl was gone.

"You still haven't told us your name, savage."

Lachlan gritted his teeth. "No, I haven't, and I'm not telling you anything."

"The magistrate will wish to know it. He might even ask you to spell it, in which case you might have a problem. Can you even read? Ever seen a pen before?"

Lachlan gazed up at the rafters. "It'll be the magistrate's problem, not mine, because he'll have to beat the information out of me—and if it comes to that, someone might get hurt."

A footman entered the tack room just then with a bottle of whisky and two glasses. The earl swiped the bottle off the silver tray, uncorked it, tipped it back, and took a swig.

Wiping his mouth with the back of his hand, he said,

"This isn't my finest, but I could hardly waste the good stuff on the likes of you."

Raonaid strode forward. "Hand me the bottle, John." She took it from him and poured a drink. "Can you lift your head?" she asked Lachlan.

He shot her a frosty look. "Wouldn't it be easier if you untied me?"

"I don't think that would be wise."

"Certainly not!" Drumloch agreed.

She ignored her cousin. Cupping the back of Lachlan's head, she held the glass to his lips. He gulped it down in one swallow. She poured another, and he gulped that down, too. Then a third. With any luck, it would dull his senses enough to forget what had happened between him and Raonaid in the stone circle.

"You certainly can drink, Highlander," she said with a hint of amusement as she stepped away from him.

"So can you, *Catherine*." He spoke her name with sardonic bite.

"Is that a fact?"

"Aye."

Without the slightest hesitation, she tipped the bottle back and guzzled.

Lachlan grinned with satisfaction. Now *there* was the Raonaid he knew—wild and uninhibited, exposing herself at last.

"Catherine, what in God's name are you doing?" The earl stalked forward and snatched the bottle out of her hands. "Don't let him manipulate you! He just wants to undermine your good judgment!"

She choked and rasped on the potent spirit, and

sucked in a few tight breaths. "He says I know how to drink. I want to see if it's true."

"Nothing he says is true," the earl argued. "He cannot be trusted."

"How do you know?"

Drumloch lowered his voice. "Because he called you a witch."

A horse whinnied somewhere nearby.

Raonaid was silent for a moment. "How do you know I'm not?"

The earl had no answer. He merely stared at her in bemused silence.

Lachlan rather enjoyed watching them quarrel. Again, it was a hint of the old Raonaid coming out of her snake hole, and the earl seemed quite taken aback.

"Because you are Lady Catherine Montgomery!" he finally replied.

"Indeed!" she shouted. "A woman who has been missing for five years, and has returned as a ruined lunatic who cannot remember a single thing about her life!"

"You are not a lunatic, Catherine. Do not speak that word again."

Lachlan watched with curious interest as Drumloch moved forward. He was about to reach out to her when the sound of hooves and an approaching carriage interrupted the sudden hush in the stable tack room.

"The magistrate has arrived," the footman said, stepping into the doorway.

Lachlan shut his eyes and listened to the ominous sound of the heavy prison coach rumbling to a slow halt outside. The horses nickered and shook in their harness while Lachlan made one last attempt to fight against his bonds.

It was hopeless, however. He could not escape.

"This isn't over," he growled at Raonaid as the magistrate and four Lowlanders armed with swords and muskets filed quickly through the door.

Chapter Three

Catherine sat before her looking glass, watching with impatience as her maid brushed and styled her hair for dinner.

It was difficult to relax. Four hours ago, the magistrate had untied the Highlander and bashed him over the head, then clamped iron shackles onto his wrists, and dragged him away. All this occurred before she could fully comprehend the ramifications of the situation.

She should never have accepted her cousin's decision to call for the authorities. Instead, she should have insisted on keeping the Highlander here until he could answer more questions—she had so many of them— but everything had spun out of control so quickly.

He was now locked up in the village prison, and she was here, dressing for dinner, still reeling from the memory of his hands on her body and his kiss upon her lips, and feeling even more separated from her sense of identity—which had been shaky and unstable to begin with.

She was supposed to be a lady of noble breeding. How was she ever to manage the disturbing prospect that she was a witch?

Before today, she had been drifting along in some kind of dull, invisible existence, believing anyone who suggested anything about the person she once was. She accepted all explanations and felt no passion for anything, no desire to change or seek something more. She knew nothing of what existed beyond this place. Her world was empty, and everything they told her made her feel like a ghost. Her soul seemed lost to her, as if it were floating around in the air somewhere over her head, just out of reach.

Something was missing.

Herself, perhaps. Her memories. Her life. That would make sense.

Or perhaps she yearned for the lover who had taken her innocence. Was he the man called Angus? The Scottish chief who, according to the Highlander, had shared her bed for a year?

If she was, in fact, this oracle called Raonaid . . . She was not yet convinced.

Reaching for the pearl and emerald earrings, she took one last look in the mirror. Tonight she wore a formal gown of dark purple silk over a wide hooped petticoat, with richly embroidered cuffs of velvet, and a fine brocade, linen-lined stomacher. At her neck she wore a pearl and emerald choker, and her hair was swept into an elegant powdered coiffure with jeweled combs.

No, she thought with absolute certainty—she could not possibly be that mad witch from the Hebrides, who put hexes on people. She was the daughter of an earl, and she looked the part. Despite everything, she *felt* the part. Perhaps the Highlander was the one who was mad. Or simply mistaken.

Catherine dismissed her maid, left her private bed-chamber, and ventured into the corridor, which was brightly lit by flickering candles in wall sconces, spaced closely together and illuminating a long row of ancestral portraits.

None of whom she recognized.

She reached the stairs, laid her hand on the rail, and decided that she would speak to John privately that evening and arrange for some sort of meeting with the Highlander as soon as possible. She needed to know more about the clan chief who had shared his bed with "Raonaid" in the Hebrides, the man called Angus. Perhaps if she met him, she would feel more confident about her past and have a better sense of what was real. She would either recognize him as her former lover—and he in turn would recognize her—or know, without a doubt, that she was not the oracle, and never had been.

Surely a woman would recognize her first lover. . . .

When she entered the drawing room a moment later, a roaring fire was blazing in the hearth and John was standing before it, sipping from a crystal glass of claret. He wore a royal blue dinner jacket with a heavy brocade waistcoat, dark knee breeches, and ivory stockings. A cumbersome French wig with a lengthy mass of brown curls framed his face.

He glanced up at the sound of her approach and gave her an apologetic smile. "My dear Catherine . . ."

She held up a hand. "Please, John, that is not necessary. I require no sympathy. The Highlander caused no permanent damage."

But the heat of his kiss was still burning in her mind.

"In that case, you look well," John said, setting his

own glass down and pouring a drink for her. She accepted it and drew in a small sip. Her cousin picked up his glass again. "It was a terrible ordeal, to be sure," he said. "I am relieved it is over."

"As am I," she replied, "but I wish to see the Highlander again. If you could please arrange it."

John faced her with concern. "*See* him, Catherine? But why?"

She had expected some opposition from her cousin. He was, after all, her guardian and protector, and the Highlander had attempted to harm her in the worst possible way.

"Surely you are as curious as I," she explained, "about what he claims to know of me. Perhaps he can unlock the mystery of my whereabouts for the past five years. Or offer some insight about my true identity."

John moved closer. "There is no insight required—and certainly not from a man like him. You are my cousin—a Montgomery!—and those are the facts. Grandmother knows it with every breath in her soul, and you know how much you mean to her. She would never make a mistake about her own flesh and blood."

Catherine swallowed over all the doubts that continued to poke at her. "Yes, I do believe she is certain that I am Catherine. But the fact remains that we do not know why I went missing five years ago, or what happened to me during that time. Do you not wish to ask the Highlander more questions? Are you not curious as to how I ended up in Italy? Perhaps he knows something that can help us fit the pieces together."

John gulped down the remaining contents of his glass and moved to sit on the sofa. "Dr. Williams would not approve. He said you must avoid situations that cause you undue stress."

She quirked a brow, and John's expression warmed.

"If it means that much to you," he conceded, "I could speak to the magistrate in the morning. We could go together."

"That would be wonderful. Thank you, John."

"But I won't let you be alone with him."

"Of course not." She quickly dropped her gaze to her lap. "Nor should I wish to be."

"And you shouldn't mention it to your grandmother."

A few moments later, Eleanor, the dowager countess, entered the drawing room. She was a short, stout woman with gray hair and spectacles, who did not often smile or show emotion—though she had wept uncontrollably when she found Catherine in the convent, alive and recuperating.

Catherine faced her.

"What are you speaking of?" Eleanor brusquely asked.

"Nothing, Grandmother."

Catherine immediately changed the subject, for earlier in the day—after learning of the attack—Eleanor had insisted they never mention the Highlander again.

They dined that evening on oyster soup, followed by a main course of roast pheasant with cranberry sauce and herbed carrots, and succulent raspberry custard tarts for dessert.

Aside from the occasional light clink of silverware against china plates, it was a quiet meal. Catherine hardly minded, for she was able to consider all the questions she would ask the Highlander in the morning, most notably the name and location of his clan chief. She hoped he would disclose that information, for he had been uncooperative when John asked him his name in the stable that afternoon. She wondered if the magistrate had fared any better.

After dinner, they returned to the drawing room for coffee and cards, though Catherine had little interest in table games. She simply could not stop thinking about the Highlander.

She remembered the words he had spoken, just before he took the pistol ball in the arm: *Look what you've done to me.* The pain in his eyes had been unmistakable. She never imagined anyone could look so tormented.

She was still thinking about that when John dealt her a rather lucky hand. Soon they began to engage in some serious play, but after a time Catherine's interest in the game waned.

"It's been an exhausting day," she said, laying her cards down, "so I shall bid you both good night."

"Good night," her grandmother replied.

John pushed his chair back, stood, and bowed to Catherine. She rose to her feet.

Deciding that a book might be a welcome distraction, she picked up a candelabra on her way out to light her way to the library.

Gingerly, she passed through the dark corridors of the manor, often glancing over her shoulder, checking every alcove along the way. Since she'd arrived at Drumloch, she often felt as if there was a presence nearby, a curious ghost perhaps, following her. It happened at all hours of the day, but was especially disconcerting at night. She had not yet told her doctor about it.

A slight chill blew through the corridor, causing her to pause while the candle flames danced. Perhaps there was an open window somewhere. She hoped there was.

At last, she reached the library and pushed the heavy oak door open. It creaked on its iron hinges. The light from her candles swung through the gloom and cast moving shadows across the bookcases. She felt the air stir against her cheek, and stopped abruptly on the carpet in the center of the room. A flash of apprehension shot up her spine.

Holding the candles high above her head, she called out shakily, "*Hello*? *Is anyone here?*"

The heavy drapes on both windows billowed softly and quietly.

She half-expected to hear the echo of her own voice, but there was no chance of that, not with so many musty books lining the walls. They were piled everywhere, on the tables and desktops, and they filled the room with the heavy scent of dust and knowledge.

She was acting a fool, she decided, as she strode to the bookcase and ran a finger along all the spines.

Finally, after a time, Catherine selected something. She set the candles down on the desk and opened the book to read the first few lines, but felt another breeze across her face. The drapes were floating on the drafts again.

She moved to check the window, but it was closed. Outside, the moon had risen high and full against a clear, starlit sky. She cupped her hands to the glass to look out at the gardens below, in full autumn bloom, then gazed farther across to the horizon, past rolling green hills and dark forests, silhouetted against the night sky. It was a beautiful night, and her senses quivered and hummed.

Again, the velvet curtain swelled beside her. She pulled the fabric aside.

There he was. *The Highlander.*

Her belly exploded in shock. How long had he been there? He had recovered his sword belt, pistol, and powder horn from the stable, but how had he gotten past the servants and found his way to this room? Was he the ghost in the corridor?

The fire in his eyes held her frozen in place, rigid with terror.

He raised a finger to his lips. *"Shhh. . . ."*

Catherine fought to suppress any sudden movement. Although she should have screamed. What was wrong with her? She was not without panic.

Suddenly she noticed the front of his shirt, stained with blood. Was it his own? One eye was black-and-blue. Had he been stabbed, or shot again?

"What happened to you?" she asked. "And how did you get here?"

He gave no answer. He simply pushed the curtain aside, whipped her around, and pressed a knife to her throat.

Chapter Four

Catherine fought against the Highlander's steely grip. She squirmed and twisted, kicked his shin with her heel, but to no avail. He was like a brick wall behind her, all rigid muscle and incredible brawn.

"It's your fault I'm cursed," he snarled, "and after getting shackled and dragged off to prison, I'm not taking any more chances with you. You'll not trick me this time."

She felt the sharp point of the knife at the base of her throat, and clutched at his muscled forearm. "My cousin was right. You *are* a brute."

"I'm only trying to survive." His breath was hot and moist in her ear. "Now stop squirming, promise you won't scream, and I'll let you go."

"I promise."

With that, he released her. Catherine swung around to face him in the eerie candlelight. Rubbing a hand over her neck, she fought to catch her breath and calm the frantic beating of her heart.

"That was unnecessary," she said. "And why on earth did you come back here? If my cousin sees you, he will shoot you dead on the spot."

The Highlander sheathed his knife in his belt. "I've been hunting you down for three years, Raonaid. I'll not give up now."

"You are still certain that I am her."

"Aye. Whether or not you're telling the truth about your lost memories I don't know, but one way or another, you're going to remember the night you cursed me. I'll find a way to make it so."

She swallowed uneasily. "How do you plan to do that? The doctor has been thoroughly unsuccessful in helping me to remember."

"Your doctor doesn't know how to apply pressure like I do."

She mulled over his meaning and spoke with seething hostility. "You're going to threaten me again with ravishment, and try to frighten the truth out of me. Is that it?"

"Whatever it takes."

She wanted to know the truth herself, desperately so, but she would not stand for abuse.

Taking a closer look at his black eye and the blood seeping through the front of his shirt, she asked, "How did you escape the prison coach?"

He put his finger to his lips again, as if he'd heard something. With light, swift movements, he crossed the library and peered out into the corridor. Reassuring himself that no one was about, he answered the question. "They tried to kill me on the way to the village."

"Who did?"

"The magistrate and his thugs. He said they were to make it look like they were just doing their jobs, so they let me out of the coach, loaded their pistols, and told me to run."

"And that's what you did?"

"Nay, I didn't *run,*" he practically spat. "I kicked the weapons out of their hands and used my fists."

She glanced down at his big hands and saw that his knuckles were nicked and bloody. "But there were four of them," she said with disbelief, not wanting to admit to herself—or to him—that she was impressed by such a feat.

"Aye," he said. "Although there might not be quite so many of them now." He peered out the door again to make sure no one was coming. "I might have killed one or two. Inadvertently."

She pointed at the wound on his stomach. "What happened there?"

He glanced down and seemed to notice for the first time that his shirt was soaked with blood. "*Ah, bal-locks.* One of them knifed me, but it's just a scratch. I'll live."

They stood for a moment, staring at each other in the tense, heart-pounding silence, until he cocked his head at her shrewdly.

"If you're thinking about screaming and turning me in," he warned, "you ought to think again. Something's not right here, witch. I believe they're using you as much as you are using them."

His eyes dipped lower, and he seemed to take in all the swells and curves of her body, awarding special attention to her neckline and breasts.

For a shaky moment she didn't hear a single word

he said, for she was growing weak in the knees under the stormy heat of his gaze. Everything about him was darkly sexual, burning with angry need, and she couldn't deny that although he frightened her and made her fear for her safety, on some basic level, he fascinated her.

Catherine shook herself out of that treacherous fog, and worked to sort out what he was trying to say to her.

"I told you before," she replied, "I am not using them." She paused and shifted her weight from one foot to the other and recalled her constant suspicion that her grandmother was hiding something from her. "But what makes you think that?"

"You're worth a lot of money, are you not? Or at least, Catherine was. Everyone in Scotland knows she's about to receive a considerable inheritance, and from what I've heard, if she's not alive to collect it, it will be forfeited to the Jacobite cause."

She nodded her head. "Yes, but I *am* alive, and it's *my* money. At least it will be in six weeks' time, when I turn five-and-twenty. You think they are using me to gain access to it? To keep it from landing in the hands of the Jacobites?"

"Someone ordered me dead today," he said, "because I know who you are. I wouldn't want the same thing to happen to you, lass. Not before you lift that curse."

"But I *can't* lift it," she insisted.

He stalked forward and caught her by the arm. His scorching gaze dropped to her parted lips. His face was only inches away; she could feel his breath beating against her cheeks. She sucked in a quivering breath.

"You're lying."

This time she did not argue. She could not even speak.

"I'll use force if I have to," he said in a low, threatening voice. "One way or another, you're going to give me what I want."

Her flesh sizzled where he touched her. She understood that it was part fear, part irrational excitement. He was stunningly handsome, bold and robust, and when she thought of how he had fought off all those armed guards, single-handedly, her body went weak all over again.

God, why did he have to be so potent and alive? She didn't want to feel any of the things she was feeling, but something about him awakened her spirit, and she was beginning to feel that he was the key to her past—that he would awaken her memories as well. Make them positively explode out of that tight, locked box.

"I told you," she replied nevertheless, lifting her chin and breathing in his musky scent while reminding herself not to become too swept up in his vigor, for he might be handsome, but he was also dangerous and volatile. "I don't know how to help you."

The sheer force of his silence held her captive as his eyes burned into hers. Then suddenly he began to wrench up her skirts and wrestle with his kilt.

"What are you doing?" she asked in horror, fighting to twist out of his hold.

"We'll do it your way then," he growled. "If you won't lift the curse, you'll have to share it with me.

Maybe then you'll be more accommodating, when *you're* the one who's staring death in the eye."

He crowded up against her until the backs of her knees collided with the sofa and she landed with a gasp on the plush cushions. He stood over her, gazing down with raging eyes, and was about to push her legs apart and descend upon her when she held up her hands and cried, "*All right! All right! I'll lift it! I promise!*"

With one knee braced upon the sofa cushion, he halted. His chest heaved wildly.

"Do it then," he commanded. "Do it *now*."

Anxiety spurted through her. Part of her wanted to cry out for help, but who would hear her at this hour, in this deserted wing of the house? And if someone did come, her cousin would most assuredly kill this man, and she would never know the truth about her life.

What if he was right? What if these people were using her to gain access to Catherine's inheritance? What if they had done something to her, to make her forget her life and cause her to unwittingly play the part of their missing heiress?

"Take me to Angus," she demanded in a rush of desperation, needing to see the man who had allegedly been such an important part of her life. The man who was once her lover. "I promise that by seeing him again, I will be able to lift the curse. I just need to remember. . . ." She fought to consider the more detailed logistics of such an arrangement and quickly added, "I won't do anything for you until you deliver me to him. *Safely.*"

The corner of the Highlander's mouth twitched.

"I need to know who I am," she continued to explain. "I cannot go on living like this. Only then will I be able to help you."

They glared at each other like two cats, each waiting for the other to pounce; then he pulled her swiftly to her feet.

"How do I know I can trust you?" he asked.

"How do I know I can trust *you*? Especially when you are always looking at me as if . . ." She paused and gestured toward his big, rampant body. "As if you want to *eat* me."

He gave her a threatening glare. "I *do* want to eat you, lass. And I can't guarantee I won't try to steal a taste of you along the way. It's been a miserable three-year famine, you see, and I'm *verra* hungry."

She could see that quite clearly for herself.

Nevertheless, she stood her ground. "No, that will not do. I'm going to need your word of honor that you will not touch me. If you give me that, I will leave this house with you quietly, without a fight. I promise."

But would she be able to lift the curse when she met her former lover again? She wasn't sure, and she knew this was a dangerous game to play.

The air sparked and crackled between them while the Highlander considered her proposition.

At last he gave her the answer she wanted. "All right, lass. I'll take you with me."

Catherine exhaled sharply with relief—a feeling that was quickly extinguished when he moved forward and spoke low in her ear.

"But know this," he whispered with sinister intent. "If you break your word to me and do not lift that curse when we reach Kinloch, I swear on my life that I will take great pleasure in killing you with it."

He took hold of her hand and led her out, while she prayed to God that she would get her memories back before then.

Chapter Five

Catherine settled into the saddle on the giant black
warhorse, realizing with some frustration that she was
still dressed for dinner. Her hair was curled and powdered, she wore formal silks and velvets, and the priceless Drumloch jewels were strung prettily around her
neck.

"I don't suppose you'd permit me to go back inside
and put on something more . . . appropriate."

The horse tossed his big black head, and his shiny
mane flung about as he whinnied and grumbled.

"Nay, lassie," the Highlander replied as he checked
his saddlebags to make sure nothing was missing. "No
time for that. Besides, I wouldn't want you to change
your mind about not turning me in."

He swung up behind her and gathered the reins in
his hands, then urged the monstrous snorting creature
out of the stable to the meadow beyond. They galloped
hard until they reached the forest; then the Highlander
drew lightly on the reins.

"Whoa." His horse slowed to a walk.

"It's very dark in here," Catherine said as they entered the pitch-black depths of the wood.

Unable to see much of anything through the silent, murky gloom, she became more intensely aware of what she could *feel*—the firm wall of the Highlander's chest at her back, rubbing up against her.

"How will we see where we are going?" she asked, struggling to ignore the vital sensation of his big, hard body, so close to her own.

"Leave that to me." The creature's hooves plodded heavily over the damp ground. "How long will it be before someone notices your absence?"

"Not until morning. Though my maid will notice later tonight."

"Will she speak up?"

Catherine considered it. "No, she's quiet and discreet. I believe she will wait for someone to question her."

Catherine's eyes adjusted eventually to the reduced light, and she was thankful at least for the full moon, which provided some illumination through the thick autumn foliage.

The horse picked his way gallantly over the leaves and dry twigs, and they soon found a narrow bridle path that took them farther away from the manor house.

"What is your name, Highlander?" she asked. "You have not yet revealed it."

"I am Lachlan MacDonald, former Laird of War at Kinloch Castle."

"Ah. A powerful and battle-seasoned warrior. I should have known."

He gave no reply, and she did not press him for one, for she had not accompanied him on this journey in order to become better acquainted. All she wanted was to meet the man who had allegedly been her lover. She had so many questions for him.

But what if she found him hideous? What if he was cruel?

What if she still loved him?

"Tell me about Angus," she blurted out, hoping to quench some of her curiosity and ease the nerve-racking fires of doubt in her belly.

"What do you want me to say?"

"Anything. Why do they call him the Lion?"

"Because he is a fierce and ruthless warrior, famous for his killing exploits during the rebellion."

"The Jacobite Rebellion?" Her family had claimed she was a passionate supporter of the cause before she went missing.

John, on the other hand, was a Hanoverian.

"Aye. His father raised an army for the battle at Sherrifmuir."

"That is particularly interesting," she said. "Catherine Montgomery's father, the former earl, died in that battle." She turned her head to the side. "Does the Lion's father still live?"

"Nay, he died for the cause, too, and now Angus just wants peace."

Catherine considered all that Lachlan had told her so far and strained to remember. She tried to imagine a ruthless, lionish warrior who fought bravely in Scottish battles, but alas, nothing seemed familiar.

"Is there anything else you can tell me?"

He leaned forward and spoke in a soft voice that was snide and taunting. "He has a beautiful wife and child."

Catherine turned quickly in the saddle. "A wife and child? Since when?"

Lachlan frowned at her, and his head drew back slightly. "You truly do not remember? Or are you just a gifted actress?"

"How many times must I say it? I do not remember a thing. I cannot even *imagine* what Angus looks like."

Lachlan regarded her with increasing frustration, and she wondered if he would ever believe her about her lost memories. Either way, he seemed disappointed that she was not throwing a tantrum about the mention of a wife and child.

"Imagine this," he answered harshly. "He looks like a lion, and has a mighty roar."

The horse lost his footing slightly over the uneven ground. Catherine slid sideways in the saddle, but Lachlan held her steady.

Again, to her dismay, his touch sent a tingling flow of excitement through her body. It was a feeling she fought hard to crush.

"You expected me to be jealous," she said, referring back to Angus and his beautiful wife. "But how can I be, when I have no recollection whatsoever of the time we spent together?"

Lachlan considered the question thoroughly. "I've never heard of anyone losing all their memories before, and I'm still not sure I believe it. So don't get too comfortable, thinking I'm convinced."

She scoffed. "Trust me, I am not the least bit comfortable with you." How could she be, when everything about him overwhelmed all her sensible thoughts?

"Clearly I did not make a good impression on you," she added, "when we knew each other before."

"Nay, you did some appalling things."

"Like what, besides the curse?" She realized in that moment that without the benefit of memory, there were no regrets. There was nothing to feel guilty about. It was like living in a constant state of innocence and purity.

And it was so very empty.

"Tell me the worst thing I've done," she said, for she wanted to know the truth, no matter how unpleasant it might be. She wanted a real life. "Perhaps it will trigger a memory."

Though nothing her grandmother told her had ever triggered anything. Not even the return to her childhood home had brought back her past.

But maybe that was because Lachlan was right: she was not Catherine and never had been.

God, help me. She was so confused and desperate to learn the truth. Desperate enough to go off into the night with a dangerous, unpredictable Highlander who despised her . . .

"Can you not answer the question?" she asked, growing almost frantic. "Or have you lost your memories, too?"

"I apologize, lass, but I don't know where to begin. The choices are endless."

She shook her head with derision. "You are a cad."

"All right, all right," he said at last. "I'll start with how you followed Angus back to Kinloch after he said good-bye to you in the Hebrides. But you better brace yourself for the whole story, because you were a villain like none I've ever known. You won't like how the tale ends."

"Enough with the suspense," she said, her heart pounding. "Please tell me what I did. I must know."

He inhaled deeply, and she found herself leaning into the warmth of his broad chest.

"You followed him to Kinloch to tell him that he had less than a month to live, and that he'd die by the noose."

She frowned. "Was it true?"

"Nay, he still lives. But you also told him that his wife—who you called a manipulative slut—would betray him, and it would be her fault that he would end up in the noose in the first place."

"Good Lord! Was that a lie as well?"

He hesitated. "It was partly true, but it's a long story. All you need to know is that you tried to lure him back to your bed when he was happily married and expecting a child, and you were the one who told his enemies that they should hang him. You were responsible for the near fall of Kinloch Castle, and another Scottish rebellion—when all Angus ever wanted was peace."

God in heaven . . . She swallowed hard, trying to manage her composure. It was a lot to take in, and if she truly was Raonaid, the oracle, she would not be proud of these things when she recovered her memories. How would she ever live with herself?

"Did I do these dreadful things because Angus jilted me?" she asked. "It sounds like I was very jealous of his wife."

"Aye, you were, and you were bitter toward me for the loss of him. That's why you cursed me."

She turned in the saddle. "What part did you play in it?"

"First, I was the one who found him with you in the Hebrides, and encouraged him to return home and reclaim his castle. That's when he left you. And when you followed, I helped convince him that you would wreak havoc on his marriage if he let you stay, and that he should banish you from the castle for good."

Evidently, she had been jealous and spiteful on more than one occasion, if she had further retaliated by placing a murderous curse on Lachlan.

"You don't suppose I have purged all my memories because of an overwhelming sense of guilt? Perhaps I could not bear what I had done, and therefore tried to erase it, or block it all out."

"That would make sense, I suppose, if you felt the least bit guilty, but I'm not sure you are capable of that." The deep scorn in his voice left her shaken. "I never met anyone more vengeful than you."

She could not accept this. She simply could not.

"And yet, your powerful clan chief lived with me for more than a year," she argued, "and we were lovers. Surely, Raonaid—or rather *I*—must have had *some* redeemable qualities."

He considered that. "Your ability to predict the future, I suppose. And you're a beautiful woman." He spoke the words in a velvet murmur and rubbed his nose across her hair. "Not even I, who hate you most, can deny that, Raonaid."

Their tempestuous kiss in the stone circle came flashing back at her suddenly, and she experienced another persistent spark of arousal, deep and heavy in her belly.

She should have been angry with herself for such a response, after he just admitted how much he hated her, but instead, she decided to accept these sensations, for at least they were proof that she was alive. She existed as a passionate being.

A light breeze blew through the canopy of autumn leaves overhead, and the moon shadows rippled like waves across the ground.

"Perhaps Raonaid is not all bad," she suggested, grasping for some hope that she could somehow redeem herself. "Did you ever really talk to her, like we are doing now?"

He laughed. "Nay! You and I despised each other with a passion. And stop calling yourself *her*. You are one-and-the-same, and when you say things like that, you sound a bit mad."

"Like a lunatic. Isn't that what I am?"

He paused. "I don't know. But I don't like it, lass, because it makes me forget who you really are."

She considered that. "I rather wish you *would* forget. Then perhaps you would be gentler with me."

"Gentler? *Me?* With *you?*"

Just then, a light drizzle began, which quickly turned to a heavy downpour.

Lachlan uttered an angry oath and steered them deeper into the forest. "This curse of yours knows no mercy," he growled.

"You can hardly blame the weather on *me.*"

He grumbled something in Gaelic, then kicked in his heels and told her to hang on.

Chapter Six

Lachlan raised his tartan over his head, but nothing could keep the water out, nor could anything be done for Raonaid, who was seated in front of him, dressed in heavy silks and velvets that were quick to soak up the rain.

Her hair—piled on top of her head in a great mountain of curls and powder—tumbled onto her neck and shoulders in a hopeless avalanche of chaos.

Not unlike what was going on inside his body at the moment.

Obviously, if he wanted the curse lifted, he'd had no choice but to bring her with him, but it was no easy task to ride behind her, with his legs straddled around her sweet, warm bottom while she swayed back and forth in the saddle, rubbing up against the insides of his thighs.

He was in a constant state of arousal and was half-tempted to stop everything, dismount, and take her heartily up against some arbitrary tree, while the rain poured down all around them and drenched them both to the bone.

It seemed his careful plan to bully and coerce her

was now a crashing wreck. She had turned the tables on him, and was now partly in control, after having set the rules in the library.

It was utter madness. He couldn't imagine how it could be worse.

And then the wind began.

"I'm freezing!" Raonaid shouted.

He wrapped his tartan around her and held her close in the saddle to stave off the chill, while he hissed a few unsophisticated oaths inside his throbbing head.

"There's a village not far from here," he said in defeat. "We'll go and dry out, and I'll get us a second horse."

He couldn't ride with her anymore. Not like this.

She turned in the saddle to look at him through the driving rain. "Are you not worried the magistrate will catch us?"

"We won't stay long." He urged Goliath into a gallop.

By the time they rode into the village, splattering through puddles of muck in the street, they were both soaked and shivering.

"Take the pins out of your hair," he said as they trotted to the stable and paused under the dripping overhang. "Let it fall loose, and give me your jewels."

"But these belong to the Drumloch estate," she replied, teeth chattering. "I am responsible for them, and they are worth a great deal."

"If you walk in there wearing them, lass, I promise you'll leave without them. Hand them over. I won't let anything happen to them."

She hesitated, then removed the pearl and emerald necklace and surrendered it. He dropped it into his sporran while she removed the earrings and handed them over as well.

Lachlan swung out of the saddle and held out his arms. She accepted his assistance without complaint, and a moment later was standing before him, letting down her hair. It fell wetly onto her soft, ivory shoulders while rainwater glistened on her lips and forced her to blink away the silvery drops of moisture pooling on her eyelashes.

Ah, fook, but she is lovely.

It was too bloody much. He wanted to hit something.

"What now?" she asked.

He removed his hands from her tiny waist and let them fall to his sides. "We go inside and get warm."

"Will we take a room?"

"Aye, but just until the storm passes."

She turned away from him and began walking toward the front door while he handed Goliath over to a stable hand.

"We'll use false names," Lachlan told her as he caught up. "And it's a good thing you look like a drowned cat. No one would take you for an heiress, looking as wretched as you do."

It would help him if he could believe it.

"Thank you so very much for the generous compliment," she curtly replied as he strode ahead to lead the way.

They entered the inn, which housed a taproom on the main floor, with dark paneling and hunting portraits on the walls. Lachlan took hold of Raonaid's hand and approached the red-bearded barkeep.

"We need a room and a hot meal."

The giant Lowlander waved a barmaid over. "Abigail, take these soggy travelers upstairs and ask them what they want to eat." He wiped a cloth over the bar. "There are only two choices," he added under his breath. "Stew and stew." He lifted his eyes and regarded Lachlan steadily. "I'm Bill Anderson, and I'll require payment in advance."

Lachlan dug into his sporran and dropped a handful of coins onto the bar.

The innkeeper's bushy brows furrowed as he counted the money. "You plan to stay more than one night, stranger?"

"Nay, but I don't want to be bothered. Do you understand my meaning?"

The innkeeper peered over Lachlan's shoulder at Raonaid, who stood behind him, wringing the water out of her hair. It splattered onto the floor.

"Someone's going to have to wipe that up," Anderson said, sounding offended.

Lachlan tossed him another few coins. "Will that cover it?"

"Aye, friend, it will. Now go with Abigail up the stairs. She'll see to all your needs."

Lachlan tossed his hair out of his eyes and waved a hand at Raonaid, who followed him across the taproom.

Upstairs, the corridor was narrow and dimly lit by a single candle in a wall sconce. The floor slanted sharply to one side, but the roof was sound, which meant they would at least stay dry.

The barmaid slipped a key into the lock and took them

into the spacious room. It had a window overlooking the
stable yard below, and a fireplace opposite a table with
four chairs. A clean blue and white quilt covered the brass
bed. It was big enough for two.

Abigail lit the lamp and soon a warm golden glow
filtered through the room. Lachlan's eyes turned to Raonaid. She, too, glowed like fire with that mass of wet
hair sticking to her gleaming white skin.

"You'd like two meals sent up?" Abigail asked as
she moved to the bed and folded back the covers.

"Aye," he answered gruffly, turning away from the
sight of that soft, welcoming mattress, and moving to
the window. "And a bottle of something. Wine, claret.
Doesn't matter." He needed to numb his passions.

She nodded and left them alone.

Raonaid crossed to the bed and sat down, but Lachlan refused to look at her. He could do nothing, however,
about the sounds she was making. His ears were attuned
to everything—the bed creaking under her weight, her
soft breathing, the rustle of her skirts. With an exhausted sigh, she removed a shoe, dropped it onto the
floor with a careless *thunk,* then removed the other one.

"I was never so happy to see a bed." She flopped
backwards onto it.

He did not share her joy, however, for it had been
ages since he was alone in a bedchamber with a woman.
And with this particular one, who was so bewitching to
him in every way, he wasn't entirely sure he'd be able
to make it through the night without doing what he'd
promised not to do.

* * *

Within minutes, Lachlan had an impressive fire blazing in the hearth. He dragged a chair across the floor for Catherine.

"Come and sit closer," he said. "Dry your clothes."

Pulling another chair forward for himself, he sat down and held his hands out to warm them.

Catherine watched him for a breathless moment, wishing he were not so . . . *wet*. His long hair gleamed strikingly in the amber firelight, and his shirt was clinging to his massive arms and shoulders, his kilt hugging his strong, muscular thighs. Ah, sweet Lord, he was a beautiful thing to behold when he was so shiny, dripping, and drenched.

He leaned back and propped both booted feet up on the opposite chair, which he had pulled forward for her. With a sigh, he crossed those big, sinewy legs at the ankles.

For the life of her, Catherine could not seem to tear her gaze away from the bulky plaid sticking to his lap, and his worn leather sporran, which rested on certain parts of his anatomy she was not meant to think about. It was all very disconcerting, and for the first time she truly wished she could lift that disagreeable curse, for what an absolute waste of manhood it was—for a man like him to be celibate.

Imagine the beautiful children he could sire.

Tipping his head back, he ran his hands over his face and yawned loudly with exhaustion. Or perhaps it was boredom. She wished she knew what he was thinking. She stared at him for a long moment, then finally shook herself out of her stupor.

Gathering her heavy skirts in her fists, she rose from the bed. "When you said to come closer, I hope you meant closer to the fire, and not closer to *you*."

She pushed the toe of his boot with her hand, forcing him to lift his feet off her chair.

"Why? Are you worried you won't be able to resist my deadly charms? Deadlier than ever," he added, "thanks to you."

She sat down. "No, I am not worried, because I do not find you charming at all. Not in the least."

It was a complete lie, of course. Everything about him fascinated her. Even when she was quivering with fear.

Especially then.

"You should be thankful," he said, lounging back comfortably, locking his hands together behind his head and making her wonder if he was some sort of dubious archangel of a man, for he intrigued her so.

"Thankful for what?"

"For that promise I made in the library, when I agreed not to touch you. Otherwise, I'd be removing your gown right now, one piece at a time—*verra* slowly— and you'd be whimpering with ecstasy and delight, begging me to undress you faster, and trying like hell to figure out a way to lift that curse."

She narrowed her eyes at him. "You're that confident?"

"Aye."

She sat forward. "But why would you even *want* to make me whimper with ecstasy? You despise me. Why not just force yourself on me, like you tried to do back at Drumloch?"

The fire danced and snapped in the grate, illuminating the golden clarity of his skin, reflecting the sparks of gold in his eyes. He leaned forward as well, so their faces were very close, almost touching, and her heart began to race with anticipation.

"Would you really like me to answer that?"

He asked the question with a teasing undercurrent of eroticism that sent wild vibrations through her body.

A knock sounded at the door just then, and Catherine sat back quickly. Abigail entered with a tray of food and a bottle of wine.

"Bowls of hot stew with dumplings," she cheerfully said, "and a basket of bread with butter and cheese." She set it all down on the table, then turned her flirty gaze to Lachlan, who observed her overall appearance. The girl was young and attractive, with dark, playful features. She grew instantly covetous while she stood there, caught up in the flattery of his attention.

"Is there anything else I can do for ye, sir?" she asked, sounding a bit light-headed as she admired him from head to foot.

"No, Abigail, that will be all." He rested an elbow on the arm of the chair, his temple on a finger. His mischievous eyes smiled at her.

The maid's lips quivered with excitement. She pointed at his bloodied shirt. "Perhaps I could launder that for ye, sir. If ye wouldn't mind taking it off . . ."

Catherine rolled her eyes, and Lachlan gave her a spiteful look, raising a brow as if to say, *See? See how you hold me back?*

"A fine idea, Abigail," he replied, returning his attention to the young barmaid. "I will place my shirt in your capable hands. Come back after supper, and I'll remove it then."

She uttered a nervous little giggle. "Very well, sir. I'll be back."

She spun around and walked straight into the wall.

"Oh my good gracious. I beg your pardon." She giggled again and rubbed the red mark on her forehead, then skipped out of the room.

Lachlan leaned back languorously in the chair and inclined his head at Catherine. He peered at her with lazy, hooded eyes.

"I'm not going to say one word about that," Catherine sighed. "Except that it turns my stomach to see a perfectly intelligent young woman behave so foolishly."

But in fact, she understood it very well and was thankful for Abigail's well-timed interruption, and the reminder that this man was a shameless rogue in plaid— for Lord knows what she might have said or done next, after he answered her earlier question. She, too, might have stood up and walked into a wall.

Feeling rather flushed all of a sudden, she rose and went to the table to eat. Lachlan remained in front of the fire, but she was intensely aware of his burning gaze while she inhaled the tempting aroma of the spicy, hot stew, and began to smear butter on both sides of her bread.

Chapter Seven

An hour later, Catherine stood at the window, peering out at the darkness beyond. The wind moaned like a ghost through the eaves. Rain pelted the glass like a pebble storm, and water streamed down the panes in shiny, jagged rivulets, like little knives of silver.

The storm showed no signs of letting up, and she could only hope that the squally weather had detained the magistrate at some point in his travels—for she did not wish to return to Drumloch. At least not yet. She wanted to recover her lost memories, and if that meant galloping into the Scottish Highlands with a volatile warrior who detested her, then that was what she would do.

It was unlikely, at any rate, that the magistrate had been able to follow their trail through the woods. The rain would have washed away their tracks, and besides, Lachlan had taken them south, rather than north, which was not what the magistrate would expect. It would take a bit longer to circle around in the direction of Kinloch Castle, Lachlan had told her, but they would reach it eventually.

Letting the curtain fall closed, she turned and faced the bed, just as he was climbing into it. *Naked.*

Her eyes darted to the hearth, where his tartan was draped over a chair, drying in front of the dancing flames. He had given his bloodstained shirt to Abigail a short time ago. He'd walked into the corridor where she was waiting for him and made a great spectacle of leaving the door open, so Catherine could watch while he pulled it off over his head.

Abigail's eyes had gone wide as saucers, and Catherine was ashamed to admit that hers had done the same, when confronted with all those lovely, rippling muscles.

But none of that mattered now, she told herself, pushing the image from her mind. What mattered was how she was going to manage her anxieties through the remainder of this storm, with a naked and powerfully built Highlander lying in the bed she'd assumed was meant for *her.*

He drew the covers up to his waist, let out a lazy sigh, and tossed an arm up under his head.

Catherine noticed the gash across his ribs. It was covered in dried blood, but he seemed oblivious to any discomfort.

"How pleasing it is," he casually purred, "to be warm and dry. Do you not agree, lassie?"

He turned his head on the feather pillow to look up at her directly, waiting for an answer.

Catherine cleared her throat.

"Is there a problem?" He asked the question with a glimmer of satisfaction in his eye, as if he knew *exactly* how he affected her and was amused by it.

A wave of excitement flooded through her treacherous body.

"Yes," she haughtily replied. "There is only one bed, and if you were a gentleman, you would let me have it."

He stared with casual indifference at the ceiling. "First of all, I'm not that sort of gentleman. I am a different sort altogether. And if you think I'll try to seduce you . . ." He paused. "*Ach,* bluidy hell, Raonaid. Just take off your gown, hang it to dry, and get in the bed."

She lifted her chin. "No, I most certainly will *not* get in that bed with you."

He leaned up on an elbow and glared at her, all amusement gone now as his eyebrows pulled together in a frown.

Clearly they were at an impasse.

Catherine glanced at her wet skirts and knew he was right about hanging everything to dry, but there was no way on God's green earth she was going to disrobe in front of him, then join him under the covers. He was naked!

She moved closer to the fire and plopped down into the wooden chair. She would sit there all night if she had to, if he insisted on behaving like a brute.

Savage, indeed.

"What are you waiting for?" he asked, rolling over onto his stomach and resting his chin on a hand.

She glanced over at him.

"You're keeping me awake, lass," he added, "and we both need our rest. We'll be heading into some rugged country in the morning."

He had already explained that Kinloch was nestled

deep in the Scottish Highlands, beyond the Great Glen. It would take at least five days to reach it, perhaps longer if the weather was foul. Once they reached Fort William, the English garrison, there would be few opportunities for hot cooked meals delivered on trays. They would be forced to sleep under the stars and eat around an open fire. She only hoped the rain would hold off after tonight; otherwise, it would be a long and arduous journey, to be sure.

"Ah, come now," he said, his voice teasing again. "Show me how brave you are. Slide in next to me, and see if you can resist any improper urges you might experience." He regarded her with challenge as he lifted the covers.

Catherine lowered her eyes to the braided rug on the floor and wondered how difficult it would be to sleep on such a hard surface. Would he even offer her a blanket or pillow?

Lachlan sat up, and his long, damp hair fell forward across his bare shoulder. "Now you're being ridiculous, lass. I'm only teasing. Think about it. Whether you are in the bed or on the floor makes no difference to me. If I grow tempted to unleash my pent-up desires on you tonight—and I haven't completely ruled that out—I will do it, here or there."

Catherine spoke sternly. "You gave me your word of honor that you would not touch me."

He gazed at her in silence for the longest time, and she could not mistake the quiet, simmering desire in those beautiful onyx eyes. He wanted to do things to her—wicked, unspeakable things. She could see it in the brooding intensity of his stare. He wanted to slake his caged-up lust on her. To pleasure her and punish her, both at the same time.

"Maybe I'll change my mind about that," he said in a low voice of sensual allure. "Because if I made love to you, lass, you'd have no choice but to lift the curse, in order to save yourself."

She shot him a threatening glare. "Go ahead. I *dare* you to do it. But keep in mind, Lachlan MacDonald, there are always choices. Perhaps I'd *let* myself die, just to spite you. Then you'd be cursed forever."

A dark shadow of surprise passed over his features. "That's insane."

She shrugged arrogantly. "Perhaps. But it's not as if I have much to live for. I have no memories, and everyone I know is using me for their own purposes—whether it's to lift a curse or get their hands on a fortune that may or may not belong to me."

She would never do it, of course. She wanted to live. She wanted that more than anything, or she wouldn't be here.

Finally, he rolled onto his back again, rubbed his eyes with the heels of his hands, and groaned irritably. "You *are* mad," he said. "Fine. If you must have your way, I will be a gentleman for the night, and take the floor."

He rose, fully nude, and reached for the folded woolen blanket that was draped over the brass footboard.

Catherine couldn't look at him. He was too attractive, too spellbinding. Instead, she turned her gaze to the fire, where the flames seemed to dance with delight as he moved across the room. When at last she heard the sound of the blanket unfolding and flapping outward to cover him, she carefully looked down.

He was stretched out on his back on the braided rug at her feet.

"Thank you." She stood up and stepped over him. "Now close your eyes and don't look."

"How you torture me so," he said with frosty sarcasm, covering his eyes with a hand while she removed her skirts and bodice and hung everything on the chair. Wearing only her shift, she dashed across the floor on her tiptoes and scrambled into the bed. Quickly she turned down the lamp and drew the covers up to her ears.

Everything was quiet in the room except for the sound of the fire snapping in the grate. She rolled over and faced the wall, and was very aware of Lachlan's movements as he, too, rolled to face the other direction.

Contrary to whatever form of torture Lachlan expected to endure while sleeping naked in a room with Raonaid (he'd had visions of waking up with his wrists tied to the bedposts while she chanted some dark spell), he somehow managed to sleep for an hour or two. When he woke, it was nearly dawn and the rain was no longer beating against the window. The fire had gone out, and the only warmth came from a few red-hot embers, pulsing like quiet heartbeats in the ash.

He rolled to face the bed. Raonaid, too, was curled up on her side, facing him. The sight of her lovely, curvaceous figure in the dim light was enough to affect the tempo of his heart. He felt yet another unwelcome surge of arousal in the pit of his stomach, which fanned the flames of his discontent, because he was sick of the torture. He was a man forced to live alone, without intimacy in any form, for if he ever made love to a woman, he would become a murderer.

As a result, he'd had very few intimate encounters since the night of the curse in Kilmartin Glen. In the early months, a few generous young lassies had been willing to pleasure him with their hands and mouths, but even that had troubled him, and he had not enjoyed the experiences.

He remembered pulling one eager lassie to her feet halfway through a session of oral frivolities, apologizing to her gruffly, then stalking off and concluding the matter with his own hand, outside in the bailey, alone in a dark corner behind a wagon stacked with empty whisky barrels. It had been a low moment.

Now, he yearned not only for sexual release, but for any form of intimacy. It had been a long time since he'd been touched by a woman. There had been no caressing, no kissing. *Nothing*—until his botched seduction in the stone circle the day before, when the floodgates had opened to a raging tidal wave of desire.

All at once, he realized he was breathing heavily while watching the rise and fall of Raonaid's ample bosom beneath the covers. It was a beautiful but dangerous thing to behold, so he turned his gaze to her face instead.

She was as lovely in sleep as at any other time, and there was something surprisingly peaceful about her, which contradicted everything he knew and remembered about her.

Strangely, that made him hate her now more than ever

for locking him up in these shackles, cursed to a life of isolation, forced to avoid the attentions of any woman who so much as smiled at him.

Another part of him, however, wanted to climb into bed with her, roll on top, and settle himself snugly between her soft, luscious thighs. He would kiss her lips, caress her, and, when she was ready, slide into her womanly depths with a profound and satisfying groan of liberation.

Lachlan shut his eyes and tried to think of something else—*anything* would do—but the effort was futile. He would have to get up.

He was about to do so when Raonaid stirred and moaned softly. She inched a little closer to the edge of the bed and wiggled her hips across the mattress. He could smell her perfume, faint in his nostrils after the storm but still present, nonetheless, and it irritated him further, due to the frustration it caused.

His mind reeled with confusion. For three long years he had dreamed of achieving vengeance against this woman. He had loathed her with every inch of his being, even imagined watching her die. He still loathed her now. But despite all that, he had been teasing and flirting, and he wanted overwhelmingly to touch her.

Which told him one thing: the flirting had to stop. It was too dangerous and vexing. He had wanted to punish her, to make her afraid, but as it turned out, he was only punishing himself.

Rising to his feet, he left the pillow and blanket on the floor. For a moment he stood over her broodingly, watching until she rolled onto her back. Then he turned his eyes away, donned his kilt in silence, and quietly left the room.

Catherine's eyes fluttered open, and she sat up quickly. A bright, hazy beam of sunlight was shining in through the window. The blanket Lachlan had used was in a jumbled heap on the floor, and his tartan was no longer hanging before the fire. The room was quiet, and he was gone.

Tossing the covers aside, she rose and crossed to the window, drew the drapes, and looked outside at the storm-ravaged stable yard below. Some of the shingles had blown off the roof, and the muddy ground was littered with leaves and broken branches that had blown down from the trees. A shimmering cloud of mist rolled close to the ground.

Lachlan emerged from the stable just then, walking purposefully back to the inn, and she was relieved to see him. He had mentioned he would secure another horse. Perhaps that was his task just now.

Catherine hurried to don her skirts and bodice. A moment later, he knocked lightly at the door, then entered without waiting for an invitation and barely looked at her as he spoke. "You're up, I see."

His dark hair was tied back with a leather string, and he looked rugged and handsome in the morning light, with his tartan pinned neatly at his shoulder, his sword belt buckled loosely at his hip. His shirt was clean and dry, and at some point he had shaved.

Catherine ran her fingers through her tousled hair, which fell in large bouncy curls to her waist, imagining that she must look a mess.

"I sent for breakfast," he told her, "but you'll have to eat quickly and fill up. We'll head east toward South Lanarkshire today, and won't stop again until we're close to Blackburn."

His tone was brisk and irritable. He would not look her in the eye.

Another knock sounded at the door. He moved quickly to answer it. "Ah, Abby, what a vision you are to behold on this fresh autumn morning." He spoke with effortless charm as the young maid entered the room, carrying a tray.

Her cheeks blushed pink as she set the tray on the table, then glanced dismissively at Catherine. "Are ye sure there's nothing else I can do for ye, sir?" she asked Lachlan. "Anything at all?"

"You're a bonny lass, Abigail. I couldn't have managed without you."

The maid beamed a besotted smile at him as he placed his hand on the small of her back and led her out of the room. He shut the door behind them, leaving Catherine behind to wonder where he was off to now, and for what purpose. Her curiosity got the better of her, and she tiptoed across the room and pressed her ear to the door.

The sounds of quiet conversation and giggles filtered through the oak panel—

Suddenly the door opened, and she jumped back.

"Eavesdropping, were you?" Lachlan asked with complete disinterest, which came as an insult after his flirtations with Abigail just now. "Why aren't you eating? Hurry up. We need to go."

He moved to the tray, picked up a biscuit, and spread butter on it. He stuffed the whole thing into his mouth, then caught her staring at him, and froze. "What's wrong with you this morning?"

"Nothing."

"Don't lie to me. You look irritated."

She moved forward and poured herself a cup of coffee. "Do women always throw themselves at you like that?"

"Aye." He glanced at her crossly. "Not that it does me much good," he added. "It's more frustrating than flattering. I've had to give them a wide berth lately."

"Because you cannot take advantage of the situation, and have your fun with them?"

"Aye. Thanks to you."

She blew on the hot coffee and carefully took a sip. "Well, for the first time I am beginning to see the merit in the curse I placed on you. At least you are learning to restrain yourself, while hundreds of vulnerable, unsuspecting young women are protected from your awe-inspiring appeal."

"*Dangerous* . . . ," he said. "I'm only dangerous because of *you*."

"And you don't think you were dangerous before? Following through on all those opportunities, no doubt breaking countless hearts without a care?"

He picked up another biscuit, slapped a thin slice of ham on it, and shoved it into his mouth. "Now you're starting to sound like your old self. Always wanting to pick a fight. And you look more like yourself, too, with your hair down, all wild and dishevelled. We're making progress, I think. Soon you'll be remembering how to cast spells and hexes, and we can be free of each other at last."

He stalked to the door, flung it open, and spoke to her over his tartan-clad shoulder. "Be downstairs in a quarter of an hour. I'll be waiting for you in the stable. Don't be late."

With that, he shut the door behind him.

He seemed especially angry with her that morning, she thought, but she supposed his anger was far preferable to his desire, for at least he couldn't kill her with it.

Chapter Eight

After gulping down most of the food on the breakfast tray, Catherine used the convenience one last time, then left the inn through the back door. She entered the stable exactly on time.

"Took you long enough," Lachlan said while he tightened the leather cinches under the horse's belly.

"You said a quarter of an hour. I am not late."

"You're not early, either. Come here, lass."

He bent forward and picked up a woolen cloak that was folded neatly on a stool. With a flick of his wrists, he shook it out.

"Where did you get this?" Catherine asked.

"From Abigail. It's not fashionable, she tells me, but her mother was willing to part with it, which was good enough for me."

"She gave this to you? How very kind of her." Catherine wondered what Lachlan had offered them in return. Perhaps he took his shirt off for half a minute and they all fell over with their legs in the air.

"It wasn't charity," he replied. "Her mother made a healthy profit on the sale. Turn around. I'll help you put it on."

He draped it over her shoulders, lifted her long locks of hair out from under, then turned her around and buttoned it under her chin. The wool, though mended in places, was soft and thick, and it boasted a wide hood that would keep her head warm and dry in the coming days.

"Thank you," she said. "That was surprisingly kind of you."

"So now you think I'm *kind*?" He gave her a skeptical frown, then turned back to the horse. "Up you go. His name is Theodore."

Catherine moved forward and mounted the handsome chestnut gelding. The saddle pouches slung across his back were near to bursting with provisions.

"Where did you get the money for all this?" she asked as she gathered up the reins. "You didn't trade my jewels, did you?"

He swung effortlessly up onto Goliath's back. "Nay, I have my own money, lass. I don't need yours."

"Are you wealthy or something?"

He gave her another look of warning that suggested she stop asking questions, then urged his mount onward.

She, too, kicked in her heels, and was pleased at least to have her own horse, so that she wouldn't have to feel Lachlan's big, strapping body rubbing up against hers every minute of the day.

By midmorning, the mist lifted. A fresh autumn breeze was gusting through the forest, bringing out the clean scent of the rain-soaked leaves on the ground.

Lachlan rode a fair distance behind Raonaid, watching those long, bouncy locks of red hair. He wondered with more than a little concern what would happen if she never regained her memories or remembered the person she once was. What would he do about the curse? How would he live? He'd be alone for the rest of his days, for if he ever let himself love a woman, he would be forced to relive the pain of his wife's death.

He simply could not bury another.

All at once, he felt a more urgent need to reach Kinloch as quickly as possible. He needed to know the truth about this woman. Was she playing him for a fool, pretending to be without knowledge of her life as a witch? Or was she truly lost and in need of his help?

Either way, he did not wish to spend any more time alone with her than was absolutely necessary, for she stirred too much chaos in his mind. She reminded him of what he could not have, and it was torture, all of it, especially because she was his enemy. It made no sense that he was attracted to her.

They trotted through a shallow burn, where the horses' hooves splashed through the rushing water.

"We need to move faster," Lachlan said, galloping past Raonaid. "Can you keep up?"

She nodded, and he led them deeper into the forest.

After a grueling day of travel with few breaks to rest and water the horses, Lachlan and Catherine stopped for the night in a quiet glade near a slow-moving river. Lachlan built a fire and warmed the salt pork in a pan while Catherine, exhausted to her core, laid out the bedroll that was tied to his saddlebags.

While the meat sizzled, she divided up the bread and poured them each a cup of wine. She sat down on the bedroll, sipping the wine slowly and rubbing the sore muscles of her thighs. "I am so tired," she said, "I can barely move."

"I'll not hear any complaints from you, lass," he gruffly said. "You wanted to come. You begged me to take you."

"I am *not* complaining," she adamantly replied. "I am merely making conversation. It wouldn't hurt you to try. The way I see it, we are both prisoners here, each of us cursed in our own way, and we have no choice but to be together for the next few days. And I certainly did not accompany you because I imagined it would be good fun. Good Lord! I came because I am desperate to know who I really am."

He sat utterly still, his eyes almost diabolical. "Do not compare your plight to mine, lass. You may not remember your past, but at least you have a future. Once you collect that inheritance, you can do whatever, or *be* whoever, you bloody well please."

She frowned at him. "Are you jesting when you imply that this is less important for me than it is for you? Or do you genuinely not understand how it might feel to have no identity, and no sense of yourself? I have been told a hundred times that I am Catherine Montgomery, and I yearn to believe it. If only I could. But in fact I believe nothing. Not in my heart. Ever since the moment my grandmother collected me at the convent, I have felt as if half of me was still missing. I see a ghost of myself in the looking glass. I have dreams that I am somewhere else, in another place, in another woman's body. I've had doubts about my home—and how am I supposed to feel about the people who claim to be my family? I feel as if they are hiding something from me—hiding the real me. So when you appeared in the stone circle yesterday, I thought my prayers had been answered. *At last*, here was a man who knew the truth!" She was growing fevered with frustration and began to shout. "A man who could prove that my feelings were justified—that I was not, in fact, the person they alleged me to be. That there was more of me, yet to be discovered! But now, sitting here with you, I am beginning to think that you don't know me at all, either, and that you, too, are mistaken. For I am certain that I cannot be a soulless witch."

Lachlan regarded her in concerned silence from under a deeply furrowed brow. Then without a word, he served up the pork and handed her the pewter plate.

She wondered uneasily if she had just confirmed everyone's fears that she was a raving lunatic, who would be better off at an asylum. Had she really just told him that she saw ghosts of herself? She wouldn't be surprised if he decided to abandon her right now and take his chances with the curse.

"It's been a long day," he said, watching her carefully while she poked at her supper. "You're exhausted, lass."

"I most certainly am."

Reaching for the jug of wine, he rose to his feet, circled around the fire, and refilled her glass. "Are you cold?"

She shook her head, but shivered. He went to fetch a blanket from one of the saddlebags and wrapped it securely around her shoulders.

"You'll have to prepare yourself for tomorrow," he told her, sitting down on the opposite side of the fire and reaching for his plate. "It won't get any easier. We'll ride around the Gargunnock Hills in the morning, stop for supplies in Kippen, and maybe get a hot meal, but once we reach the Great Glen, we'll be sleeping and eating under the stars. Will you be able to manage?"

She looked down at the bedroll, then across at him in the firelight, taking some comfort in the fact that he was, to some extent, concerned for her well-being.

"I suppose if I have come this far," she heartily replied, "I can survive the rest, for the sake of recovering my memories. It hardly matters anyway, where I rest my head. My joints are groaning with agony; my eyes feel like they are full of sand. Even if there were cannons going off over my head, I'm quite sure I would sleep like a baby."

"Good." He stared at her for a moment, then dug into his supper. They spoke no more after that.

Later, after washing the dishes in the creek, Catherine returned to the fire and lay down on her side. The last thing she remembered as she drew the blanket over her shoulders was the sight of Lachlan on the other side of the fire, lounging back on an elbow, sipping a cup of wine, watching her through the iridescent flames with those smoldering dark eyes, before her own weary lids fluttered closed.

Sometime during the night, Catherine tore the blanket off and scrambled to her feet. *"Get off me!"* she shrieked, slapping at her cheeks and arms, spitting out the dirt she could still taste on her tongue.

She was aware of the campfire and the trees, and part of her knew that she was somewhere in Scotland, traveling with Lachlan MacDonald, the Highlander who had attacked her in an ancient stone circle—and that she'd had a dream. But the effect upon her mind was so vivid and disturbing, she could not yet escape it. Her heart was racing with terror. She felt as if she were suffocating. She couldn't get the dirt off her sleeves!

Suddenly Lachlan was there, holding her steady by the arms. "You're dreaming, Raonaid. Wake up. Look at me!" The deep timbre of his voice compelled her to focus on his eyes, darkly luminous in the night.

It took a moment for her to accept that there was no dirt on her. Still feeling panicked, she held on to him, her hands curled tightly around his forearms.

"Are you all right?" he asked when he seemed certain that she was fully awake.

"I dreamed someone was trying to bury me," she said, "as if I were dead. I was lying in a grave, and dirt was being shoveled onto my face. It felt very real."

"It wasn't," he said. "No one was trying to bury you."

"Am I going mad? I fear that I am. The nuns in the convent thought I was haunted by the devil. If my grandmother hadn't come to claim me when she did, they might have sent me away, to someplace terrible." Her body began to tremble.

Lachlan regarded her with concern in the moonlight. He was completely drawn in.

Was this a trick? he wondered, working hard to shake himself out of the spell. Was she making it up in order to convince him that she was truly in need of help?

It had occurred to him more than once that she

might simply be seeking another chance to return to Kinloch and destroy his cousin's marriage. She had been obsessed with Angus before, to a murderous degree. Perhaps she was out to finally seize everything she wanted—a dead heiress's fortune and the powerful Chief of Kinloch as well.

A tear spilled from the corner of her eye, rushed down her soft, pale cheek, and all thoughts of theft and treachery tumbled from Lachlan's mind.

"There's no need to cry," he heard himself saying as all his protective instincts came surging to the fore. "You're going to be fine. I promise."

"I'm *not* crying," she insisted, lifting her chin, but she looked so frightened, he couldn't bring himself to abandon her just yet.

He gently wiped the tear away from her cheek and looked into her eyes. *It would just be for this one night,* he told himself. He would give her the benefit of the doubt until she went back to sleep.

She placed a shaky hand on his chest, on top of his shirt, and he allowed her that liberty, covering it with his own to keep it warm. When at last the fear in her eyes began to subside, he led her back to the fire.

"Lie down now," he said. "You need to rest."

Catherine obeyed Lachlan's quiet command, for she couldn't seem to think clearly enough on her own. Dropping to her knees, she arranged her skirts, then curled up on her side and faced the fire. Lachlan covered her with the blanket.

"Do you think it was a memory?" she asked. "It felt very real."

"Dreams often do."

To her surprise, he knelt down and curled up behind her. He tucked the blanket in all around her and laid his heavy arm across her hip.

"You'll be all right now." His voice was unexpectedly soothing.

"After I was missing for two years," she confessed, "I was presumed dead. My family gave up the search. Perhaps that's why I dreamed such an awful thing."

She felt his warm breath against her hair at the back of her head. Soon her fears began to diminish, and she closed her eyes, taking comfort in his warmth—and his surprising, unexpected tenderness as he brushed the hair away from her forehead and stroked a light finger back and forth across her brow.

"You seem very different now," she whispered, looking over her shoulder at him, as confusion welled up inside her.

"Don't get used to it," he softly replied. "We are still enemies, Raonaid."

Yet he snuggled closer, tucking his hips tight up against her bottom, while holding her securely in his arms. She could feel the beat of his heart against her back and realized he was breathing very fast. So was she. Butterflies fluttered in her belly.

For a long moment he did not move, and it seemed as if the whole world went quiet and still. Then he nuzzled her hair and lifted his head. He paused a moment and slid away from her. "This isn't wise," he said.

"Why not?"

"You know why, lass."

She felt all the warmth and blissful serenity pull

away from her as he stood and returned to his own bedroll. Again he watched her from afar with those sweltering dark eyes, until at last she drifted back into a dark and dreamless sleep.

Chapter Nine

Drumloch Manor

John Montgomery galloped down the drive to the groomed path at the lake, where Aunt Eleanor always took her morning stroll. Rain or shine, she packed her two silly lapdogs into the coach, drove to the bridge, where she was let out with her walking stick, and circled once around the lake.

This morning there was a crisp autumn chill in the air, and John sniffled before he trotted up beside his aunt. The dogs yapped and barked at him, and his horse reared up and nearly threw him.

"Quiet, you rascals!" the dowager commanded, pointing her stick at them. "Or I'll boil you both for dinner."

The dogs continued to growl at John and his skittish mount, but anything was better than their incessant yapping.

"Have you come with news?" the dowager asked, shading her eyes to squint up at him.

He dismounted and walked beside her. "Nothing yet. Not a single word from anyone."

They had sent a few of their own men in various directions to search for Catherine, and the magistrate had his people searching as well—those who had survived the Highlander's escape.

"I am confused, John. How could our girl go missing *twice*? You don't suppose this Highlander is the same one who abducted her before? Perhaps it is a scheme to hold her for ransom, now that the inheritance is finally within reach. But no one ever asked for money the last time."

"It's impossible to say," John replied, "for we haven't the slightest idea what happened five years ago, or how she ended up in Italy. You have your theories, of course."

"That she simply ran off, for some kind of wild adventure?"

He removed a handkerchief from his jacket pocket and dabbed the perspiration on his brow. "Yes, but that does not explain her memory loss. Nothing seems to explain it, other than a spell of madness."

"But we mustn't ever say such a thing to others. It's enough of a scandal without adding talk of lunacy. If she is declared mentally unfit . . ."

"The inheritance will be lost."

The dowager tapped her walking stick lightly along the gravel path. "Are you paying Dr. Williams well enough?"

"Aye. More than enough, and he knows it."

"That, at least, is helpful."

The horse nickered and tossed his head behind them, and they walked on in silence. John watched the two dogs scamper ahead of them, then turned his gaze to his aunt. She had a stern face, lined with years of bitterness and hostility. As a child he had always found her intimidating, and he continued to feel that way now, even though he was earl.

He stopped on the path. "Aunt Eleanor, I must be frank."

She stopped and turned, and the dogs circled back to wait at her side.

"You know how I feel about Catherine," he said. "I want nothing more than to bring her home, safe and unharmed, but I cannot accomplish that if I do not know the whole story. For that reason, it must be said . . . I sense there is something you are not telling me."

His aunt regarded him with chilly disdain. Her lips curled into a thin, hard line, and the dogs began to bark and snarl. She lifted her walking stick and jabbed him with it, hard in the chest, so that he was forced to take a step back.

"There is *nothing*," she said harshly, "that you need to know. Leave me be now. I must walk."

With that she stalked off, and the dogs growled at him viciously before turning to follow her, tails wagging in the morning sun.

John mounted his horse. The corner of his mouth twisted in annoyance. Catherine was out there somewhere, most likely in the clutches of a brutal Highlander with dangerous intentions. John had seen what the dirty savage tried to do to her in the stone circle, and he'd heard the particulars of the Highlander's violent escape from the prison coach.

Meanwhile Catherine's inheritance was at risk as well. If anything happened to her, the funds would be sent to Edinburgh, forfeited to the Jacobite cause.

That John could not allow.

As he galloped off in the other direction toward the manor house, he wondered if it was possible to physically shake the truth out of his wretched old aunt. Someone needed to stand up to her for once. And those exasperating little dogs, too.

Chapter Ten

On the night that followed Raonaid's strange awakening from the dream, Lachlan could not sleep.

Throughout the day, he had watched her with silent, broody fascination, becoming less consumed by his physical desire for her and more curious about her peculiar state of mind. She had mentioned on more than one occasion that she felt as if she were going mad, and had even referred to herself as a lunatic.

He'd always known Raonaid to be deranged and lacking in what he would call a *normal* human conscience, but somehow the woman before him—wrapped in a heavy blanket and sleeping in the grass—no longer fit that description.

After two full days of riding with her, he no longer felt that she was the embodiment of pure evil. He felt quite the opposite, in fact, and far less certain that she was lying to him about her memory loss. All he wanted to do now, as he sat awake by the fire and watched over her while she slept, was *help* her, and it confused the hell out of him.

How could he possibly feel this way about Raonaid, the oracle, after loathing her for years, hunting her down with an obsession that bordered on madness, and giving up everything—*everything*—to achieve some sort of vengeance against her?

Suddenly she stirred and whimpered softly in the night. The sound of her voice was velvety and erotic.

Lachlan sat forward, resting an elbow on a knee, watching as she rolled gracefully onto her back.

A light breeze whispered through the grasses and fluttered the bottom of her blanket. He felt a shiver of need rush through him, though he didn't want to bed her. Not exactly. He just wanted to lie with her and hold her as he had the night before. To feel her soft, lush body against his own, to smell her hair. To experience the intimacy and closeness. It all seemed like a dream to him now. He had not known anything like it in such a long time.

Raonaid lay very still and quiet in the dark chill of the night; then suddenly, without warning, she sat up—her back straight as a spear.

Lachlan did not speak. He remained utterly still, though his heart began to pound like a wild thing in his chest.

Tossing the blanket aside, she rose to her feet, gathered her skirts in her fists, and started walking away from the camp.

"Wait!" he quickly said, shaking himself out of his stupor and rising to follow. "Where are you off to? It's dark, lass. You'll get lost."

Ignoring the warning, she trudged with purpose through the damp, tangled grass, straight ahead, as if she knew exactly where she was going.

Lachlan hurried to catch up. He walked briskly beside her. "Raonaid . . ."

She continued to ignore him.

"Are you dreaming?" He studied her profile in the bluish light from the moon. "You need to wake up. You're walking in your sleep."

He hurried a few steps ahead of her, then turned to walk backwards in front, keeping a steady pace.

Though her eyes were open, she did not see him. There was a strange barrenness in those bottomless pupils. It was as if she were not even present in her body. He waved a hand in front of her face. She showed no awareness of him.

Curious as to where they were heading, he followed until she began to run. He stopped for a moment and spotted the striking silhouette of a single standing stone at the crest of a hill, with the full moon behind it.

Raonaid ran faster, as if drawn to it by some invisible force. When she reached it, she fell to her knees and sat back on her heels.

Lachlan was out of breath when he caught up. He bent forward and rested his hands on his knees, watching her. He glanced at the stone, then sat down in the grass beside it.

Raonaid stared blankly at the standing stone for a full hour. Soon it became increasingly difficult for Lachlan to keep his eyes open. He wanted to sleep, his lids felt heavy, but he could not rest. Not yet.

At last, she reached out and touched the rough gray ridges of the rock, running her fingertips lightly across the surface, picking at the grooves with her thumbnail.

Sitting forward, Lachlan studied her vacant eyes more closely, then turned to the stone. Was she trying to spell a word?

She began to slap her open palm against it, as if it were a locked door and she needed to escape through it, but no one would come and open it. She smacked it hard with all her might, over and over, then sat back on her heels again and stared at it, frozen in silence like a statue, for another hour.

Lachlan did not wake her.

When the first light of dawn brightened the sky, she gathered her skirts and stood up, then made her way back to the camp. Without uttering a word, he walked beside her and stood over her as she climbed back into her bedroll and calmly went back to sleep.

Catherine woke to the smell of salt pork sizzling in a frying pan.

Groggily she sat up, and within seconds became aware of a terrible stinging sensation on the palm of her hand. She held it up in front of her face and frowned when she noticed that it was chafed and red. "Did I burn myself?"

Lachlan set the frying pan down on a rock. Without answering right away, he picked up the coffeepot and poured her a cup, walked around the fire, and handed it to her.

"Why are you looking at me like that?" she asked, squinting up at him in the bright morning sunshine. She tossed the blanket aside and accepted the hot coffee, careful not to wrap her sore hand around it. "Now you're scaring me."

"Well, you deserve it, lass. You gave me a bit of a scare last night."

"How?"

He returned to the other side of the fire, but remained standing. "Do you not remember anything?"

She looked down at the coffee and searched her memory, which was usually a futile exercise. This morning, unfortunately, was no different.

"No," she replied, "but I hope you will be able to tell me something. I cannot cope with any more mysteries about my actions or whereabouts."

He poured a cup of coffee for himself. "You walked in your sleep. I couldn't wake you, so I just followed you."

A slow surge of apprehension made its way through all her nerve endings. "What did I do?"

"You walked to a standing stone on that hill"—he pointed—"and sat in front of it, staring at it for most of the night. You scratched at it with your fingers and smacked it with your whole hand, which is why you're sore this morning."

She stared up at him in disbelief. "That is very disturbing." Her stomach began to roll with nausea. "To think that I was out there, wandering around in the dark, pounding on a stone . . ."

He grimly shook his head. "You weren't just wandering. You knew exactly where you were going. You were drawn to that stone."

Catherine frowned. "But how? Why?"

He looked at her squarely. "I cannot answer that. It's not something I ever understood, but I can tell you this: Raonaid always had her most powerful visions at the stone circle at Callanais. Angus said she was drawn to it, and he would follow her there. That's where she saw his triumph at Kinloch, and sure enough, he later reclaimed his castle from the enemy invaders who took it from his clan."

"What are you saying? That I was having some sort of vision? But I don't remember anything. I didn't see the future. . . ."

"Nay, I don't think you did," he agreed. "It's why you were pounding on it. You seemed frustrated."

Catherine stared at him mutely. "So this is proof . . . that I really am her."

She should have felt some relief to know the truth at last, but all she could feel was a wretched loneliness and a terrible grief, as if someone had died.

"You look disappointed," Lachlan said.

"I suppose I am. Perhaps I have been holding on to some sliver of hope that I was not that vengeful person who put curses on people, and that my family truly was my family, and they were not using me for their own unscrupulous gain." She looked across him. "I didn't want to be her," she admitted. "I wanted to be Catherine."

There was a spark of some indefinable emotion in Lachlan's eyes as he regarded her in the morning light. "I'm sorry."

Catherine lowered her gaze and finished her coffee.

"What will happen when we meet Angus?" she asked. "He will identify me, that is certain now, but will he ever forgive me for all the things I did to him?"

"I cannot answer that, either."

"Maybe we should turn around," she said, looking

up hastily. "I'm not sure it's in my best interest to go there."

Lachlan drained his coffee cup and shook the last few drops into the fire. When he spoke, there was a resurgence of hostility in his voice, and his eyes clouded over with something almost threatening. "You'll not change your mind now, Raonaid. You gave me your word, and you must get your memories back."

"So that I can lift the curse."

"Aye."

Of course, that was why he had come to Drumloch in the first place. It was why he had taken her with him. He wasn't here to *rescue* her. Like the Montgomerys, he wanted something from her.

Either way, she still needed her memories back, and for some reason she could not explain, she was certain she would find them at Kinloch. Or at least find something . . .

"I cannot deny that you have helped me," she confessed, remembering also the promise that she had made. "You've solved one mystery at least. I now know that I must be the oracle. So I suppose I owe you this in return: I will do my best to find a way to lift the curse."

There was a tingling in the pit of her stomach while his steady gaze bored into her with scorching, impatient resolve.

"Pack up," he said. "It's time to leave."

Chapter Eleven

If Catherine thought the first two days of their journey into the Highlands were an impossible trial of physical endurance on horseback, the days following proved to be a cruel test of human fortitude, deserving of a shiny gold medal.

They woke early each morning, ate quickly, packed up the saddlebags, and rode into parts unknown with a relentless fury, as if the devil himself were hunting them down with his pointy pitchfork and burning flames of wrath.

The horses could not keep up a constant frenzied pace, so they spent much of the time plodding through forests and glens, galloping sporadically, stopping often to eat and drink. In the end, all the hours of the journey seemed to merge together into a single, endless dash toward the absolute outer edges of the world.

On the fifth day, as they trotted through a lush green glen with a river snaking through the center, Catherine looked up at the cloudy sky and tried to shift in the saddle to sit more comfortably, but her legs were as stiff as logs. Her skin felt grubby, and when she looked down at herself she realized that her fine silk and velvet gown had lost all its richness and shimmer beneath a nasty film of grime. She might as well be wearing a homespun rag.

And her lustrous red hair felt like a dirty haystack hanging down her back.

As they crossed the river, the horses fought the current in an onerous struggle to reach the other side. Catherine's skirts floated on the surface. The icy water reached up to her knees—and she began to wonder if her memories were worth all this effort and turmoil.

Quite a distance ahead of her now, Lachlan climbed the steep side of a ridge, reached the crest, and reined in his spirited mount. The wind gusted through Lachlan's thick dark hair, and the circular shield at his back bounced upon his broad shoulder blades. His tartan fluttered wildly in the breeze.

He was her only anchor in this storm, she supposed, as she kicked in her heels to join him at the top. He was the only thing keeping her from drifting away into that strange, mysterious dreamworld of stones and spirits.

A moment later, she caught up with him and took in the vast panorama before them—a vista of Highland hills and forests, lakes and streams.

"There it is," he said, pointing to the distant foothills, their peaks shrouded in a heavy mist that shifted and rolled across the landscape. "Kinloch is there. Do you see it?"

Catherine squinted and picked out an impressive stone bastion of massive proportions, with four corner towers and battlements all around. To the east there was a village with a market square. All of it was difficult to make out, however, on account of the mist.

"I do." Sitting back in the saddle, she experienced a tremor of apprehension. They had come a long way, and she was about to meet the man who might know all the answers to her past.

Her former lover. A man she had betrayed.

"How long a ride?" she asked, her own horse lathered and winded.

"We'll be there in time for supper if we keep up this pace. Are you able to continue?"

She patted Theodore's neck and nodded gamely, though she could barely comprehend the notion of what might transpire when they rode through the castle gates. How would she feel when, God willing, she finally remembered all the details of her life as a witch?

Lachlan said the oracle had been jealous and spiteful. Surely the Lion's wife would not welcome her. The woman might want to scratch Catherine's eyes out.

"Will the Mistress of Kinloch allow me to enter?" she asked. "You said I called her a manipulative slut. Did I say that to her . . . directly?"

"Aye, you did," Lachlan said with a wry chuckle, "just before you shoved her out of your guest chamber and slammed the door in her face."

Catherine gazed across the distance at the mist-shrouded castle. "Good gracious, what was I thinking? She was my hostess."

His smile faded, and he frowned. "I am beginning to think I kidnapped the wrong woman."

"First of all," she said with a defiant toss of her head, "you did *not* kidnap me. If anything, I commandeered *you*. But why would you say such a thing? I must know."

"Because Raonaid would never care about such rules of etiquette."

She regarded him warily.

He clicked his tongue and walked his horse down the other side of the ridge.

Catherine watched him for a moment, then followed carefully, wondering again with despair if she should ever have embarked upon this grueling journey. Perhaps it had been a terrible mistake. From everything Lachlan had told her, the oracle was not the least bit likable.

It was a disturbing thought indeed, to realize you could not possibly like yourself. It was equally disturbing to feel utterly disconnected from your own soul.

Horns blared from the tower battlements the instant Lachlan walked his horse out of the forest. He was not surprised to hear them. He knew the protocol. He had written most of it himself three years ago, after he and Angus stormed these gates with an army of MacDonald warriors and reclaimed the castle from an enemy clan.

In the months following, Lachlan had devoted his life to the defense of these walls, in anticipation of a retaliatory attack. Then the worst occurred. Their enemies found a way back in—no thanks to Raonaid.

Angus the Lion had triumphed in the end, and Lachlan had celebrated at his side. But that was a long time ago. Everything had changed since the curse. Lachlan had not fulfilled his duties as Laird of War. He had abandoned his cousin and his post in search of the oracle, and at the present moment, he was not entirely sure he would not be shot upon arrival.

Raonaid trotted up beside him. "The horns are intimidating, I must say. How soon before they recognize us?"

He darted an uneasy gaze from one corner tower to the other and took note of a panicked sentry dashing back and forth, calling out orders. "I think they already have, lass, and it might be a problem. You're at the top of their list of mortal enemies. At least you were when I left here a year ago."

"Wonderful," she said. "They're not going to shoot me, are they?"

"I sure-as-Jesus hope not. You'll not be much good to me six feet under."

As they crossed the damp field and approached the bridge, the iron portcullis began to lift. The sound of the pulley and chains rattling through the wheel relieved some of Lachlan's trepidation, for someone had at least given the order to permit them to enter.

What would transpire on the other side of the gate, however, he did not yet know, for he had not spoken to Angus in over a year. They had not parted on good terms.

The wide oaken doors swung open for them, and they passed under the shaded arched gateway to the open square bailey beyond.

There was a frenzy of activity—grooms rushing up to them, servant women stopping to stare and gossip. Three armed guards dashed forward and aimed muskets at them. The sound of the hammers cocking made Lachlan's blood run cold, for he was an enemy of Kinloch now.

Dropping the reins, he slowly raised his hands into the air.

"Put your hands up," he said to Raonaid.

"But I thought this was your home," she replied as she obeyed his grave command, "and that Angus was your cousin. Is this how he treats family?"

"I *used* to live here," Lachlan clarified. "And aye, Angus is my cousin, but the last time we saw each other I nearly killed him in a sword fight."

She shot a look at Lachlan. "And you neglected to tell me this?"

"I forgot."

"How could you forget about almost killing your chief?"

He glanced over his shoulder at her. "I was drunk at the time. And you're a fine one to point fingers, lass. You can't even remember your own name."

"Lachlan MacDonald, is that you?"

Catherine's eyes lifted at the sound of a woman's voice, deep and confident, echoing across the bailey from the battlements above.

"Aye, my lady!" he called out with his hands still in the air. "Will you be so kind as to call off your guards? I come ready to eat humble pie—if you'll let me live long enough to reach the feasting hall!"

Catherine observed the woman on the rooftop above. She was dressed in a simple blue-and-white-striped skirt with pale yellow stays laced over a loose white shift. Her wavy jet-black hair was swept up at the sides, but fell down her back in loose, flowing locks. She was beautiful and charismatic—the Lioness of Kinloch, no doubt. Their hostess. The one Raonaid had once called a slut.

Gwendolen MacDonald waved a hand at the guards, and they lowered their weapons. Catherine exhaled with relief.

Lachlan leaned forward on the pommel and spoke casually to the young clansman standing in front of his horse. "It's good to see you, Andrew. You've grown a beard, I see. Looks good on you."

"Do you really think so, sir?" Andrew replied, stroking his bearded chin. "The wife says it makes me look like her father, and she doesn't like it much."

Lachlan chuckled and leaned even closer, over the horse's mane. "Then you ought to shave it off. You must keep your priorities straight, lad, and a wife's pleasure should be at the top of your list, always."

The young clansman smiled. "I always imagined you would say that, and if there's any Highlander a man should listen to when it comes to a lassie's pleasures, it's got to be you, sir."

The other guards murmured in agreement as they lowered their weapons to their sides.

Lachlan leaned back. "Well, it's too bad I cannot practice what I preach."

An uncomfortable silence ensued while the others glared up at Catherine with looks of bitter malice. She was tempted to explain herself and say that the curse wasn't really her fault, but decided it would be best not to enter into a debate about a life she could not remember.

Gwendolen, the Mistress of Kinloch, emerged from

the tower staircase. She crossed the bailey toward them.

Lachlan dismounted and walked to meet her. They embraced with affection while Catherine waited uneasily on her horse.

Despite the earlier orders, one of the guards raised his musket again and aimed it at her head, as if he expected her to try to murder his chief's wife in the next few seconds.

Clearly Catherine was not going to be forgiven quite so easily as Lachlan.

"I wasn't sure we would ever see you again," Gwendolen said as she withdrew from the embrace. She looked up at his face, and her eyes pooled with tears. "I've missed you, and you know I never blamed you for what happened. It was an accident. We all survived it."

Catherine assumed she was referring to the sword fight.

"Thank God for that," Lachlan said. "But what of Angus? You are by nature a forgiving creature, Gwendolen, but the Lion's emotions are often forged of steel. Has *he* forgiven me?"

She inclined her head apologetically. "I think you should speak to him about that, not me. He's in the village, but I suspect he heard the horns, and will be back at any moment." She squeezed Lachlan's arm. "But I will say this at least—what stands between you is not the fact that you nearly killed him in a contest of skills. It is the fact that you left without a word, and we have not heard from you in over a year."

Lachlan was quiet for a long moment. "I have much

to apologize for." He looked up at the sentries on the rooftop. "Has he replaced me with another?"

"Another Laird of War?" she blurted out. "Good heavens, no. There was never anyone he trusted enough, or respected more than you. He is his own laird when it comes to the defense of these walls."

"At least it has been a time of peace," Lachlan mentioned, "more or less, since I left."

Gwendolen shook her head. "I'm afraid not. There have been some developments lately. Speaking of which . . ."

Gwendolen's piercing brown eyes lifted to lock on Catherine's, whose skin prickled with unease. She felt trapped in the woman's inquisitive stare.

Angus the Lion might be away from the castle at present, but clearly his wife was more than competent to assume command.

"I see you brought someone with you," she said. "Is she here as a friend, Lachlan, or as your prisoner?"

Lachlan gazed up at Catherine as well. She felt like a squirming insect in a glass case.

"I wouldn't exactly call her my prisoner," he replied, "for she came with me willingly. But she's not my friend, either."

Catherine's stomach knotted at the unexpected venom in his tone. When they entered the bailey, she had felt secure in the knowledge that he was her escort and protector, but the look in his eye now crushed that sense of security.

But it was more than just that. Over the past five days, they had become partners in this journey. He had been surprisingly kind to her at times, especially after the nightmares and sleepwalking. But now suddenly he was regarding her with derision, and everything seemed different. She was no longer the lost Drumloch heiress. She was the spiteful witch, Raonaid—and she felt a deep ache in her chest at the notion that she must take on this dark identity.

"I should think not," Gwendolen said. "Otherwise I would be inclined to suspect that she put another spell on you."

The Lion's wife strolled closer to Catherine's horse. She stroked Theodore's nose while keeping her shrewd brown eyes fixed on Catherine's.

"I have allowed you to pass through these gates," Gwendolen said, "only because you are with *this* man, and he means a great deal to me. But know this, Raonaid: if you say or do one thing that displeases me, you will soon find yourself banished beyond these walls. Do you understand me?"

Catherine bristled at the chill in the woman's tone, but spoke with an equal measure of authority. "Mistress MacDonald, I understand you have reason to mistrust me, but I request an opportunity to explain myself, if you will be so kind as to hear my plea."

"Explain yourself?" Gwendolen scoffed. "Three years ago, you tried to steal my husband by luring him to your bed, then you colluded with his enemy and tried to have him killed. Nothing you say or do will ever change how I feel about you, Raonaid. Nor will it earn my trust. *Ever.*"

Catherine squared her shoulders. "Regardless, I

wish to explain myself. Whether you believe me or decide to pitch me over the castle walls is entirely up to you."

While Gwendolen stroked Theodore's forelock she looked up at Catherine for a tense moment.

Gwendolen turned to address Lachlan. "What do *you* say, Lachlan? Is it worth my time to hear the tale she wishes to spin?"

He strode closer. "I believe so, Gwendolen, but whether you believe her or not will depend on how open-minded you are."

Gwendolen backed away from Theodore and signaled to a groom to approach. "You both look weary," she said to Lachlan. "How long has it been since you've eaten?"

"If it's a kitchen-cooked meal you're speaking of," Lachlan replied, "it's been too long. We've been eating out of our packs for five days."

"Then come with me, the both of you. I'll take you to the day parlor and have something sent up straightaway, while rooms are prepared."

Catherine dismounted, and the groom led Theodore to the stable.

Gwendolen looked her up and down from head to foot, taking note of her soiled hemline and tattered bodice. "Is that all you have to wear?"

"Yes," Catherine replied. "I apologize for my appearance, madam. I realize it's hardly an appropriate traveling costume, but we left Drumloch Manor in such a hurry, shortly after dinner. There wasn't time to change, or even pack a brush."

Gwendolen regarded Lachlan with bewilderment. "Drumloch Manor?"

"It's a long story," he said, "and a strange one. Can we eat first?"

She glanced back and forth between the two of them, then nodded and led them to the Great Hall.

Chapter Twelve

After enjoying a hearty plate of boiled vegetables and roast mutton, drowning in a thick, spicy gravy, along with a large goblet of wine and fresh warm bread, Lachlan was summoned to the solar to speak to Angus, who had come galloping into the bailey a short time after he and Raonaid arrived.

Lachlan had not seen his cousin in over a year, and the last time they spoke, Angus was down on one knee, bleeding from the stomach and accusing Lachlan of being a miserable drunkard who couldn't hold a sword.

Angus was right. Lachlan had been stewed to the gills that morning, and most other days, too. The second year of the curse had been the worst. It sent him into a downward spiral of bitterness and rage. He had seen no way out of it, other than to leave Kinloch and hunt down his enemy. The person who had cursed him to a future that would continually repeat the past—for if he ever loved a woman, he would be forced to listen to her screams on the birthing bed, as he had with Glenna, and when he buried her, he would know that he had killed her. Her death would be his fault.

And so Lachlan had left his post as Kinloch's Laird

of War and gone off in pursuit of the witch who had cursed him to this particular dimension of hell, reliving his wife's death every time he so much as smiled at a woman.

He reached the solar and stood outside the door in the vaulted stone passageway, wondering if his cousin would ever forgive him. Angus had almost died from his wounds that fateful morning. Lachlan had waited only long enough to learn that Angus would survive; then he'd walked out of his chamber, saddled a horse, and simply galloped away.

He paused a moment under the archway, then breathed deeply and entered the room.

The great Lion of Kinloch was seated on a stool, his elbows on his knees, his hands clasped together, his head bowed down. When he heard Lachlan enter, he looked up. Lachlan froze on the spot.

Very little about his cousin had changed. He still had the same thick, tawny mane of hair; his pale blue eyes were as icy and forbidding as ever. Apparently, even the joys of fatherhood had not softened the steel in his eyes. It was part of who he was, Lachlan supposed, and his lioness would never try to change him. It was part of his allure, as far as she was concerned. She had always admired his ferocity.

"I didn't believe it when they said it was you," Angus said, rising to his full, towering height. "I heard the horns blaring from the village and thought we were under attack. Maybe we are, for all I know. They say you brought Raonaid and that she is here now, in my home, eating my food, drinking my wine. I am half-tempted to call for my guards and lock you up as a traitor."

"I do not deny it," Lachlan replied. "I have brought her here, but not to cause trouble. She is here to lift the curse."

A dark shadow of condemnation passed across Angus's golden features. "She convinced you that the only way to lift it was for you to bring her *here*? And you believed her? She is a cunning witch who conspired to have me hanged, Lachlan. What were you thinking?"

Lachlan strode forward. "That's not how it was. I practically had to kidnap her to get her here, and you have not given me a chance to explain."

Angus made a visible effort to calm himself by resting his hand on the hilt of his sword and crossing to the other side of the solar. "Go ahead then. Explain."

Lachlan worked to gather his thoughts, to put them together into some form that made sense.

"You have not yet seen her," he said, "but I am almost certain that the woman who rode through the gates with me today is Raonaid."

Angus faced him with a grimace. "*Almost* certain? What are you telling me? That she denies being the oracle? That she claims to be someone else?"

"I know it sounds ridiculous, but aye, she has been deemed the lost Drumloch heiress. Do you know of whom I speak?"

"Of course I know," Angus replied, striding forward. "Before she went missing she was to become one of the wealthiest women in Scotland. Her father was a great war hero. He died at Sherrifmuir."

"Aye, that's correct, and she has been missing for five years. But last spring, she finally reappeared in a farmer's stable in Italy, and was taken to a convent, where it was discovered that she had no memory of her former life. Her grandmother, the dowager countess, insisted that she was Catherine Montgomery, and I heard tales of her discovery. From the descriptions and rumors about her being an imposter, I had to see for myself that she was in fact the true heiress."

Angus moved closer, both curious and suspicious. "You believed that she was Raonaid, masquerading as Catherine Montgomery, in order to steal the inheritance?"

Angus had always been swift to put two and two together. "That's right. At first, I believed it was a clever ruse. If anyone could pull off such a deception, it would be Raonaid. But after spending time with her since leaving Drumloch Manor, I've had my doubts. Now I don't know what to believe. She's had visions, you see. I witnessed one myself. But she is not the venomous, conniving creature I remember, and I think she may be telling the truth about having lost all memory of her former life. Which is part of my problem, for she does not remember anything about the curse."

Angus began to pace back and forth across the brightly lit room. Then he paused and regarded Lachlan with curiosity. "Gwendolen said you thought Scotland was at peace."

Lachlan shifted uneasily. He was Angus's former Laird of War and had always kept abreast of political developments, but over the past year he had become so absorbed in his own personal affairs, he had ignored the rest of the world and its politics.

"Are we *not* at peace?" he asked, feeling rather ridiculous to be so completely uninformed.

Angus went to the sideboard and poured two glasses of whisky. "There have been rumors of another rebellion, which is why your story seems like a bit of a lark."

"What sort of rumors? And what do they have to do with my situation?" Lachlan accepted the glass his cousin held out.

"According to my spies, and confirmed by my friend Duncan MacLean, there is another Jacobite uprising in the works. Plans have been afoot all summer long."

"Who is behind it?" Lachlan asked, feeling a surge of annoyance, for his countrymen had fought too many deadly battles, all to restore the Stuart King to the throne of England. Too much blood had been spilled. He was sick of it, and like Angus, he wanted peace.

"My mortal enemy and brother-in-law," Angus replied, "Murdoch MacEwen—with his lover at his side." Angus swallowed his whisky in a single gulp, then bared his teeth at the fire blazing down his gullet.

"Who is his lover?" Lachlan asked as a dark tremor of apprehension moved through him.

"I have been told he has become enraptured by a beautiful mystic who is encouraging him to raise his sword again for Scotland, and fight for the old king. She is promising him that by doing so, he will gain great power and fortune."

Lachlan frowned. "And you believe this beautiful mystic is Raonaid?"

"Who else could it be?" Angus replied. "They know each other. She gave him what he needed to enter my castle three years ago and put a noose around my neck—all in the name of the Stuart cause."

"But are they *together*?" Lachlan asked, feeling the

fires of his passion rising explosively. "Sharing a bed, I mean?"

The image of it plowed straight through his tremulous self-control. Raonaid and Murdoch? Lovers? He clenched his teeth together and fought to keep his breathing under control. *Bloody hell! It could not be true.*

"I do not know," Angus replied. "Raonaid does not move in polite society. She has always been an outcast, and is rather like a night creature in that way. Difficult to find."

"It is quite possible then," Lachlan was forced to accept, "that she could have been living at Drumloch Manor, masquerading as the heiress, then traveling here with me to get back inside these castle walls, while secretly planning an uprising with Murdoch? As his lover?"

Ah, Christ. . . . A blinding rage was searing through his brain. He wanted to hit something.

Angus locked eyes with him. "There is only one way to find out. Bring her to me now. I lived with her for a year. I bedded her countless times. I will know straightaway if she is Raonaid. And I will also be able to tell whether or not she is lying about her lost memories."

Lachlan downed the rest of his drink and set it on the sideboard. "Wait here." He stormed out of the room, determined to unearth the truth about the woman who had completely bewitched him. "I will be back at once."

Chapter Thirteen

"Do you believe *any* of what I have told you?"

Catherine had just relayed to her hostess the entire
story of her five-year disappearance and memory loss—
along with how Lachlan had attacked her at Drumloch
Manor and brought her here to lift the curse.

Gwendolen's eyes darkened with suspicion, and she
rose from her chair to pace about the room.

"It's quite a tale," she said, "but I'm afraid it will take
far more than your word to make me believe it. I look at
you, and all I see is the woman who was once my husband's lover. There is no doubt in my mind that you are
the one who entered my home and poisoned my husband's mind against me. You were a jealous, conniving
vixen then, and I see nothing different about you now.
You can pretend to be a tragic heiress until you draw
your last breath, but I will believe none of it. So do not
look to me for friendship or support. I will not be your
ally. If anything, I will talk sense into Lachlan. You
have done him enough harm. I will not stand by to see
him hurt again."

Catherine stood up. "I have no intention of hurting
Lachlan, so you needn't bother yourself." She knew in

her mind that Gwendolen had every right to be mistrustful of her, but her words were difficult to accept, for Catherine did not remember doing any of the things that aroused such hatred in the Lioness. "I am disappointed that you cannot forgive me for past wrongs," she continued. "But I also understand my actions were deplorable. I will therefore leave Kinloch Castle as soon as possible. I have no wish to remain where I am not welcome."

Lachlan entered the room just then, and they both said his name at once.

"Lachlan . . ."

He halted in the doorway. "What's going on here? I see cheeks flushed with anger. Both of you."

"We were just catching up," Gwendolen told him with an obvious stroke of anger.

"She does not believe a single word of my story," Catherine explained.

He approached and gave her a vicious look. "We'll find out soon enough. Come with me now. Angus is waiting to see you."

Her heart turned a somersault inside her chest. It was what she wanted of course. She had come here to meet her former lover, in the hopes that her memories would materialize and she would remember her old life.

Her hostess approached her. "What's wrong, Raonaid? You look pale. Are you worried that my husband will confirm that you are attempting to deceive us all, and that he might confine you to the dungeon?"

Catherine felt sick to her stomach. "I am, in fact. And if that is his decision, I will accept my fate, but I will not rest until you at least believe that I am repentant."

A look of surprise flashed across Gwendolen's face, and she turned her eyes to Lachlan, who frowned and said, "Do you see my dilemma? She is not the same."

With that, he gestured for Catherine to follow him out of the day parlor. When they reached the curved staircase at the end of the corridor, Gwendolen came running.

"I am coming with you," she said, moving past them and leading the way up the stairs. "I must bear witness to this."

"Did he forgive you for what happened a year ago?" Catherine whispered to Lachlan as they approached the solar, where Angus was waiting for them. She was seeking to calm her anxieties and wished to know if the great Laird of Kinloch was capable of forgiveness.

"We did not speak of that," Lachlan replied.

"But you were gone for quite some time. What *did* you talk about?"

"You."

That did not help the rickety state of her nerves, for she knew all the terrible things Raonaid had done. If Angus confirmed her as his enemy, the next few minutes could prove perilous—for according to Lachlan, she had tried to have Angus killed.

Oh, God, she should never have come here. It had been a terrible mistake.

As they rounded the corner and walked into the bright, sunlit solar, Catherine looked around at the bank of windows on the opposite wall. There were only two wooden chairs by the door, a sideboard with a decanter and glasses, and a stool in the center of the room. A single tapestry adorned the east wall, but other than that, it was a bare room, and Angus the Lion was nowhere in sight.

Lachlan turned to her. "I've done what you asked. I brought you to Kinloch to see my chief. You'd better be true to your word and lift this blasted curse, or I am sure I can convince him to hang you from the gallows."

Her stomach careened. Where was the generous warrior who had held her after her nightmares? He was looking at her now with malice and accusation . . .

Footsteps entered the solar. They all turned toward the door.

Catherine knew instantly that the Highlander before her was the great Lion, Angus MacDonald, Laird of Kinloch. There could be no mistaking his imposing presence or the cold expression of command in those ice blue eyes.

He was a tall, flaxen-haired warrior who wore the MacDonald tartan with pride. His hair was long, golden, and loose upon his broad shoulders, his face handsome in the blinding light beaming in through the leaded windows. He unnerved her immediately and caused the hairs on the back of her neck to stand on end.

Was this man her former lover? Had he touched her body in intimate ways and taken her innocence?

She faced him directly, determined to show herself, to let him see her and recognize her. Though part of her did not want him to. This man terrified her. How could she survive even the memory of being deflowered by him?

"*It's you,*" he said in a quiet, ominous voice, laced with malice. "What game are you playing now?" he growled, crossing toward her with murderous intent.

Catherine sucked in a breath and took a step backwards. Her heel kicked the stool, and she stumbled. It all seemed to happen in a strange suspension of time and existence. Then she felt herself falling. . . .

Fear burned through her body, and she experienced a flash memory of tumbling backwards into an open grave. Just like in the dream.

"*No, stop!*" she blurted out.

The whole world went black.

When she opened her eyes a second later—or perhaps it was a number of moments?—she was lying on her back, blinking up at Lachlan, Gwendolen, and Angus.

She realized that Lachlan had been lightly slapping her cheek.

"You hit your head," he told her. "You've been unconscious."

"For how long?"

"Just a minute or two."

Angus glowered down at her with a passionate loathing, then rose to his feet and offered his hand.

Reluctantly, she accepted his assistance and stood.

"Well?" she boldly asked. "What is your conclusion? Am I the witch? And if I am, what will you do with me? Burn me at the stake? If so, be done with it, sir, for I have had enough of this intolerable treatment."

She was angry now, and uncontrollably so.

Angus's gaze burned into hers; then he quickly shook his head. "Something's not right."

Her knees began to tremble, and her breath came short.

Lachlan grabbed hold of Angus's arm and spoke insistently. "What are you saying?"

The Lion's eyes searched her face, her hair, her breasts, and traveled up and down the length of her body. He circled around behind her. "I need to see the back of your neck."

Catherine was about to protest, but thought better of it. Angus stepped close to her—*terrifyingly close*—and swiped a big, battle-scarred hand up under her hair. He twirled her locks in his big fist and lifted them up over her head. Her skin erupted in gooseflesh as he put his nose to her neck and smelled her.

"What are you doing?" Lachlan demanded.

"She's different," Angus said. "She looks the same, but something is not right. Raonaid had a birthmark on her neck . . ."

She felt his fingers at her nape, pushing the fallen strands of hair out of the way. His hands were warm as they slid close to her scalp and combed through her hair, moving it this way and that, while he bent at the knees and tilted his head, searching for the mark. . . .

At last, he let her hair fall from his grasp and stepped back. She spun around to face him.

Where his eyes had been cold and steely before, they were now flashing with agitation. "God help us all if this is some kind of sorcery," he said.

"What are you saying?" Lachlan asked. "That she is not Raonaid?"

Eyes narrowing, Angus continued to stare at her; then he nodded. "The resemblance is uncanny," he said. "Everything is the same, and yet it is not, which leaves only one explanation."

Catherine turned to Lachlan and somehow managed to remain on her feet, when it felt as if the floor were giving way beneath her. "I am Raonaid's twin."

Confused and bewildered, she could barely breathe.

"What?" Lachlan grimaced and shook his head, seeming unable to accept it.

But neither could she. "A twin?"

She looked down at the floor and realized in a rush of anguish that her dreams of a ghost, her awareness of some other spirit self, had stemmed from some intrinsic knowledge of this lost sibling—a soul who had shared the womb with her. It had always been beneath the surface of her perception.

"This changes everything," Lachlan said.

Catherine knew exactly what he was thinking. How could she not? It was written all over his face. "Yes, it does," she replied. "I am not Raonaid; therefore I will not be able to lift your precious curse."

He frowned at her. *"Precious* curse? Are you mad? And why did you make that promise to me at Drumloch? You said you would lift it if I brought you here, yet you were not in a position to barter."

"What did you expect me to do!" she argued. "I told you a dozen times that I did not know how to help you, but you were going to force yourself upon me! I did what I had to do, to ensure my safety!"

He winced at the words. A muscle flicked at his jaw. "I didn't know who you were," he ground out. "I thought you were *her.*"

"Oh!" Her temper exploded like a powder keg. "So

it would have been perfectly all right for you to rape my *sister*?"

His expression grew tight with strain. "I should never have brought you here." Turning toward Gwendolen, he said, "Will you see that she is looked after?"

"Of course," the Lioness replied, looking startled and ashen faced.

With that, he left Catherine in the solar, as though he had no more use for her, as though she existed only to serve his need to rid himself of the curse.

It was quite some time before she was able to bring her anger under control. Then at last, she found the strength to turn and face her hosts.

As Lady Catherine Montgomery, heiress of Drumloch.

Lachlan burst through the solar doors and raked both hands through his hair, clenching his teeth in a frenzy of disbelief as he stormed through the winding corridors of the castle. He didn't know where he was going. He only needed to exert himself, to use his body to relieve some of the tension that was turning him into a raving madman.

He could not believe it. And yet he could. He'd known from the first moment that there was something wrong about her, that the lass was different from the witch he remembered and reviled, even though she looked the same.

He thought of his immediate attraction to her, how he had become so aroused when he touched her in the stone circle, and was strangely relieved that he had not fallen under some other kind of spell. What he'd felt for her was natural and explicable, for the woman was innocent. Pure of heart. And oh, so incredibly beautiful.

He stopped and laid a hand on the wall to steady himself. He pounded a fist up against it. *Bloody hell!* What had he just done? She was not Raonaid! She was Lady Catherine Montgomery, and she had learned for the first time today that she had a twin sister, and he had been unthinkably cruel. He had thought only of himself and how he could never have her.

Especially not now.

He grabbed his hair in both fists and pressed his back to the wall, then slid down to sit on the cold stone floor. He realized in that moment that the only thing that had kept him sane over the past five days was the underlying belief that he despised her. All the desires he felt and fought against . . . He'd convinced himself they were some form of sexual madness because of the curse.

But none of that was true. He could no longer depend on his hatred to prevent him from surrendering to his desire.

She was not Raonaid.

She was an innocent, forlorn heiress, who needed help and protection. And what had he done in her worst hour of need? He had let her down.

Because he wanted her so badly, he could not bear to be near her.

Chapter Fourteen

"I suppose this confirms that I am Lady Catherine Montgomery," she said, working hard to recover her composure as she turned to face Angus and Gwendolen in the solar. "But how is it possible that I have a twin who is widely regarded as a witch? My family never mentioned such a thing."

"What did they tell you?" Angus asked.

"That my mother died in childbirth and my father never remarried. As far as I knew, I was his sole heir and he left his entire unentailed fortune to me."

Gwendolen approached and touched her arm. "You should sit down, Lady Catherine. You've lost all your color."

She realized suddenly that the room was spinning. She feared she was going to be ill.

Angus went to pour her a drink from the sideboard while Gwendolen led her to a chair.

"Permit me to apologize to you," her hostess said. "I will never forgive myself for how I treated you earlier. I was wrong not to believe you."

"It was a misunderstanding, that is all."

Catherine sat down, but declined the drink Angus offered while all the sounds in the room grew muffled, as if she had just dunked her head underwater.

It was one thing to learn she was not a deranged witch when she had spent the past five days preparing herself to accept such a fate. It was quite another to learn that she had a sister. A sister who, evidently, was separated from her at birth and had turned out to be a mystic.

If that was true, no one at Drumloch seemed to know of it. Or if they did, they were all keeping it a well-guarded secret.

"A room has been prepared," Gwendolen said. "I will take you there now."

"But I must decide how to proceed," Catherine argued.

On top of everything else, there still existed the question of where she had been for the past five years and why she could not remember any of it.

And what of her strange behavior at the standing stone? Did she have the same gifts as her sister, and if so, had she had them all her life?

Gwendolen laid a hand on her shoulder. "We can decide that later. For now, let me show you to your chamber. You must be terribly distraught, Lady Catherine. I hope you will take some time to rest and absorb this news."

Catherine finally agreed, and Angus accompanied them to the door.

"You will dine with us this evening," he said, "and we will discuss what must be done. Rest assured, Lady Catherine, that as chief of the MacDonalds of Kinloch, I am at your service. No harm will come to you."

"Thank you." She was indeed reassured, knowing that she was in the care of the great Scottish Lion, and that he no longer considered her his enemy. It was something, at least, to be thankful for.

She and Gwendolen exited the solar together and headed toward the tower stairs.

"Will Lachlan dine with us as well?" Catherine asked as they began their spiraling descent.

She imagined him, at this moment, preparing to leave Kinloch again, to continue his quest to find the woman who had cursed him.

She might never see him again.

"I cannot say," Gwendolen replied. "Angus is not pleased with him. Aside from the fact that he cut him with a sword a year ago, then left without a word, he has just committed a crime by bringing you here."

"How so?"

"You are worth a great fortune, Lady Catherine, and I am sure your family did not sanction your removal from Drumloch. In their eyes, he kidnapped you, which implicates my husband as well. I expect there will be some angry words exchanged between the two of them in the next little while."

Catherine followed her hostess down the curved staircase and into a wide stone passageway, lit by a number of torches.

"I do not wish for him to be punished," Catherine said. "You must inform your husband that there was no abduction. Lachlan did not plan it that way. I *asked* to be taken."

Gwendolen regarded her with an arched brow as they walked side by side down the long corridor. "I am surprised you are defending him, considering how he treated you just now."

Catherine, too, was surprised, for he had wounded her deeply. But it did not change the fact that he had delivered her to Kinloch Castle without incident, and he had kept his promise to her—that he would not endanger her life by slaking his lust on her.

"I cannot help myself," she replied. "He did all that I asked of him."

"Perhaps." Gwendolen was quiet for a moment. "May I be frank with you, Lady Catherine?"

Catherine regarded her warily. "I wish you would be."

The Lioness sighed. "You've been through a terrible ordeal, and Lachlan is . . ." She paused and glanced both ways, up and down the corridor. "He has a certain way about him. He is handsome, and women are drawn to him."

"What are you trying to say?"

Gwendolen took a moment to better articulate herself. "His path is littered with broken hearts, and not just because of the curse. Even before that, he was not the kind of man a woman should ever fall in love with." She hesitated. "I would not wish to see you hurt more than you have been already. It would be best if you returned to your home, and did not think of him again."

Catherine's stomach clenched tight with distress, for she feared it might be too late for such warnings. She might not be in love with Lachlan, but she was somehow swept away.

"Do not worry for me," she said nonetheless. "I am not a fool."

Yet she did not want him to leave the castle. She wanted—she *needed*—to see him again, though she did not want to explore too deeply the reasons why.

Gwendolen took hold of her hand. "I am pleased to hear it. Now let us deliver you to your bedchamber. You will need time to rest before dinner."

After summoning Lachlan back to the solar, Angus spoke harshly. "So it appears you kidnapped the wrong woman. An heiress worth ten thousand English pounds. Bloody hell, Lachlan, I hope you covered your tracks."

"I did," he replied. "We spent the first night at a coaching inn to the south of Drumloch, then doubled back to the north and kept to the hills. And I did not kidnap her."

Angus palmed the hilt of his sword. The air between them sizzled with tension. "I still want to thrash you senseless. For more than just what occurred here today."

It was time, evidently, for Lachlan to pay the piper for what he did on that fateful morning a year ago.

At least he was ready. He had replayed, in his mind, the details of their contest a hundred times over.

"I won that fight fair and square," he said. "You can call me a drunkard if you like, but the fact remains, you weren't quick enough to block my maneuver, unsteady as it was. On the battlefield, you would be dead. And drunk or sober, I would be the victor."

Lachlan and Angus had been cousins and friends since they were young lads, racing around the castle with wooden dirks in their belts, pretending to be warriors. As men they had continued their competitive games, using each other to practice and hone their skills for battle. They had always been equally matched, until that fateful day.

"Is that your way of apologizing?" Angus asked, eyes narrowing. "Or are you looking for another fight? Because I will gladly meet you in the Hall to even the score. Simply name the day and the hour."

Lachlan regarded his cousin in the bright afternoon light shining through the windows, and felt a deep regret for all the days since his departure, knowing how he must have disappointed his chief, whom he respected more than any other Scotsman alive.

"I don't want to fight you," Lachlan replied. "I only want to tell you that I regret the day I rode away from here. It might have been a fair fight, but I should not have left, and you would be well within your rights to thrash me senseless. God knows I deserve it."

"Aye, you do. You were my Laird of War, Lachlan."

He lowered his gaze to the floor. "Not a very good one in those last few months. You were fortunate there were no unexpected attacks. I might have lost you your castle."

Angus moved to a chair and sat down. He was quiet for a long time.

"What was your plan, coming back here?" He regarded Lachlan coolly. "Did you expect me to confirm that the heiress was actually Raonaid? Did you think I would force her to lift the curse, so that you could go back to your old life? Shagging lassies you barely knew?"

Lachlan looked toward the windows. "That would

have been a simpler outcome." He ran a hand through his hair. "But nothing seems simple now."

Again he thought of Catherine, and wished he had been less cruel, from the first moment he found her in the stone circle.

"By coming here," Angus continued, "you have dragged me into a very complicated hole. What I ought to do is turn your sorry arse over to the Lowland authorities and save myself from being implicated as your accomplice."

"Is that your intention?" Lachlan asked, half-expecting his cousin to answer in the affirmative—in which case he would be forced to ride out of Kinloch as quickly as possible, leaving Catherine behind, of course.

She would be better off, without a doubt.

Angus approached him. "No, I will not turn you over. You are my cousin, and despite a few recent errors in judgment, you have, for most of your life, been a loyal member of this clan. God knows I have made my own share of mistakes in the past, but I have been blessed with forgiving friends. For that reason, I cannot hold a grudge against you. I owe you that."

In the long pause that followed, Lachlan counted his own blessings—and felt quite undeserving. "In that case, I will say what I've wanted to say to you for the past year."

Angus waited patiently while Lachlan labored to collect his thoughts and find the right words to convey his true feelings.

"I'm glad I didn't kill you," he said at last.

Angus's eyes narrowed coolly. "As am I."

The great Lion did not often smile, and today was no different from any other. He acknowledged Lachlan's apology with a mere nod, then headed for the door.

"Go and get some rest," he commanded, "and for pity's sake, Lachlan, take a bath. You reek like the arse end of a bull. We'll dine at eight."

Lachlan followed him out, but when they were about to part ways in opposite directions, he stopped. "Angus . . ."

His cousin halted in the torchlit passageway, waiting for him to speak.

"What chamber is she in?"

"The heiress?" By the knowing look in Angus's eye, it was more than apparent that he recognized Lachlan's burning need to see her.

"Green one," he said. "South Tower. You owe her an apology, Lachlan, but you'd better not try anything else with her. You've done enough damage as it is. I've forgiven you once, but I will not clean up any more of your messes." He turned and disappeared down the twisting staircase.

Lachlan did not go to Catherine's chamber straightaway, however, for Angus was right, about one thing at least.

Lachlan needed to bathe. And he hoped—somewhere beneath all this dirt and grime—there might exist a small kernel of the charmer he had once been. For that was the man he wanted to be, when he asked for the lady's forgiveness.

Chapter Fifteen

An army of chambermaids arrived at Catherine's door within minutes to fill her bath, followed by an experienced lady's maid who brought her a clean white shift to sleep in and a gown to wear for dinner. The woman was a MacEwen, and after the bath she explained to Catherine, while she brushed out her long curling hair, that the MacEwens had once ruled at Kinloch. Angus MacDonald had stormed the gates, however, and taken command, which was how he and Gwendolen became husband and wife. Gwendolen was the daughter of the former MacEwen chief.

"So they were enemies once?" Cathcrine asked with some surprise. "I would never have known. They seem very well suited."

"Aye, Lady Catherine. That's because they fell in love."

"Well," she cynically replied, "I suppose that means there is hope for anyone." Though she did not truly believe it, not when she thought of Lachlan and how coldheartedly he had behaved when he learned she was not Raonaid.

Later she slipped into the bed, fluffed up the feather

pillows, and dismissed the maid, who indicated that she would return in time to assist her in dressing for dinner.

The door closed with a gentle click, and the room fell silent. Catherine gazed up at the green canopy above and thought of her twin.

Over the past six months, since Catherine's return to Drumloch Manor, she had assumed that the emptiness she felt stemmed from the fact that she had no memories of her loved ones and was therefore—in her own mind at least—alone in the world.

Now it seemed that in infancy she had suffered a terrible loss—that of a sister who had shared the womb with her. A sibling who was severed from Catherine's life the same day they lost their mother. It was a double tragedy, an inconceivable loss. How grief-stricken she must have been. And though Raonaid was a stranger to her, and quite likely a villain, she felt a deep and agonizing grief for her as well.

Her sadness quickly turned to anger.

Who had done it? Who had cast out her infant sister? Was it her father? Or her grandmother? Or someone else Catherine had yet to meet?

A light knock sounded at the door just then. She rose up on her elbows, but it opened before she had a chance to respond.

In walked Lachlan.

He wore a fresh kilt and a clean, loose-fitting white linen shirt. The brooch at his shoulder was polished to a fine sheen, and he was without his usual weaponry. His hair was wet, sticking damply to his muscular shoulders in shiny disarray.

He circled around the bottom of the bed and stood at the foot of it, one hand on the corner post, his gaze dark and troubled as he observed the length of her body beneath the covers.

Something prompted her to raise her knee, and his eyes lifted keenly to meet hers.

"Why are you here?" she asked, still angry with him for what had occurred in the solar, while at the same time her insides were careening with both trepidation and desire. She hated herself for feeling that way, after all that had happened.

"Lady Catherine . . ." His tone was quiet and seductive, and the sound of it matched perfectly with the erotic spectacle of his muscular warrior's body. His big hand opened and closed around the bedpost. "Do you *really* want to know why I'm here?"

Catherine inched upward on the pillows. *"Yes. . . ."*

The word spilled past her lips in a breathless sigh, and she wanted to strangle herself with her own stockings, for she was not some smitten young barmaid in a village inn. She was a lady of noble breeding, and she would not be so easily seduced by his charms.

"But I don't care what you have to say to me," she quickly amended. "I will never forgive you for your reprehensible behavior in the solar. You were a selfish brute."

"Indeed I was," he agreed, surprising her by lifting a knee and climbing onto the bed.

Her belly swarmed with nervous butterflies, but she fought the urge to blush or stammer. "And that's all you have to say to me?"

"No, that is not all." He stretched out on his side

beside her, propped up on one elbow, and cupped her cheek in his hand. "I owe you an apology, lass. I should have listened to you in the stone circle when you denied my accusations. I should never have taken you from your home. And while we were traveling, I suspected something was wrong, that you were not the woman I despised, and yet I pushed on. I should have listened to my instincts—and to you—and for that I am deeply sorry."

Catherine regarded him with shock in the pale afternoon light, and tried to ascertain if he was sincere, or simply trying to charm her into forgetting that he'd treated her like a witch and deserved to have his head soaked in brine.

All her instincts told her that he was genuine, but she wasn't sure she could trust those instincts—not when her foolish body was melting into a puddle of infatuation at the wonderful nearness of him.

"What about your beastly behavior in the solar just now?" she added, working hard to sound impervious to his apology when she knew how difficult it must have been for him to come here and essentially get down on his knees to grovel. But after everything that had happened between them, she *wanted* to see him grovel. It was only right. "Do you have anything to say about that?"

He looked into her eyes, then down at her lips. His thumb brushed across her cheek, and she felt a passionate fluttering in her belly.

"That, too, was wrong," he softly said. "I was selfish and harsh, when I should have been sympathetic. None of this was your fault, yet I have been a scoundrel with you since the beginning, never more so than today. My only excuse is that I desired you, and when I learned that you were not the woman I hated, I could not confront those desires. You have to understand, lass, that I've spent the past three years pushing such feelings away. But today, it was cowardly of me, and you deserved better. So I will make my apologies to you, Lady Catherine, and beg for your forgiveness."

Her heart began to hammer against her ribs as she pondered the fact that he'd just confessed desire, when she'd presumed he felt nothing for her but malice and loathing.

Despite everything, she desired him, too; there could be no denying it. He had lit a fire in her body that first day, kissing her senseless in the stone circle, and she had not been able to quench it since.

Now, here he lay, touching her cheek, begging for forgiveness, and confessing mutual desire. . . .

Catherine rested her hand on his chest and felt the beat of his heart. He allowed it only for a moment, then took hold of her hand and set it between them, back on the bed.

"It's been a long time since I've let a woman touch me," he said.

"What about the night I woke from the dream?" she replied. "I touched you then, and you touched me, too."

"Aye, but I could not stay long beside you."

A swarm of butterflies fluttered in her belly as she looked at his soft mouth and dreamed of how it would feel to be kissed by him again.

Lachlan gazed languorously into her eyes, and she wet her throbbing lips. A hot ache pulsed in her belly.

How was it possible that the mere power of his gaze could fill her with such feverish desire? She wanted overwhelmingly to touch him.

"There is another reason why I am here," he explained as if he sensed her yearnings and knew he had to interrupt them. "I have information about your twin. Angus told me that Raonaid has been living in Edinburgh."

Catherine leaned up on her elbow. "He's certain?"

"Aye. Do you want to meet her?"

"Yes, of course," she replied.

He reflected upon that for a moment. "As you know, I have my own reasons to see her again," he said, "so I will be leaving very soon. If you wish to accompany me, I will deliver you to Edinburgh safely, and do whatever it takes to protect you, and help you regain your memories. Perhaps Raonaid can be of some assistance to you. She is a mystic, after all."

"But if she truly has such powers and sees things in visions, why has she never known that she has a twin? Angus was her lover for a year and she did not reveal it to him. Do you think she knows about me?"

"I wish I could answer that," he replied; then he laid his head down on the pillow.

Exhaustion soon washed over Catherine, and her eyes began to flutter closed.

"I should go," he whispered.

"Please don't," she blurted out. "It brings me comfort to know you are here. Please stay until I fall asleep."

She was surprised when he nodded and brushed the hair away from her face.

The sound of his breathing soon lulled her into a

deep slumber, filled with colorful dreams of the Highlands. She flew over valleys and mountains, then swooped down into a glen, over the rooftops of a stone cottage with a stable. There was a vegetable garden, and hens clucking nearby. She flew through the stable door, as if riding a fast gust of wind.

Hours later, she woke groggily, and Lachlan was gone. She sat up in a daze as the reality of her life settled into her consciousness.

It was safe to assume now that she was indeed Lady Catherine Montgomery, but she still did not have her memories back, nor did she know where she had been for the past five years, or why she was not a virgin.

Who had she been with, if not Angus?

Part of her did not want to know the answer to that question. She wished it would stay buried in the past.

When it came to her twin sister, however, she felt the opposite.

Of Raonaid, she wished to know everything.

Chapter Sixteen

Blue Waters Manor, south of Edinburgh
Same day

Raonaid was just finishing the afternoon milking when the stable door blew open and a strong wind stirred up the loose hay that was strewn across the floor. The hogs squealed and the chickens outside squawked and flapped their wings.

Heart suddenly racing, she stood up and knocked over the milking stool. "Who's there?" Her gaze darted all around. "I know you're in here!"

It was a presence she had felt all her life, even as a child, alone and frightened in bed. The spirit had never caused her harm, however, so Raonaid had learned to push the fear away. Over the past six months, however, the spirit had come more frequently and Raonaid sensed its agitation.

It blew around her in rapid circles, lifting strands of hay off the floor.

"Speak to me, ghost!" Raonaid said. "Why do you haunt me?"

I'm not a ghost.

Raonaid dashed forward with surprise, for it had never spoken to her before. She turned in circles and looked up at the rafters. "What are you, then?"

I'll come for you.

Another fierce gust blew out the stable door, knocking it back on its hinges; then the air went still. The animals calmed and grew quiet.

A second later, the cow lifted her head and let out a raucous, shrieking, *Mooo!*

Panic like Raonaid had never known before welled up in her heart. She grabbed the bucket of milk and ran outside, slamming the door shut and lowering the bar. She ran past the vegetable garden to the house and burst through the back door. Setting the bucket down on the worktable, she hurried through the parlor to the stairs.

Murdoch was seated at his desk. He looked up from his papers. He was dressed in his kilt today, which was unusual. His dark hair was tied back in a leather cord.

"Raonaid!" he shouted.

She halted at the bottom of the stairs.

"You look like you've seen a ghost."

"It wasn't a ghost," she replied. "I don't know *what* it was."

His eyes narrowed with curiosity as he rose and stalked toward her. "Was it some kind of vision?"

"I am not certain."

He grasped her arm and hauled her around to face him. "Well, you best figure it out, lass. Scotland needs a king, and I must know when to act and who to trust. You promised me another vision by now, and if this opportunity passes, there may not be another."

"Why does it matter so much to you?"

His cheeks flushed with passion and vigor. "We cannot allow the English to continue to subjugate us. If they had their way, they would banish us all to the north, then eventually push us into the sea. You don't understand anything, do you?"

She wrenched her arm away from him. "Don't tell me what I do, and do not, understand. I know how it feels to be banished. I've been branded a witch all my life, and now I am rejected by *you*—who will not even be seen in public with me."

"People fear you, Raonaid. Your gifts make them uneasy."

She arched a brow and spoke to him with dangerous accusation. "Do my gifts make *you* uneasy, Murdoch? Does my wickedness make you nervous?"

He took a moment to consider how best to answer the question; then at last, he cleared his throat and stepped back. "You're my woman. I'll not cast you out, like others have done."

She scoffed bitterly. "You only keep me as your woman because you think I can change your future. You want to triumph over the Hanoverians, and you think that if I see it in the stones, it will make it so."

"You saw a great triumph for Angus the Lion," he argued. "You predicted his invasion at Kinloch Castle." When she gave no reply, Murdoch's voice softened and he laid a hand on her shoulder. "But that's not the only reason I want you, Raonaid. You know that. You're a beautiful woman."

She glanced down at his hand, thought of the mysterious spirit that haunted her, then gave him a spiteful glare. "I don't know why you think so. I am spiteful and malicious."

It's why she had been alone all her life. Everyone feared her. Some believed she was the devil.

Murdoch carefully removed his hand from her shoulder and let it fall to his side.

"There, now," she said mockingly. "That's more like it, for I cannot abide lies." She turned away from him and climbed the stairs to her chamber.

Chapter Seventeen

Kinloch Castle

With her young maid as an escort, Catherine entered the twisting tower staircase. They climbed up one level, then made their way down another long, torchlit passageway.

"Is this the right direction?" Catherine asked, uncomfortably aware of the distance they had traveled through the castle. "I thought we were to dine in the East Tower?"

"Aye, milady, but I was given instructions to bring you here first."

They reached another staircase and climbed all the way to the top. The maid gestured with a hand. "He's waiting for you here, milady. He'll take you to supper himself."

Hoping her maid was referring to Lachlan, Catherine stepped onto the stone rooftop and looked up at the night sky. The stars were twinkling. The air was still. Wispy clouds floated in front of the moon. She glanced from east to west, wondering how long she would have to wait here alone.

"Lady Catherine." That familiar husky voice reached her from the other side of the tower stairs.

At last, Lachlan stepped into view, darkly handsome in the moonlight. Her knees nearly buckled beneath her, and she felt giddy with excitement.

"Why did you summon me here?" she asked, determined to reveal none of that.

He dug into his sporran. "I wanted to give you these, and I didn't dare come to your bed again."

He withdrew her heavy pearl and emerald necklace and held it up. The stones gleamed brilliantly in the moonlight.

"I believe there are some dangly earbobs in here as well," he added, patting his sporran.

Catherine reached for the necklace, but he quickly drew it back. "What will you give me for it?"

There was a charming playfulness in his eyes, which again surprised her. He had not shown this side of himself before.

"You are a terrible tease." She attempted to swipe the jewels from his grasp, but he hid them behind his back. "I should kiss you like I did at Drumloch," she said, "just to punish you."

The playfulness in his eyes vanished instantly, and his tone grew serious.

"Those are dangerous words. Please, allow me." He moved behind her to drape the pearls around her neck and fasten the clasp. "I've never been called a tease before," he said while she tingled at the sensation of his warm hands gracing her nape. "It was always the other way around, where women were concerned."

"But our situation is not like anyone else's, and I am

not like most other women." She was referring to her memory loss, of course.

He moved to face her again. "No, you are not. You are more beautiful, and a thousand times more intriguing."

Lord help her, she felt as if she were floating in a sea of heavenly bliss.

"May I have my earbobs now?" she asked, holding out her hand.

He kept his eyes on hers while he dug into his sporran again, pulling out one earring at a time. He handed them over and watched her fasten them to her lobes.

"Now you look like a proper heiress," he said.

She lifted an eyebrow. "I am hardly proper. You should know that better than anyone, for you have slept with me under the stars for five days straight, with no chaperone in sight."

"Now who's being a tease, reminding me of such a thing?" His eyes smiled in a way that made her pulse thrum.

"It takes one to know one, sir."

He grinned. "Aye, and if I were not half-dead from lack of excitement over the past three years, I would show you how dangerous it is to tease a man like me. I am attracted to shiny things, you see, and *you*, my lady, are quite dazzling."

Catherine inclined her head at him. "I appreciate the compliment."

But it was so much more than that. She loved the fact that he was flirting with her and allowing her to see his famous charm, which he had kept hidden from her until now.

He held out a hand. "May I escort you to supper?"

"That would be delightful," she replied. "I am absolutely ravenous."

For more than ten years Lachlan had managed to avoid permanent relationships with women. He could spot a frisky lassie at twenty paces, and such women, in turn, seemed able to recognize in him a mutual inclination for involvement without commitment. They recognized that he did not seek or want love. He'd had it once, with Glenna, and when she died he decided there would never be another to replace her.

Over the years, no woman had come close to making him feel the things he had felt with his first real love—the tragic adolescent longing, the willingness to sacrifice everything for that one person, who seemed destined to be one's only mate forever. The power and poignancy of his brief love affair and marriage had never touched him again after Glenna.

He had, in subsequent years, been faithful to her—not in body, but in heart. He had sought intimacy through sexual dalliances with women who did not require more from him than mere physical pleasure.

Until the curse, of course, which had exiled him to a life of celibacy and a complete absence of intimacy of any kind.

Tonight, however, as he escorted Catherine into his chief's private dining chamber, he felt all sorts of unbidden emotions stirring within. Emotions he found both disturbing and enticing, for he wanted her with something more than just physical desire.

As they walked side by side through the corridors of the castle, he breathed in the intoxicating scent of her flowery perfume. Everything about her challenged his capacity for restraint—her gleaming red hair and soft cherry lips; her ample breasts, spilling out of her tight bodice in a luscious burst of temptation. It all made him feel reckless, and that worried him, for she was not a frolicsome tavern wench with loose morals. She was something else entirely.

At last, they entered Angus's private dining chamber, where a hot fire was blazing in the massive stone hearth. The mahogany table was polished to a fine sheen and adorned with silver candelabras and colorful bowls of fruit. The walls were paneled in dark cherry oak, the windows covered in heavy velvet drapes.

Angus and Gwendolen turned to greet them in the glow of candlelight. A servant brought a silver tray and offered them wine in gold-plated, jewel-encrusted goblets.

"Lady Catherine, the gown is stunning on you," Gwendolen said. "I hope your chamber is sufficient to meet your needs."

The conversation continued in a light vein, for it was not every day that a famous Scottish noblewoman from the Lowlands came to dine at Kinloch, and certainly not under such bizarre circumstances of mistaken identity and possible kidnapping, depending on who was describing the events.

They dined on bowls of spiced beef broth, followed by fresh roast goose bathed in a thick cream sauce, and boiled greens.

When the servants came to take away their plates, Angus lounged back in his heavy chair and signaled for more wine.

"Have you decided," he asked Catherine in his deep Scottish brogue, "how you wish me to proceed in regards to your current predicament, my lady? We can have you escorted back to Drumloch at first light, if that is your wish."

"I am grateful to you, sir," she replied, "for your kindness and hospitality. I will wish, of course, to be reunited with my family, but what I desire most of all—aside from meeting my twin—is to recover my memories and learn where I have been for the past five years. You have helped immensely by confirming my identity and the existence of my twin. I had not known of it, and I long to know the truth. If I were in possession of magical powers, I would summon my grandmother to this table tonight, so that I could ask her directly about the circumstances of my birth, but alas, I am without such magic, so I will have to be patient, until I am reunited with her."

Angus leaned forward. "What do you require, Lady Catherine? I can send a man tonight with a written letter if you wish. Or as I said, I can make the necessary arrangements to deliver you back to your family."

Catherine sat back in her chair and considered the options presented to her, then turned her eyes to Lachlan.

He nodded once at her, to indicate that he, too, was at her service. Whatever she needed, he would provide it.

"Perhaps a letter would be the best thing," she decided. "I want my grandmother to know that I am safe and in the care of good people. Also that I chose freely to leave Drumloch and travel here in order to learn about my past." She regarded Angus again. "Then—if you could arrange it, sir—I wish to travel to Edinburgh to meet my sister."

He took a deep breath. "I will see to all of it. Every detail."

"Thank you. But I have one final request, and that is for Lachlan to be my escort. He has brought me this far, and I trust him to see me safely to my destination."

Angus turned to his wife, who picked up her goblet of wine and took a slow sip, regarding her husband warily over the rim of the cup.

Gwendolen turned and addressed Catherine. "I understand your desire to meet your twin," she said, "but I must warn you that you may be disappointed. She is not like you, Lady Catherine. She has lived a life apart from the world, and she has lashed out at me and my husband, and Lachlan as well. We will not stop you from traveling to Edinburgh, of course, but please keep your wits about you. Do not become too hopeful. She is not to be trusted."

Catherine gave her a melancholy smile. "I thank you for your honesty. I will certainly heed your advice, and I hope that one day I will be in a position to repay you both for your generosity. You have been very kind."

Dessert plates with sugar cakes and buttered cream were placed before them, and the conversation turned to other, lighter topics.

Afterward, they all went together to the Great Hall, where musical festivities had begun. Gwendolen took Catherine across the Hall to meet a group of prominent clanswomen while Lachlan remained with Angus.

Lachlan picked up a tankard of ale from a passing

servant. "Does everyone know that she is not Raonaid?" he asked. "Because if someone makes that mistake, they will need to be corrected."

"Everyone has been informed," Angus replied. "I suspect she will become an object of fascination," he added, "especially among those who have met Raonaid in person."

Lachlan took a deep swig of the ale. "Identical twins, yet opposite in every way. Gwendolen was right to warn her against becoming too hopeful, and believing she will discover a true loving sister in Raonaid. I'll not leave Catherine alone with her, that is certain."

Angus glanced at him sharply. "It is true," Angus said, "that Raonaid is volatile, but do not forget that she was my lover once, for a full year. I would not say this to my wife, Lachlan, and if you repeat a word of it to her, I will knock your head off your shoulders. But I am not sure what would have become of me if Raonaid had not taken me to her bed that first night when I arrived in the Western Isles, after being forsaken by my father. I might have kept riding straight into the North Atlantic."

Lachlan regarded his cousin with disbelief. "But she betrayed you. She provided your enemies with information that resulted in an attempt on your life. You were poisoned and hung from the battlements, and she tried to frame Gwendolen for it."

"She did so because she felt abandoned."

Lachlan regarded him with dismay. "How can you defend her? She was malicious and vengeful. I became a victim of her malice myself, when I wasn't even the one who jilted her."

"You were the one who came to her home and stole me away."

Lachlan turned and watched Catherine converse with the other clanswomen. She was Raonaid's identical twin, but when he looked at her he did not see the witch.

"What are you trying to say to me, Angus?"

His cousin finished his ale and set the tankard on a table. "I know how much you despise Raonaid, but your pretty heiress might not take your side if you go to war with her sister. Be prepared for that, Lachlan. Be prepared also for the fact that her family would never approve of you. They would rather see your neck in a noose than have you as a son-in-law."

"Who said anything about marriage?" Lachlan asked.

Angus studied his eyes. "I saw how you looked at her at dinner." He paused. "Be careful, Lachlan. This curse of yours . . . it has more power over you than you know."

"You don't need to worry about me," he replied. "I've survived this long, haven't I?"

"It's not *you* I'm worried about. It's her. And since I have given my oath to ensure her protection, I intend to send an armed guard with you to Edinburgh. A few of my best men, extra horses, supplies, and a cook."

"That's not necessary," Lachlan told him.

"I will decide what is, or is not, necessary, for by bringing the Drumloch heiress here, you have involved me in her disappearance. Not just now, but five years ago. I will therefore spare no expense in assuring her safe return to her family."

A lively reel began, and members of the clan rose to dance.

"When you reach the town of Killin," Angus continued, "hire a coach and a reliable driver. Stop as often
as she wishes, and when you are finished in Edinburgh,
take her home to Drumloch by coach. Purchase a vehicle if you must, but see that she arrives home in luxury.
And if Raonaid lifts the curse, for God's sake, release
your pent-up lust on someone else, Lachlan, not Lady
Catherine. She is not for you."

Angus turned and left him standing alone, uneasy
with the notion that he might not possess the discipline
it would require to obey *all* of his chief's commands.

The music in the Hall seemed to grow louder and
livelier while the dancers moved faster, their heels
pounding across the floor.

Lachlan pinched the bridge of his nose, then grimaced through all the noise and chaos, his eyes searching only for Catherine.

Chapter Eighteen

Catherine danced a reel in the Great Hall, and by some miracle, remembered all the steps without having to think. Though she could not remember anything about her life, she somehow knew how to dance, how to ride a horse, and she could recite the Lord's Prayer perfectly well.

Her cheeks were flushed with heat when the dance ended, and she fanned herself with her hand. She was still laughing when she turned and saw Lachlan on the other side of the Hall, standing under a stone archway, watching her with passionate intensity.

Their eyes locked on each other, and a spark of excitement lit in her belly. In the glow of the candlelight, he leaned one broad shoulder against the stones, and with his strapping form and powerful stance he flaunted a breathtaking masculinity that was unmatched by any other man in the room. The fine, chiseled features of his face, and his dark probing eyes, only served to increase his allure. No other Highlander could rival his extraordinary beauty.

The fiddle music roused her spirits as she became embroiled in a flood of heated emotion. It was too much. Too overwhelming for her heart and mind. She was forced to tear her gaze away from his awe-inspiring image and instead went to the table, in search of something to eat.

She picked up a bright red apple and bit into the juicy flesh, reminding herself that Lachlan did not welcome her attentions. He had made that abundantly clear when he was lying on her bed that afternoon. He did not want her to touch him. And yet he had not taken his eyes off her in the past few minutes since she finished the dance. He may have been watching her the entire time for all she knew.

She glanced over her shoulder at him again. He was still watching her. A hot pulsating thrill coursed through her body.

Did he know? Could he see how she responded to him? Could he sense her desires?

In that heart-pounding instant, he pushed away from the stone archway and began to shoulder his way through the crowd, keeping his eyes trained on hers the entire time.

As he walked toward her, everything about him exploded with erotic allure, and she wondered if all the other women in the room were melting with desire, as she was. Or was she the only one who could feel it?

It didn't matter. She did not care—and she wasn't about to take her eyes off him to look at anyone else.

He reached her at last and held out a hand. "Walk with me." The deep timbre of his voice sent a hot thrill through her bloodstream, and she placed her hand in his.

He led her across the crowded, festive Hall.

"Where are we going?" Though it hardly mattered. She would follow him anywhere.

"Not far."

He took her through a wider arched doorway and pushed through a pair of planked oaken doors that creaked and groaned on their enormous hinges.

Outside in the bailey, the night was illuminated by a bright three-quarter moon that cast long shadows across the ground. The air was crisp and cool on her cheeks.

"I can see my breath," she said, stopping to tip her head back and close her eyes.

He was still holding her hand, and when she opened her eyes again, he was watching her expression with interest.

"There is something about you," he said, "that makes me feel . . . *different*."

"How so?"

His dark eyes scrutinized her. "I'm not sure how to describe it, except that tonight I felt young again. Sometimes you make me forget certain things that have cast a shadow over my life."

"Perhaps my memory loss is contagious," she said with a hint of a smile.

His eyes warmed. "I would not be sorry," he replied, "if I could forget certain elements of the past and begin again. I think it would be a very pleasant way to live."

"What would you wish to forget?" she asked, wanting to know him better. She longed to know every last detail about his life.

"I would forget my wife's death, and all the pain that followed."

Catherine drew back in surprise. "You were married?"

"Aye."

She could not believe it. Lachlan MacDonald, the charmer, the flirt, had taken a wife?

"It was more than ten years ago," he explained, "and she died giving birth to our first child."

All Catherine's emotions flooded to the surface, and again she longed desperately to touch him. She reached out and cupped her hand around his arm. "I'm so sorry, Lachlan. I didn't know."

Catherine fought through the cobwebs of confusion in her mind. She had thought this man incapable of true intimacy or commitment, but it seemed he had once loved a woman deeply enough to marry her and had not been able to love again after the loss of her. In more than ten years, he had engaged in only superficial affairs, hence the legend of his reputation as a heartbreaker.

The details of the curse came hurling toward her suddenly, and she frowned. "Did my sister know about your wife?" The possibility turned sour in her stomach.

"Aye, it's why she chose that particular curse. She knew how to hurt me in the worst way, and she did so on the tenth anniversary of my wife's death."

Catherine fought to control the effect of that horror on her heart. That anyone could inflict such cruelty upon another was unthinkable to her.

"You have indicated many times that my sister has a vindictive side, but this is very disturbing to hear. It is beyond malicious." She inclined her head at him. "I am almost afraid to meet her now. You and everyone else seem determined to prepare me to meet a wicked hellion who might fly into a rage and put a deathly hex on me. Maybe it's true. She sounds like a person without a conscience. Perhaps I should not go to Edinburgh."

"Raonaid does lack a human conscience," he replied. "At least from my experience." His eyes slowly gentled, and his shoulders rose and fell as he took a deep breath. "But Angus reminded me tonight that she was his lover once, and that he genuinely cared for her. I could never imagine why, but if she is your sister, there must be a trace of decency in her. I will try to remember that when I see her again. I owe that to you, lass. I want you to know it, and I believe you must resolve this missing piece of your life."

Catherine regarded him in the moonlight and felt as if she were falling from a very high place.

Lachlan looked away, toward the main gate, and his voice dropped to a hush. "You look beautiful tonight. I watched you dance, and all I wanted to do was find a way to be alone with you."

"And here we are," she replied with a seductive purr in her voice that came completely unbidden. "Together and alone."

His dark eyes locked with hers, and she felt breathless, panicked under the sudden fever of his expression.

"I need to touch you," he whispered.

A small involuntary whimper escaped her as he strode forward, took her by the hand, and led her across the bailey into the stable, where the scent of hay and horses was thick in the air. A startled groomsman looked up from his task of pouring water into a trough, and Lachlan pointed at the door.

"Leave us," he said in a gruff, commanding voice.

The groomsman dropped the wooden bucket with a clatter onto the hay-strewn floor and ran out. Lachlan smoothly pushed Catherine up against the wall.

"All night I've been fighting the urge to kiss you," he said, "and hold you in my arms."

"Please don't fight it anymore. It's just a kiss. Surely there can be no danger in it."

"There is danger in what it would lead to."

She wet her lips, trembling with anticipation, while he kept her pinned up against the wall, his hungry gaze sweeping over her whole face.

Catherine's voice shook with need. "Today, you said it's been forever since you let a woman touch you. Why not let *me*? I will not ask you to make love to me, and I trust that you will not try."

Something dark flared in his eyes, and he needed no further pleading. In a flash of heat and aggression he covered her mouth with his own in a deep, open kiss of extreme sensuality and slid his big hands down the front of her gown.

Oh, at last . . . At last . . . Her body exploded with pleasure and delight.

He wrenched her closer, so that his pelvis squeezed against hers, and her breath caught in her chest. With blinding need and trembling hands, she grabbed at his shoulders and clutched at his shirt, gathering the heavy linen in her fists and pulling him closer.

The damp, open pressure of his mouth upon hers sent a fresh flood of desire into the pit of her belly, and she raised a knee to rub the inside of her thigh along the outside of his.

He took her face in both his hands, dragged his lips from hers, and spoke against her cheek. "If it were not for this bluidy curse, I'd be inside you by now."

He pressed his lips to hers again with a passion that was unbearable, for there could be no more than this. He could kiss her and caress her with his beautiful, masterful hands, but it could never go any further. With or without the curse, she was not some happy-go-lucky tavern wench. She was the daughter of an earl, and a wealthy one at that. One day there would be offers and negotiations for her hand in marriage, and this reckless moment up against a stable wall with a wild Highlander would not improve her already-damaged reputation.

"I want so badly to have you," he whispered as he blazed a trail of damp, openmouthed kisses down the side of her neck. "I want to run my hands over your sweet naked flesh, and taste you everywhere with my mouth."

"You can," she told him, and though she knew it was risky, she whispered, "I want you to."

His fingers brushed lightly over her skin, just above her neckline, and he followed their path with a series of small, tender kisses. His tongue darted and probed under her low neckline.

"No, I can't. . . ." The sensation of his hot breath in her cleavage thrust another flood of lust straight to her toes. "I want you too much, lass. I wouldn't be able to stop myself from taking you fully, and I don't want to hurt you."

He kissed along her collarbone and she shivered with sweet, intoxicating pleasure.

"You won't hurt me just by kissing me," she argued

while she ran her fingers through his heavy hair. "It feels so good, Lachlan." She closed her eyes and tipped her head back against the wall.

"Aye, it does. Too good. It's dangerous."

He took her face in his hands again, cupping her jaw and running the pads of his thumbs across her chin before he drank in her open mouth, kissing her deeply and passionately.

Catherine melted into his arms. He kept talking about danger, but she was not afraid. She was filling up with joy and ecstasy.

He ran his hands across the front of her stomacher, and she wished she could rid herself of the constricting garment and feel his bare hands on her breasts.

"We need to find your sister," he growled, still kissing Catherine's neck. "She must remove the curse. I cannot live like this."

She clutched at his shoulders and held him tight. "If we find her, and she lifts it, would you make love to me then?"

Straining against her, he shut his eyes and bowed his head to rest on her shoulder. "*Ah, hell, lass,*" he groaned. "You should not say things like that. It's the worst kind of torture."

She lifted his face so he was forced to look her in the eye. "Not for me. It excites me."

He shook his head. "It's not that simple. Even if there were no curse, I could not have you. You are the Drumloch heiress, and a woman like you does not give herself to a man like me."

" '*A woman like you . . .*' That implies that I am like every other nobleman's daughter, but we both know I am not, and all the world knows it as well. I was missing for five years and eventually presumed dead. I am already ruined by that scandal. But I am still one of the richest women in Scotland, and young enough to bear children, so one day very soon some well-titled—and most likely impoverished—gentleman will negotiate with my cousin for my hand in marriage, and he will not care whether or not I am untouched. He will marry me for my money."

Lachlan's eyes darkened, and his tone grew serious. "*Are* you untouched?"

It was a bold question, and a shocking impropriety to ask such a thing.

Catherine lowered her gaze. She had never been ashamed of her situation—it was beyond her control—but this, the loss of her virginity, was something more.

At last she looked up and shook her head. "No. I am not a virgin. But I don't know why, or with whom, or how. All I know is what the doctor has told me. So you see, you would not be taking anything of any great value if you made love to me. No one would even know, because my virginity has already been taken by another, and my family knows it."

He took a step back, and the sudden distance between them robbed her of all warmth.

"Do not make it sound like that," he said. "I've never wanted a woman like I want you now, so it would mean *everything* to me. But none of that matters, because it cannot happen between us. Do not forget, you are under my protection. I have vowed to escort you safely home, and that is what I intend to do."

Catherine swallowed uncomfortably and realized

she was breathing very hard. Her chest rose and fell, tight up against her gown, and it made her head swim. She wanted him so badly, but he was not in a position to give her what she desired.

And she was not entirely sure that what she desired would be good for her. As he said, they came from different worlds.

Truthfully, she didn't care about that. She would be perfectly happy wearing a homespun skirt and living here in the Highlands as his wife, gathering eggs and milking her own cows, if that were possible. Perhaps the old Catherine might not have felt that way, but the person she once was no longer existed. That person was gone. From the moment her grandmother collected her at the convent, she had felt like a fraud, like she did not belong in that world—until the moment Lachlan arrived.

"We should return to the Hall," he said, glancing impatiently over his shoulder and offering his hand.

Catherine let him lead her out of the stable and across the moonlit bailey, where the distant sound of fiddle music and cheerful singing penetrated the silence of the night and seemed to contradict the heaviness she felt from within.

"Are you angry with me?" she asked when they reached the Hall, for he had not spoken a word while they walked.

"No," he answered. "You've done nothing wrong. I just need you to give me some space when I ask for it."

He wasted no time leading her back to Gwendolen, who was sitting with Angus at the head table.

"We'll be leaving for Edinburgh in the morning," Lachlan said to them.

"So soon?" Gwendolen replied.

Lachlan turned his heated gaze to Catherine and let go of her hand. "Aye. Lady Catherine must meet her twin. There are questions she needs answered, and then, she must be returned to her family."

No one dared suggest that he had his *own* reasons to meet Raonaid again.

"Good night, Lady Catherine," he said, bowing to her. "I will leave you in the care of our hosts."

With that, he strode away and left her standing there, shaken and disoriented, until she felt Gwendolen's hand on her arm.

"Please join us. Warm sweetbreads are on their way."

"No, thank you," she shakily replied. "You are very kind to offer, but I must retire for the night. I will need my rest for the journey in the morning."

She watched Lachlan leave the Great Hall and was about to follow him out when Angus spoke up.

"What about your letter to your family?" he asked. "They must know you are safe."

She swallowed uneasily. "Yes, of course. I will write to my grandmother tonight, and I will tell her that I am on my way to Edinburgh. If you could see to its delivery . . ."

"I will," the Lion replied. "Sleep well, Lady Catherine."

"And the same to you, sir. Your kindness will not be forgotten."

Chapter Nineteen

Drumloch Manor

John Montgomery handed his horse and riding crop over to a groomsman and strode purposefully back to the house. He had just come from the magistrate's office in the village and learned that they were calling off the search for Catherine. There had only been one clue about her disappearance—her possible stay at an inn on the first night of her capture. Beyond that, the magistrate implied that she had simply disappeared into the mist, which was not an uncommon occurrence when a Highlander was involved. The magistrate had suggested that John hire a few resourceful men who knew their way around the north country.

Quite ridiculously, the man seemed to think there was some mysticism involved, but John knew better. The Highlander who had abducted Catherine had known something. Either he had information about her whereabouts over the past five years or he knew something about this family—perhaps what John's great-aunt refused to reveal.

John pulled his gloves off and slapped them against his thigh as he climbed the steps. The front door opened a few seconds before he reached it, and he found himself stopping under the wide portico, staring at his butler as if he were seeing him for the first time. John observed the man's tall, thin frame and his neatly combed white hair.

"How long have you been at Drumloch, Smythe?" he asked, stepping inside and removing his hat. "Forever, it would seem."

"Not quite that long, my lord. I began here in '86."

"That's long enough. It's thirty-five years."

"Indeed, my lord."

John watched him steadily. "Follow me, then. I have questions to ask."

John led the way into the library. "Close the door, Smythe. Very good. Now what secrets do you know about this household—specifically in regards to Lady Catherine, and her disappearance five years ago? She is about to turn five-and-twenty, and will come into her inheritance, but if she is not alive at that time, the funds will be forfeited to the Jacobite cause, and we cannot have that." He studied the butler with suspicious eyes. "I understand you were very devoted to my uncle, the former earl." He paused. "I also know that he was a staunch supporter of King James and his claim to the throne, but those days are gone, Smythe. You must know that. It is a hopeless cause and I do not wish to see this family's fortune lost to it. This is a Hanover house now, and we are loyal to King George. So tell me what you know. There must be gossip below stairs. There always is. Where is Lady Catherine? Where would she go, and what the bloody hell is my aunt hiding from me?"

The butler went white as a sheet but quickly recovered his composure and spoke with indifference. "I regret to say that I know nothing, my lord. Lady Catherine's disappearance five years ago remains a mystery to us all, and if the dowager is hiding something from you . . . I daresay she has always been very discreet about family matters. There has never been any talk of secrets or gossip of any kind below stairs. With respect, my lord, I do not permit such indiscretions."

John had no doubt that Smythe would manage the servants with a firm hand, and that Aunt Eleanor would not likely confide in him. John doubted she would confide in anyone.

"The housekeeper . . . ," he said on a whim. "How long has Mrs. Silver been serving this family?"

"Longer than I have, my lord. She began in the kitchen, but established herself at a young age and has risen accordingly."

"She earned everyone's trust, did she?" John circled around his desk and sat down. He leaned forward and removed his spectacles. "Tell her I wish to see her at once, and warn her that her position is at risk if she does not earn *my* trust. Go now. I do not wish to be kept waiting. There is a great deal of money at stake, not to mention the welfare of my dear cousin, Catherine. We must get her back. She has been through enough. She needs our protection."

"Very good, my lord." Smythe turned and left the library.

* * *

Smack! The sharp sting of the dowager's hand across Mrs. Silver's face caused both dogs to lift their chins from their slumber in front of the fire.

"You have betrayed me," Eleanor said. "You wretched woman. You have behaved intolerably! I would shoot you dead if I could, but I will have to settle for ending your employment, and I promise you—no other decent family will ever accept you into service after this. You will soon find yourself destitute or scrubbing pots in some village alehouse. If you're lucky."

Mrs. Silver lifted her chin and glanced down at the growling dogs with a cool, derisive expression. "I'm afraid not, milady," she said. "The earl has promised me employment here indefinitely, and he has rewarded me with a substantial increase in my wages."

The dowager scoffed. "So your loyalty was bought for a better price? Is that it, Mrs. Silver?"

"Aye, milady. The earl was very kind, and concerned for Lady Catherine's welfare. She was abducted by a Highlander. I could not, in good conscience, keep information from him which might result in her rescue."

The dowager swung her cane through the air like a whip and knocked over a vase of fresh flowers. "He is concerned for her money, you fool! He doesn't give a fig about her welfare! She has already been ruined in every way. What is the point in saving her now, except to hold on to her inheritance? And as for being concerned . . ." She paused and pulled her lips into a thin line. "I was concerned once before, and traveled all the way to Italy to bring her home, only to be disappointed by her yet again. She is a disloyal, ungrateful gel. This is the second time she has run off, and I am through with her. I am done with you, too, Mrs. Silver. Get out of my sight."

The dowager whistled, and the dogs followed her into her dressing room, where she waited for the door to close behind the wretched, unfaithful housekeeper. For a long moment the dowager sat in silence.

Though the room was quiet, her heart was pounding in her ears like heavy claps of thunder. She could endure it no longer. She fell to her knees and collapsed into a fit of despair.

"Damn her!" she cried. "Damn that wayward child! How could she have left us like this?"

Chapter Twenty

"Tell me what I need to know about Murdoch and Raonaid," Lachlan said to Angus as he tossed a loaded saddlebag over the back of Catherine's horse. "Where are they living, and will he think I have come to seek vengeance for his invasion of this castle three years ago?"

"He is living outside Edinburgh," Angus replied. "Directly south of the castle in a stone manor house called Blue Waters, which he has let from a sea captain. Murdoch will speak with you if you tell him you are there on behalf of his sister. We have agreed on a truce, he and I, since we cannot escape the fact that we are brothers by marriage."

"What are the terms of this truce?" Lachlan asked.

Angus leaned a shoulder against the side of the stall. "Murdoch has agreed never to come within a ten-mile radius of Kinloch."

"And what have you agreed to?" Lachlan asked as he buckled the saddlebags.

"I've agreed not to hunt him down and kill him like the dirty dog that he is. To this day I believe I got the lesser end of the bargain."

Lachlan regarded him keenly. "Well, I suppose there must be sacrifices. You are married to his sister, after all, and I doubt she'd be pleased if you dirked her own brother. Even if he does deserve it."

"Aye, and my wife's pleasure has always been my primary concern."

Lachlan nodded with a grin. "I remember. But are you sure you don't want me to take care of him for you? I could make it look like an accident."

The corner of Angus's mouth curled up in the smallest hint of a smile. "Your offer is very tempting, Lachlan, but I'm a man of my word, so I will keep to the truce."

"So will I, then," he replied, "unless he pulls a dirk on me, or tries to put a musket ball in me, in which case I will consider the terms null and void. Anything else I should know?"

"Aye. There is the issue of Murdoch's renewed interest in another rebellion. It might cause trouble for you."

"How so?"

Angus glanced over his shoulder as if to ensure there was no one about. "Catherine's father might have been a loyal Jacobite, but her cousin, the earl, is a stanch Hanoverian with no love for Highlanders."

"You don't have to tell me that. He shot me in the arm."

"Did he, now? Well, you might want to keep that to yourself. It only serves to prove that Catherine may be an enemy. She certainly stands in the way of a great deal of money for the Jacobites. We all know what will happen to her inheritance if she does not live long enough to see her twenty-fifth birthday."

"According to her father's last will and testament, it will be forfeited to the rebellion."

"Aye, and the situation is especially sensitive these days, since the attempt on the young prince's life. Many Scots are shouting for justice, and they look at every Hanoverian as a murderer. The fact that Catherine was recovered in Italy does not reflect well on her, since the Stuart court is currently in Rome."

Lachlan stopped what he was doing and faced Angus with a frown. "What are you speaking of? Do you mean Charles, the son of King James? He is an infant in the cradle. Are you saying someone tried to murder King James's newborn son?"

Angus regarded him with disbelief. "You truly *have* been obsessed with your curse, Lachlan. You've not seen what's been happening all around you."

Instantly frustrated, Lachlan swung around and yanked at the saddlebags to ensure they were soundly in place. "Well, that's about to change."

He could no longer continue to live for his vengeance alone. If Murdoch and Raonaid succeeded in raising another rebellion, more of his countrymen would die.

And who the devil tried to kill young Prince Charlie?

"What do you want me to do?" he asked Angus pointedly, facing him again. "I could try to talk sense to Murdoch. Perhaps discourage him from starting another war."

Angus moved forward and stroked Theodore's neck. "That won't be necessary. My good friend Duncan MacLean, the Earl of Moncrieffe, knows the right people, and he is planning a trip to Edinburgh very soon. He will take on that challenge. He has no love for Murdoch. But *you* . . ." Angus's blue eyes narrowed. "Just keep Lady Catherine safe. Use false names at all times. Do not stay long in Edinburgh, and keep your presence there a secret. After you've met with Raonaid, deliver Catherine home to Drumloch as quickly as possible to collect the inheritance. Once it belongs to her, it will no longer be a temptation for the Jacobites."

"It won't be easy to keep our presence a secret, once we meet Raonaid."

Angus nodded. "I understand your concern, but I know Raonaid. She will not betray a twin."

Lachlan eyed him carefully. "What if you're wrong?"

"Then do what you must to keep her quiet. Whatever it takes."

Four other clansmen entered the stables just then, and Lachlan turned. "Good morning," he said, forcing himself to focus on the task of leading these men into the Lowlands and delivering Catherine safely back to her family. "Are you packed and ready to go?"

"That we are, sir," Roderick replied. "You remember my brother, Rodney?"

Indeed, Lachlan had known these men for many years. One was tall, dark, and lanky; the other was short, big boned, and fair-haired—their differences due to the fact that they had the same mother but different fathers.

"Aye, good to see you again," Lachlan replied as they shook hands.

"This here is Gawyn MacLean," Roderick said. "He'll be doing the cooking for us."

"He's one of Duncan MacLean's men," Angus mentioned. "We fought together at Sherrifmuir and wreaked havoc together for a few years afterward. He's an expert swordsman and fast on his feet."

Gawyn was a tall Highlander who sported a shaggy mane of red hair and a matching beard. His freckled face was marked by a diagonal scar. He stepped forward to pump Lachlan's hand.

"And this is Alexander MacEwen," Roderick continued. "He knows every loch, glen, and glade from here to the bottom of the Scottish Borders. He'll keep us heading in the right direction, won't you, Alex?"

The fourth clansman reached out to shake Lachlan's hand as well. He was a good-looking young lad with brown hair and gray eyes.

"Are you new to Kinloch?" Lachlan asked. "I don't remember your face."

"Aye, sir," Alex replied in a polite tone. "I'm second cousin to the chief's wife. I came up from Glasgow six months ago, took a shining to the place, and never left."

Angus gestured toward Alexander with a toss of his golden head. "He's a good man, and I'd trust him with my life. He and Gwendolen grew up together. He's a fast rider, and good with a sword."

"Ah," Lachlan replied.

A shadow passed across the open stable door just then, and Catherine stepped into view, wearing the shabby old cloak he had purchased from Abigail. Beneath it, she wore a modest blue skirt with green plaid trimmings, and green stays over a white shift. Her hair was swept up into a loose, untidy knot.

It was all part of the disguise—to prevent her from looking like an heiress—but he wasn't sure how much good it would do. She was still breathtakingly beautiful. All the men, including the great Lion himself, went speechless for a moment while she stood before them in the doorway.

Lachlan approached her. "Good morning, Lady Catherine." He respectfully offered his arm.

Her expression warmed at the sight of the same chestnut gelding he had purchased for her at the inn where they spent their first night.

Patting Theodore's nose, she whispered, "We meet again." She ran her gloved hands down the smoothly muscled length of his neck. "Well groomed, I see." She stroked his shining mane, and he responded by nuzzling her ear.

One of the stable hands hurried forth to hold Theodore steady while she mounted and settled her pretty bottom into the saddle.

"Well, gentlemen? I am ready to depart. Shall we venture onward?"

Lachlan looked up at her, sitting proudly and cheerfully in the saddle while she looked down at all of them with a charming enthusiasm that sparked around him like fireworks.

After a decade of seducing countless, nameless women who wanted nothing more from him than a quick tumble in a haystack—and never once becoming besotted with a single one of them—this feeling in his gut plagued him. His desire for Catherine was insatiable, and it was dangerously distracting.

But somehow, *somehow*, he had to find a way to accept that he could not have her. He certainly could not make love to her, and he didn't think he could manage all the other things without it eventually coming to that. Which created a problem. For although he was a renowned Scottish warrior who faced death and doom without hesitation on the battlefield, he did not know if he was strong enough, or brave enough, to resist the tempting allure of Lady Catherine Montgomery.

Clearly, she was the greatest challenge of his life.

He had never wanted her more.

Chapter
Twenty-one

The first full day of travel passed quickly, the moments weaving together into an impressive tapestry of changing landscapes, which were as beautiful and moving to Catherine as any grand opera or priceless work of art.

Earlier in the morning, when the cool Highland mist hung low over the dewy grass in the meadows, they had trotted across the castle bridge, galloped over the field toward the east, and slipped gingerly into the cover of the forest, where autumn leaves detached themselves from the treetops and floated lightly to the ground all around them.

Alexander, the youngest clansman and closest to Catherine's age, had ridden ahead to scout out their route, and returned after an hour to discuss the best options with Lachlan, who rode several yards in front of Catherine.

The other three Scots rode behind her, and though there was no one to talk to, she could not complain of boredom—at least not yet—for the journey itself was enough of a challenge and distraction to keep her mind occupied.

Late in the afternoon, they were forced to cross a

fast-moving river, and Catherine had to coax and wheedle Theodore down the slick muddy slope to reach the water. They slipped and skidded at the bottom, and together plunged into the icy river with a heavy, shocking splash that pulled a gasp from her throat.

Theodore kept his footing over the slippery rocks below the surface while the cold water swirled around them and penetrated Catherine's skirts to the tops of her thighs. At least the sound of the rushing water drowned out Theo's panicked whinnies.

When they reached the other side and galloped up the bank, she ran her hand down his russet neck, gentling him. "Well done," she said. Her own heart was racing, and she was relieved to have made it across.

She looked up then, to find Lachlan watching her intently.

"Are you all right?" he asked, waiting for her just ahead in a grove of junipers.

"We're fine." She urged Theodore into a light canter and rode past Lachlan, to lead the way. He soon caught up with her and trotted alongside.

"Do you know which way we should be going, lassie?" he asked.

"I haven't a clue," she confessed, "but I am confident that you will rein me back in if I lead us astray."

He glanced over his shoulder to check on the others, who were out of sight, though Catherine could hear them shouting as they crossed the river.

"We shouldn't ride together," Lachlan said. "The others will be watching us, and they will soon suspect something. They will see what is obvious and know that I have taken certain liberties with you, which I had no right to take. We must guard your reputation from this moment on."

Catherine's mood dipped sharply at his sudden penchant for propriety. "I told you last night that my reputation is already in ruins. I don't care what anyone thinks."

"But I have no right to your affections, lass. Nothing can happen between us, and you know that."

Her temper flared unexpectedly, for she had been waiting so long just to be with him. She had hoped to secretly flirt during the journey, perhaps sneak off and be alone. She'd dreamed of being kissed in the moonlight, like she was kissed in the stable the night before. She had thought of little else since the moment he left her in the feasting hall, but now his words wounded her. She wanted to shout at him but somehow managed to keep her voice steady.

"Why would you say such a thing? You have every right to my affections, if I wish to bestow them upon you."

"But you should *not* wish to. That is the point. It's not wise." He lowered his voice, glancing over his shoulder again. "I will not lie to you, Catherine. You know I desire you, but Angus was right to send the others with us. They will keep me in my place."

"Is it because of the curse?" she asked. "Because soon we will reach Raonaid, and I will do whatever it takes to convince her to set you free."

He shook his head. "It's not just that. It's *everything*. I shouldn't have kissed you last night. I shouldn't have come to your bed yesterday. All of that was wrong. It will only make things more difficult."

A frosty chill hung on the edge of his words, and she reacted with anger at the rejection. "What things? You talk about it as if it is all about you, and *your* choices. Do I not have any say in this?"

His dark eyes bored into hers. "You can say whatever you like, lass, but it will not change the fact that we cannot be . . ." He stopped. "I cannot be anything to you, other than your escort to Edinburgh, and eventually back to Drumloch."

"What if I don't *want* to go back?" she blurted out in a sudden flash of anger.

Something wild blazed in his expression, as if he was tempted in that instant to steal her away forever, to throw her over the back of his warhorse and gallop off into parts unknown.

But then his eyes turned cold again and he kicked in his heels. "Then I'd think you were very foolish."

He took off in a quick gallop, then slowed to a walk just ahead, leaving her behind to ride alone.

Catherine sucked in a breath and fought to crush the heavy aching sensation inside her heart. This was not fair. None of it. She didn't care that she was a nobleman's daughter with a sizable inheritance. She didn't want the money or the jewels or the gowns or anything else that came with her privileged social position. All she wanted was to be a normal person, to remember her life, to perhaps know the sister who had been torn from her at birth. She wanted to love whomever she wished to love. And she wanted to help Lachlan rid himself of that wretched curse that was keeping him from her.

Perhaps her twin would be able to help her with a few of those things.

She wondered uneasily how Raonaid would react to seeing her own mirror image for the first time.

Did she even know she had a sister? And would she be welcoming?

"Would you like to stop for the night, Lady Catherine?"

Catherine started at the appearance of Alexander MacEwen, the young scout, who trotted up beside her when she had been, quite frankly, in danger of drifting off to sleep and toppling off her horse onto the grassy moor. They had been riding for many hours, and her muscles were aching. She felt clammy all over.

Shaking herself awake, she strove to smile. "I beg your pardon, Alex. I did not hear you approach. I suppose that means I am in need of a respite. Perhaps it would be prudent to stop. I'm sure the horses could use the rest as well."

"I'll ride ahead and speak to Lachlan," he replied.

Catherine shifted uncomfortably in the saddle while he galloped off. He spoke to Lachlan briefly, then wheeled his horse around and galloped back.

"I know a cave not far from here," he explained as he slowed his horse to walk beside her again. "Lachlan is familiar with it. We'll stop there for the night, and Gawyn will cook us a hot meal."

"That sounds wonderful." She was eager to stretch her legs and feed her groaning belly.

She and the young Highlander rode in silence for a few minutes across the wide moor, flanked on both sides by grassy mountains. A wolf howled somewhere in the distance.

"How is it that you know this country so well?" she asked Alexander.

"I used to hunt a fair bit with my father, and I did some scouting during the uprising. I learned quickly how to avoid the redcoats and get from one place to another without being seen. I found all the best places to hide away for a night or two."

She studied his profile in the dusky light. He was a handsome young man, slender, with a clean face and strong-looking hands. His hair was shiny and brown and cropped short, unlike most of the other clansmen, who wore bushy beards and unkempt hair.

"I see why Angus sent you along with us," she said. "You seem very capable."

He surveyed the moor judiciously. "I'd do anything for the great Scottish Lion. He's a good husband to my cousin, and he's a fair chief to the MacEwens."

"And what about Lachlan?" she boldly asked. "What do you know of him?"

Alexander glanced the other way when he spoke. "I'm afraid I don't know much about him, my lady, other than the gossip I've heard."

Her heart thudded against her ribs. "And what, exactly, have you heard?"

"That he's a highly skilled warrior and very brave," Alex quickly replied. "But he also has a reputation with the lassies. I'm told they all swoon when he walks into a room. I've also heard there's some sort of curse that keeps him from taking a wife." He awkwardly cleared his throat and shrugged. "But what do I know of it? I only met him for the first time this morning. He seems like a decent enough fellow. Angus is loyal to him, and that's good enough for me." He glanced at her curiously. "What about you, Lady Catherine? I understand you have no memory of your life. That cannot be easy. It's no wonder you are out here, searching."

"Searching." She inhaled deeply and looked up at the dusky sky. "Yes, that is exactly what I am doing. I continue to hope that something will happen that will spark a memory. Without any recollection of the things I have seen and done, my life seems rather meaningless."

He spoke with a kindness that touched her heart. "I am sure your memories will come back to you, my lady. I often forget things," he added, "and then one day, somehow as if by magic, I remember. You just have to relax, and try not to force it."

He turned in the saddle and whistled to the other Highlanders who were following at a short distance. They urged their horses into a canter.

"I'm going to ride ahead with Gawyn," he told her, "and set up camp. The others will see you there safely."

"Thank you, Alex."

He galloped off, but she did not watch him ride. Instead, she squinted through the pink twilight, wondering if Lachlan would share a private moment with her later, as Alex just had.

They ate supper in a small cave beneath a rocky outcropping, all sitting around the fire on beds of fur that covered the cold, earthen floor, and would later provide a soft place to sleep for Lady Catherine.

Lachlan announced that the clansmen would sleep

just outside, guarding the entrance, but when he spoke the words, he experienced an ache of discomfort at the thought of Catherine sleeping alone in this cold hole in the mountain while he was outside, also sleeping alone.

Well, not alone exactly. With the others. But they were invisible to him. Everyone and everything was invisible when Catherine was near.

He hated the fact that they had argued that day. Hated that she was so lovely in the firelight and was glancing at him frequently, but looking away whenever their eyes met.

She was punishing him, he knew, for how he had pushed her away after the river crossing. But what else could he do? Treat her the way he treated other women? Smile and flirt, and flatter her?

God help him, he couldn't even look at her without wanting to hold her.

Everyone sat down to eat, and he was pleased at least that Gawyn MacLean had put together such a tasty meat stew, which he'd boiled in an iron pot over the fire and served with crusty rye bread and a full-bodied wine in fine pewter goblets. Lachlan would have to thank Angus for sending such a functional fellow.

He would not thank him, however, for sending Alexander, for the lad had pushed his way into the circle to sit beside Catherine on the fur, and now they were eating their suppers together, laughing and engaging in light conversation while the others looked on and listened.

Alexander told her, in painful detail, about his schooling in Glasgow, and now he was asking her questions about her own upbringing, trying to help her remember things.

He was too polite. And helpful. And wholesome looking.

Lachlan didn't like him.

Catherine, on the other hand, seemed to have taken a fancy to him. They had ridden together across the moor for near a quarter of an hour that evening.

Ach! Lachlan tossed his plate aside, for he had suddenly lost his appetite. He had made a noble effort that afternoon to do the right thing and put some distance between them, and the very next minute this boyish upstart was slinking up beside her, working a little too hard to charm and impress.

The lad reminded Lachlan of himself in his younger days, and that did not sit well in his stomach.

Downing the last of his wine in a single gulp, he tossed the goblet into a bucket and stood. "Alex! I need you outside to help groom the horses before it gets too dark."

The young Highlander looked up in surprise, leaped to his feet, and tripped over the corner of the fur as he dropped his plate into the water bucket.

"Aye, sir." He strode purposefully out of the cave.

Catherine frowned up at Lachlan. "It could not wait?" she said. "Poor Alex wasn't finished his supper."

"He looked done to me."

They stared at each other for a tense moment while the others shoveled stew faster into their mouths. A starving bunch they were, apparently.

Catherine shook her head at him in a somewhat scolding manner, and he wanted very much to ask her what was so special about Alex MacEwen that she couldn't bear to see him go. But that would reveal to everyone that he was jealous and that this woman was getting under his skin, so he simply walked out.

After supper, Catherine lounged back on the soft fur with a second goblet of wine and looked toward the mouth of the cave. Alex and Lachlan had not returned since they went outside to tend to the horses, and she was beginning to worry that Lachlan had sent the young clansman on a fool's errand in the dark—to scale and scout the mountaintops on the other side of the moor or to measure the depth of the next raging river they might need to cross.

She stood and excused herself from the others. Outside, away from the warmth of the fire, the air was cold and damp on her cheeks. It smelled of winter.

The chill penetrated the fabric of her gown. Gathering her shawl more tightly about her shoulders, she peered through the darkness but could see nothing through the shifting mist, which hovered in brooding silence over the moor. If not for the sound of the horses nearby, munching on grass, she might have thought she was alone and that the rest of the world—mountains and all—had been swallowed up by the fog.

"You should go back inside," a voice said, husky and low and *oh,* so familiar.

She spun around and spotted Lachlan. He was a shadowy figure leaning against the outside wall of the cave. His tartan was pulled up over his head and wrapped around his shoulders like a cloak.

"Where is Alexander?" she asked, feeling some concern for the young clansman, who had been very kind to her and was only trying to help pass the time by striking up conversations.

"I'm up here, my lady," he keenly replied from an overhanging rock above.

Catherine lifted her gaze. The lad's legs were swinging back and forth over the edge.

"Oh, there you are." She felt rather foolish all of a sudden.

Lachlan lowered his hood. "Do you need something, Lady Catherine?"

Even through the darkness, she could feel the heat of their shared awareness of each other. The silky cadence of his voice sent a tremor of longing through her veins. It also revealed the desire he could not hide. At least not from her.

He wanted to keep her at bay, of course. He had made that abundantly clear. He wanted to behave properly in front of the others, but she could sense, deep in the workings of her body, that he was not pleased about it.

"Yes, I do need something," she replied. "I wish to speak with you privately, Lachlan. Alex, would you excuse us?"

It was a bold request. Lachlan was probably gritting his teeth at her blatant disregard for his earlier command—to hide what existed between them—but she didn't care if the others knew. She felt no need to hide the truth. Why should she?

She realized suddenly that her memory loss had erased any inhibitions she might have felt if she'd had a real life and a reputation worth caring about. But she did not. As far as she was concerned, anything before six months ago simply did not exist; therefore, her persona had no genuine value to her. In that way, she was perhaps a bit reckless.

Alex hopped down from the ledge. "I'll join the others by the fire."

As soon as he was gone, Catherine spoke in an angry whisper. "You didn't have to treat him like that."

"Like what? I didn't say a word just now."

"He's intimidated by you."

Lachlan merely shrugged. "He's just young, that's all."

"And how old are you? You've never told me."

His eyes lifted briefly, as if he was surprised by the question. "Three-and-thirty."

In her mind, she worked out the details of his life. If he had been cursed for three years and the curse had begun on the tenth anniversary of his wife's death, he would have been less than twenty when he married.

"Will you walk with me?" she asked. "I want to speak with you, and I don't want the others to hear."

"It's dark," he replied. "The moor is rocky. You'll fall and hurt yourself."

"Or *you* will."

Lachlan let out a breath of annoyance and pushed away from the wall. "You don't give up, do you, lass? Pick up your skirts. We'll stay close to the hillside, and we'll just go far enough away that we won't be heard. Will that suffice?"

"I suppose it will have to."

He took her by the hand and led her away from the

cave entrance, past the horses. He sat down on a big boulder and raked his fingers through his hair.

"Is it that much of a chore just to talk to me?" she asked, wishing she did not feel so hurt by his frosty demeanor, but there it was.

He looked up. "Aye. It's the worst chore imaginable. You know how I feel, Catherine. You know all the things I want to do to you, but this curse prevents me from doing anything, so I just wish you would let me be and let me get through this trip to Edinburgh without making things harder than they already are."

Oh.

Her breath sailed out of her lungs. She had been so absorbed in her own need to be close to him—to feel the way she had felt the night before, when he kissed her up against the stable wall—that she had ignored the fact that he was not actually rejecting her. It was quite the opposite, in fact. She understood it logically, she supposed, but her heart only felt one thing: the agony of being apart.

She sat down. "This is difficult," she said. "To be honest, I wish the others hadn't come. We would have been fine on our own, just as we were before, and I would have been happier, not having to hide how I truly feel."

"Do not say it," he growled. "I've been in hell all day. I want to touch you and hold you—but I can't. And tonight that young MacEwen . . ." He flung a hand through the air. "All I wanted to do was drag him out of the cave by the ear, toss him up onto his horse, smack the animal's rear flank, and send him galloping back to Kinloch—just for talking to you."

It was not quite a vow of everlasting love, but it was enough to make Catherine smile, for he had just confessed that he was jealous.

"Do not shut me out," she implored, trying to move past all of that. "You are the only person with whom I feel I can be myself. Even if we do not kiss or touch each other like lovers, I still need you. Please ride with me tomorrow. That is all I ask. I am alone, and lonely, and you were hurtful today."

She wished she could see his expression, but his face was shrouded in the murky gloom of the night.

"I didn't mean to hurt you, lass," he softly said, and all at once he was back inside her heart, as a hazy sensuous heat flared between them. "That's the last thing I wanted to do. But we both need to forget about certain things we've done. There's no future in it."

"I have no regrets," she told him. "I never will."

He bowed his head and said nothing for a long while, and when he finally spoke his voice was firm with resolve. "I must say something to you, lass, and I hope you will take it to heart." He gazed at her directly. "I believe the only reason I fire your passions is because you cannot remember anyone else in your life that you might have cared for in the past. You said it yourself. You're alone, and you're lonely. So don't make too much of what happened between us."

"I could say the same thing to you," she replied. "That you only want me because you haven't had a woman in three years, and you are perpetually . . . *aroused*."

He inclined his head at her, as if to suggest it was a dangerous thing of which to remind him.

In a flash of movement he reached out and pulled her close. He crushed her body against his and wrapped his arms around her, keeping her warm as he feathered his lips across her cheek.

"You're right," he whispered in a low, seductive voice. "I've been aroused since the moment I met you, but I have not felt that way in a long, long time—because when you're celibate long enough, you eventually begin to forget how it feels to even *want* it."

"I wouldn't know about that," she shakily replied, fighting against overpowering desires that left her trembling with need. "I don't remember how I felt about my first time. It disturbs me greatly to think that I have lost that part of my life."

He nuzzled her ear, and she knew in the depths of her soul that he understood her meaning.

"You don't have to talk about it, lass."

"I might want to someday."

"If you do, I will listen."

She snuggled closer to him, burrowing into the warmth of his body, the soft wool of his tartan, and the clean, musky scent of his skin. There was nowhere on earth she would rather be than right there on that rock, with him, where she felt safe, protected, and cared for, even after he had told her to keep away.

Catherine lifted her face to look up at him. "Will you ride with me tomorrow?" she asked. "There is no reason why you shouldn't. We'll be on horseback. There will be no touching."

His head dipped lower, and she could feel the curve of his smile when he spoke. "You say that while your hand is rubbing my chest and your sweet breath is beating upon my neck."

"I can't help it," she replied with laughter. "I'm cold, and you are so warm. I need your heat."

He gathered her closer, bracing both feet on the ground to keep them from sliding forward, supporting her legs across his lap. "Is that better?"

"Yes. I only wish we could stay like this forever."

They sat together in the rolling fog, their breaths creating steam, while Catherine gloried in the sensation of his hand toying with the locks of hair at her temple, cupping the side of her face.

"We should go back," he said after a while, brushing his lips across her forehead.

"Not yet. Please, just a few more minutes. This feels so good."

"You shouldn't say things like that, Catherine."

She didn't plan it or think about it consciously, but somehow her hand slid down his chest to his hard stomach, along the side of his hip, and lower still, across the front of his kilt.

He was fully erect, and she buried her face in his shoulder. All she wanted was to feel the shape of him, to know the contours of his body, but he quickly seized her wrist.

"Not a wise idea."

She swallowed hard, frustrated by the sudden wall that came crashing down in front of her. "I didn't mean to start anything."

They stared at each other tensely in the wintry chill.

"It's time to go now," he gruffly said, rising to his feet. "I'll take you back."

Catherine slid off his lap while her blood pumped hotly through her veins, sending a rush of unfulfilled desire straight to her core. She felt light-headed and dizzy. It was a wonder she did not faint dead away at his feet. "Are you angry with me?"

He shook his head. "It was my fault."

"No, it was mine."

Again, like the night before, he escorted her away—to leave her in the care of others. It was the gentlemanly thing to do, of course, but it left her wanting so much more.

"Will you ride with me tomorrow?" she asked again when they reached the cave entrance.

He leaned very close—so close she felt the scratch of his whiskers on her cheek. "I don't think you know what you're asking of me." He whistled at the others to indicate that it was time to leave the cave. "Out, now!" he shouted. "Lady Catherine needs her rest."

But rest was not what she needed, and just before Lachlan turned away, he gave her a look that indicated he knew exactly what it was that she required.

And that particular thing . . . He needed it, too. Far worse than she did.

Chapter Twenty-two

Lachlan did not ride with Catherine the next day, nor did he sit with her when they stopped to eat a light lunch at noon. Instead, he sat on the other side of the cook fire with Rodney and Roderick. Afterward they practiced a few maneuvers with their claymores while Gawyn cleared away the food and eating utensils.

They stopped again later in the afternoon to water the horses at a shallow burn and eat a light meal of bread and cheese, but Lachlan went off alone while the others took care to see that Catherine was looked after.

Not a moment passed where she was not aching to be with him, but he made every effort to avoid her and maintain a certain distance at all times. Their eyes rarely met—he seemed determined not to acknowledge her existence—and it was all Catherine could do not to march straight up to him, pound her fists on his chest, and demand that he talk to her.

By nightfall, she was more frustrated than ever and determined to crush her unbidden desires for him. She would not continue to yearn for a man if he did not welcome her attentions. She would move forward and forget him. She had a sister to meet after all—a twin. That would be enough.

The sun was setting in the sky by the time they rode onto a pebbly beach, where Gawyn was already waiting for them with a roaring fire, an open jug of wine, and a sizzling skillet that gave off a succulent meaty aroma.

"It smells delicious, Gawyn," Catherine said to him as she dismounted and led Theodore to the water's edge, where he drank thirstily.

Feeling tired and clammy, she looked down at the water lapping up onto the shore at her feet and wondered how cold it would be, for she longed to take a bath. She looked up at the clear evening sky, blew into the air to see if her breath was visible in the chill—*it was*—then wondered when they would reach a village where they could enjoy a full night's rest in a warm and cozy inn, before reaching their destination.

"I appreciate the compliment, Lady Catherine," Gawyn called out to her. "I only hope it tastes as good as it smells."

She tossed her head and smiled to indicate that she had every confidence in his culinary abilities, then heard footsteps crunching across the pebbles, approaching from behind. It was Lachlan, leading his horse to the loch for a drink. He came to stand directly beside her.

Their eyes met in the pink haze of the setting sun, and all at once the anxieties of the day went quiet and still in her head. She could almost hear the gentle rush of her blood, whispering through her veins. She felt frozen in time, at rest and peaceful. He was so impossibly handsome, and everything about him made her feel safe and euphoric—but she willed herself to maintain her good sense. She simply had to.

He peered at her sideways, assessing her mood, and she decided to speak frankly. "You were very rude today," she said.

"It was for the best, lass. We both know it."

"Yes, after today, I have come to realize that. There is no need to repeat it."

Thirst quenched, Theodore lifted his head. Thankful for his convenient timing, Catherine turned away and led Theo back to the edge of the forest, where he could nibble on the tall grasses. Roderick greeted her there.

"I'll take him from here, Lady Catherine." He proceeded to remove Theo's saddle and lead him away to be groomed.

Farther from the beach, within the shelter of the trees, Alex and Rodney were assembling a tent for her to sleep in.

Catherine approached Gawyn, who was shaking the sizzling skillet to and fro over the fire.

"How soon will it be ready?" she asked.

"It's ready now, my lady," he replied.

Somehow she managed to paste on a polite smile while glancing briefly over her shoulder to watch Lachlan lead his horse into the woods.

Shortly after midnight, Catherine woke from another frightening dream to discover a hand covering her mouth.

Eyes wide, heart pounding like a drum, she realized it was Lachlan. He was using his body to pin her down while she wildly thrashed about.

"*Shh*, lass, calm yourself," he whispered into her ear. "You're dreaming again."

She could not seem to think clearly enough to form words. Perhaps she had cried out. It was likely that she had. What had happened? She was out of breath now, and perspiring.

Slowly he withdrew his hand, and she lay very still, staring up at him, bewildered and disoriented, while the warmth of his body helped to calm the fires of her anxiety.

He relaxed as she did, and inched back slightly. "Are you all right now?"

She labored to catch her breath. "I think so. Did I wake everyone?"

"No, just me. Luckily it was my turn to be on watch. The others are sleeping on the beach. The sound of the waves would have drowned out the sound of your voice." He pushed her damp hair away from her face. "Was it like before?"

"Yes. Only this time, I saw a wee bairn. It's a dream I've had before."

"What sort of dream?" His brow furrowed with concern.

"I saw myself smothering the life out of an infant boy, or attempting to. They were my own hands on the pillow, and it was always the same—blue with white fringe. I could not seem to stop myself, even though I knew it was wrong."

The features of Lachlan's face contorted into a frown, and he sat back, recoiling from her. "Whose baby was it?"

"I don't know."

Oh, God. Was it her own? Did she have a child? Had she tried to kill it?

The possibility of such a hideous act flooded her mind with horror, and she scrambled away from Lachlan, rising in a flash to her feet.

"Light the candle," she whispered. "Please hurry." She could not bear to be in darkness.

He moved to the table, found the flintbox, and struck a flame. A flickering golden light illuminated the tiny shelter.

I am a madwoman . . .

The unwelcome thought shrieked through her brain.

Or a killer. Perhaps I should run!

Catherine stood in a panic, astonished, and let her hands fall away from her face and drop to her sides. Her eyes darted to the tent flap.

Lachlan held up a hand as if she were a frightened animal in the forest who might spook and dash. "It was just a dream," he said. "It might be nothing. Maybe it was a vision of something—something that has nothing to do with you. Remember your sister."

"Raonaid. Yes. She sees the future."

"Aye, she has a gift. Clearly you have one, too. Maybe what you saw was something else."

Catherine sucked in great gulps of air. He was suggesting that there might be other explanations for the disturbing images that haunted her sleep. It would be a comfort to believe he was right, but alas, she suspected otherwise. . . .

"I think I may have done something very wrong," she said. "I fear I will be caught."

His voice lowered to a hush. "That's how they found

you, isn't it? In a farmer's stable, huddled and shivering in a corner, terrified out of your wits? You wouldn't let anyone touch you."

"I was running from something."

Time seemed to stand still for a moment. Their breaths puffed into the air, for it was cold inside the tent. Catherine hugged her arms around herself and shivered.

In the next instant, Lachlan was gathering her into his arms and holding her against the solid warmth of his body. His breath was hot and moist against her neck. "Let's get you warm."

He led her back to the bed of fur and knelt down on one knee, but her arms tightened around his neck. She gathered the wool of his tartan in one fist, his linen shirt in another, and pulled him closer to prevent him from drawing away.

"Please stay."

Still down on one knee, leaning above her, he glanced over his shoulder. "I don't want the others to know I'm here."

"Tell them I had a nightmare, that I was frightened to be alone. It's the truth."

He hesitated and cupped his forehead in a hand. "It's not really their opinions I worry about, lass. It's what might happen between us."

She moved to make room for him on the makeshift bed. "I trust you."

At last, he stretched out beside her. He wrapped an arm around her, and she rested her head on his shoulder.

"There is something you should know about that dream," he whispered as he nuzzled his lips across her ear. "It might be disturbing for you to learn of this, but

I cannot keep it from you, for you need to know what is happening in the world. If there is some connection between your dreams and these events, it might help to restore your memories."

She leaned up on one elbow. "What events?"

His eyes focused closely on hers. "Before we left the castle, Angus told me something about your sister, Raonaid. She has formed an attachment to his enemy, Murdoch MacEwen, Gwendolen's own brother, who was responsible for the siege on Kinloch three years ago. Murdoch was a passionate Jacobite then, but something has happened that has reignited his ambitions to reclaim the throne for the Stuarts."

Catherine took a breath and braced herself. "Tell me what it is."

"Are you aware that King James's wife gave birth to a son last December? They called him Charles."

"Yes, I know of it."

"He is the heir to the Stuart dynasty," Lachlan continued. "But not long after his birth, there was a plot to murder him in his cradle—obviously to thwart any future threat to the Hanover throne."

Catherine frowned. "What are you suggesting?"

His hand cupped her cheek. "The child was born in Rome, where the Royal Family is in exile. That is where the plot was hatched and discovered."

"They never found the culprit?"

"No."

"And I was found in Italy, not far outside of Rome." She pressed her hands to his chest and looked him in the eye. "You think I was involved in the plot to kill the prince?"

"I didn't say that."

"But you are thinking it, as I am. What if it is true? What if I was a spy using my father's reputation and friendship with King James in order to gain entrance to his court and kill his son?" She sat up abruptly. "It cannot be true. I would never try to kill a child, and surely my grandmother would have known if I was a member of the Jacobite court abroad, yet she claims to know nothing of my whereabouts over the past five years."

"Are you sure she can be trusted? She did not tell you about Raonaid."

Catherine considered it. "Perhaps she never knew about her."

Lachlan sat up. "What about your cousin, John? He is a staunch Hanoverian."

"Yes, but he has never shared his political ideas with me. Since my return, he has always been careful to avoid the issue of the succession, and I assumed it was because he did not wish to enter into a heated debate with me, for I was a passionate Jacobite in the past. At least, that is what they tell me. But what Jacobite would ever want to kill the Stuart heir?"

A gust of wind swept across the roof of the tent, and the canvas whipped noisily. Lachlan reached for the heavy woolen blanket she had kicked off during her sleep. It was balled up at her feet. He shook it out and wrapped it around her shoulders.

"Is that better?" he asked, sitting up beside her, rubbing her cold hands between his and blowing into them.

"Yes."

He kissed her on the forehead and lay down beside

her again. The fur was soft and warm beneath her body, and his presence in the cold night was a soothing balm to her anxieties.

"What would I do without you?" she asked. "You have come to my rescue more than once, and have taken such good care of me."

"One could argue the opposite. I took you away from the safety of Drumloch, and *now* look at you—having nightmares in the wilds of Scotland, sleeping outdoors beside a cursed Highlander who may be more of a danger to you than anything else you might envision in your nightmares."

She snuggled close to him, praying that he would not, in the next few minutes, decide to leave her. She wanted him to stay. He was her lifeline out of this empty void of her existence, where her past was merely fodder for speculation. He was an anchor of true human connection.

"As bad as it feels to imagine that I might have been involved in such a twisted plot, what if it's not that? What if I simply had a child of my own, and I tried to harm him?" The notion made her stomach roll with nausea.

"I do not believe you would do such a thing," he replied. "Not under any circumstances."

"How can you be sure?"

"It is not in your nature, lass."

She wondered how he could speak with such confidence about her nature when neither of them knew a thing about her behavior in the past, before her grandmother found her in Italy.

She gazed at Lachlan, sprawled out beside her, his rugged beauty a constant reminder of her frustration at not being free to love him. How could she when she did not know who she was?

"It would be best," he said, "if you did not tell anyone about your dream. Your own sister is at the center of this new rebellion, and if Murdoch suspects you of being a spy, involved in the plot to kill the Stuart prince, they might not . . ." He paused. "They might not welcome us with open arms."

"If I am guilty of such a crime against Scotland," she said, feeling increasingly uneasy, "would you not feel an obligation to turn me in?"

He turned his head on the pillow to look at her. "My only obligation is to protect you."

She chose her words carefully. "But if I tried to murder a child, I would not be worthy of your protection."

"You *didn't*," he said. "And nothing will convince me otherwise."

Chapter Twenty-three

For a few hours they slept soundly in the tent, until Lachlan stirred, shortly before dawn. Half-dozing, he grew conscious of Catherine's warm body, snuggled close to his in the darkness. He breathed in the enchanting fragrance of her hair and wallowed drowsily in the forbidden bliss of an early-morning arousal. She felt like heaven lying next to him, her soft, lush body conforming perfectly to his, and he sighed with pleasure, shifting his hips ever closer.

Still bleary with sleep, he moved his hand slightly and explored the engaging, provocative contours of her thigh, before journeying upward to the alluring curve of her slender waist. His thumb stroked across the smooth ridges of her rib cage, and he bided his time, waiting for wakefulness, while he resisted the urge to cup her whole breast in his palm.

Her blue eyes fluttered open, and she blinked at him sleepily, without uttering a word.

"I should go now," he whispered, wanting her with a dangerous urgency that thundered unbearably through his mind. He moved to sit up, but she reached out to stop him.

His eyes narrowed, for he could feel the tide of his self-control shifting while desire drowned out the more rational part of his brain that was warning him not to stay. Not to let go.

"Please don't leave yet," she pleaded in a velvety voice that touched him through the darkness. "Why not let me help you? Surely there are ways I can give you pleasure without evoking the curse. Just tell me how to touch you. Tell me what feels good."

He had no control over his erection, which responded quite favorably to her offer, while the rest of his body flooded with alarm.

Even in the murky shadows of the dawn, her beauty was pushing him over the edge, and he was painfully aware of her full, moist lips begging to be kissed.

"It wouldn't be wise," he whispered in a voice that shook.

"Why not?"

He swallowed over the torrent of passion building up inside him. "Because I say so. It's taken me a long time to learn how *not* to feel certain things, and it's best if I maintain that discipline."

"But why should you suffer like that, if I am willing to give you pleasure without asking for more? All you have to do is lie back and tell me what you like."

Her provocative words fed his engorged desires, and he shifted uncomfortably. She brushed a hand over his knee with a light and feathery touch, inched her body closer, testing his resolve. His heart throbbed lustily, and he clenched his jaw, fighting against an overpowering onslaught of physical sensation, as she slid her warm hand up under his kilt and massaged the thick muscles of his inner thigh.

He was overcome suddenly with a surprising rush of despair, for this represented all that he could not have—physical intimacy with a woman he wanted desperately.

And she was not just any woman. She was *this* woman, and he wanted her with a frenzy that made him shiver. His breath caught in his chest.

"Just relax," she whispered as she slid her hand farther up and finally reached his aching manhood. He was tempted in that spiraling moment of ecstasy to grab hold of her wrist and yank it out from under his kilt, but he resisted and instead let his eyes roll back in his head.

Pleasure trembled through him, potent and penetrating, while she stroked his heavy balls.

Senses attuned to her slightest movement, he listened to the sound of her mouth—her tongue licking across her lips—and uttered a deep groan of need. It took every ounce of strength he possessed not to rise up, seize control, and flip her over onto her back.

Catherine sat up just then and swung a leg over him, straddling over his knees and raising his kilt to expose his erection. Their eyes met. He was hungry for her. He wanted her with a recklessness that was burning through him like a fireball, out of control. He knew he should stop, but he could not refuse what she offered. He *would* take it. He would take all of it.

Carefully, she unfastened his brooch and slowly slid his tartan off his shoulder. Next she tugged his loose shirt out from under his belt. He raised his arms, and she pulled his shirt off over his head, then proceeded to remove his kilt. Everything was done with steady, measured movements. She did nothing in a hurry, and soon he was completely naked. The cool air upon his body inflamed his passions, and again he had to struggle to remain on his back when he wanted to rise up and take command of the situation, to undress *her*, to touch *her*.

Still straddled over him, Catherine bent forward to kiss and lick the quivering muscles of his stomach. Her tongue probed insistently into his navel, and the muscles in his legs began to shake. He brushed her hair to one side, out of the way, and rose up on an elbow to look down at her in the muted light.

To see a woman's head down there, so close to the core of his need, was enough to make him explode before she even touched him.

Ach! He wanted to tumble her onto her back right now and plunge himself into her hot, downy wetness! But he smothered those urges and reminded himself that if he had the will to resist all forms of sexual pleasure for three years, he could restrain himself from making love to this woman now.

Her lips found his mouth and she kissed him deeply, luxuriously, sighing with her own pleasure at the damp heat of their mingling tongues.

Lachlan reached up to hold her face in his hands, thrusting his hips forward, knowing there was no danger of penetration, for she was up on all fours above him, a safe distance away from his genitals.

"Tell me what to do," she whispered.

Her eagerness aroused him further, and he shivered with need.

"Do what comes naturally, lass. Just remember, I can't be under your shift when I come."

She nodded, and her thick, gleaming hair swept across his face. Lachlan stroked it back, so that he could see her eyes. She leaned forward to kiss him again. Her lips were damp and swollen with desire, and as her tongue met his, he understood consciously that this was dangerous for both of them, but the blinding force of his need could not be ignored. He wanted her with a fierce abandon that was beyond anything he'd ever known before. He had proven himself remarkably formidable over the past three years, but this was not the same.

Catherine dragged her mouth from his and eased back onto all fours while she kissed down the front of his neck and stroked her hands up and down his bare torso.

Kissing and licking his nipples with the silky flick of her tongue while her hands strayed downward to his thighs again, she smothered him in breathless, flame-hot kisses.

He lifted a knee and bumped into the sweet luscious haven between her thighs, the place he wanted to touch and penetrate, but could not.

In the next moment, she licked her palm and wrapped it wetly around him. Lachlan gasped and twitched beneath the skilful stroke of her hand. It had been so long since he'd been touched. He wasn't sure he could survive the pleasure of it.

She stroked him with a firm squeezing grace, then began to pump furiously, fast and quick. It was more than he could take. He felt like an untried adolescent. Something took hold of his senses. He lost all control, forgot who and where he was, as a blistering orgasm began to tremble and quake through his body. He tried to grab hold of Catherine's hand to slow her down, to hold off the crashing wave of fulfillment—because it was too soon, too fast, and he had never surrendered to a climax so quickly before. But almost immediately he found himself writhing on the bed of fur, clenching his jaw and gritting his teeth in abandon.

Abruptly he sat up, then flopped back down again and shot his seed onto his stomach in an explosion of lust that brought him right off the ground.

His eyes flew open, and he looked at Catherine to make sure she was not in a position that might risk her safety.

Thankfully she was not. At some point she had rolled off him, and she was now lying beside him.

"There, you see?" she said in a teasing, seductive voice. "There are *some* things we can do."

"Aye, darling," he wearily replied, dropping his head back down, feeling dazed and delirious, still shuddering with sensation. "And you did them very well. I never came so fast in my life. If news of this gets out . . ."

She smiled. "I promise it will be our secret."

He admired her beguiling beauty in the morning light and yearned to feel again the pleasure that had accompanied his surrender just now, but feared he might become addicted to it.

She reached for a towel in the supply pack.

"I need to go down to the loch and swim for a bit," he said, watching her face while she took great care in wiping his stomach.

"But it's so cold."

"I'm a Highlander," he said. "I'm accustomed to it."

And the shock of it would do him good.

She tossed the towel into the washbasin, then laid her head on his shoulder again.

For a long time after that, they lay together in the quiet dawn, just holding each other.

When the morning grew brighter, Lachlan reluctantly rose to his feet. Peering out of the shelter to make sure no one was about, he bent to pick up his shirt. He donned his tartan and buckled his belt, often glancing down at Catherine to make sure she was not offended by his hasty exit.

She did not appear to be. In fact, she seemed quite pleased with herself.

"You are the most handsome man I've ever seen," she said. "I cannot tear my eyes away. I love to look at you."

Her words filled him with a mixture of joy and unease, for he felt the same way about her, but he was not accustomed to such intense feelings and knew not what to do with them. In the past, if a woman spoke in such a way, he would simply kiss her on the cheek and thank her for her charming words, and tell her in return how lovely she was, before backing out of the room with a teasing smile.

He was about to leave now, but found that he could not summon such superficial endearments. He looked down at her, his expression serious and honest.

"I love to look at you, too," he replied. "I love everything about you."

She stood up, approached him slowly, and wrapped her arms around his neck. The tenderness of her embrace touched his heart, and he fought an irresistible impulse to change his mind about leaving and carry her back to the bed of fur.

"How soon will we reach Edinburgh?" she asked, dropping lower, for she had been standing on her toes. "I want more than anything to meet my sister, and I promise you, when I do, I will demand that she set you free. If that does not work, I will get down on my knees and beg. I will do whatever it takes."

He cupped her cheek. "I appreciate the offer, lass," he said, "but I can handle Raonaid myself."

"I want to help."

He shook his head at her. "I thought I was to be *your* champion, delivering you to safety, but it seems you wish to be mine."

"Yes, I want to be everything to you. I want to take away all of your torment. If only you would let me."

But could he? For more than ten years he had lived a life of shallow flirtations and emotional solitude, never giving his heart to another. He had held true to a vow that Glenna would be the only woman he would ever love, but that seemed a very long time ago now. It was another life. So much had changed. He had been with many women, few of whom he remembered, but he would never forget Lady Catherine Montgomery.

In this moment, he did not want to let her go. He would have to of course, for he was still cursed, and everything that existed between them seemed to be in a state of anarchy.

"Will you come to me again tonight?" she asked, still resting her hands on his shoulders.

"Tonight we will reach Killin and take a room there. You'll be more comfortable."

"But will you come and stay with me?" she pressed. "I don't care what the others think. Can you not command them to secrecy? Or perhaps you could climb through my window."

All of a sudden, he felt lighthearted and adolescent again. "You're a wild one, aren't you? Have you always been so keen for adventure?"

"I have no idea," she replied. "I am a mystery, even to myself."

He pushed a lock of her hair behind her ear. "And you think that meeting Raonaid will solve everything."

Perhaps he was jaded, but he was not so sure.

"I can only hope."

He couldn't help himself. Slowly, he bent his head and touched his lips to hers. It was not a kiss to satisfy his lust, however. It was a tender show of affection—and his desire to simply dissolve into her tranquility hit him very hard.

He stepped back and held her away from him. "I will scale the walls if I have to," he said, referring to their upcoming sojourn at the inn and feeling rather shaken by his readiness to make such a promise. "But I must go now. Go back to sleep for a little while." He backed out of the tent and felt the dawn's chill on his body.

It was a good thing. He needed it.

Running a hand down over his face, he experienced a flash memory of the orgasm and wanted very much to reciprocate. There were many things he wanted to do for Lady Catherine, and he would do at least some of them tonight.

He turned toward the loch and took off in a purposeful jog.

Chapter
Twenty-four

Edinburgh

Raonaid raised the hood of her cloak over her head as she stepped out of Murdoch's coach and collided with a rainy, blustery wind. The gusts whipped through her skirts and tugged at the empty basket she carried. Usually the streets of Edinburgh were bustling with activity at this time of day, but the foul weather had kept most sensible folk indoors by their fires.

Raonaid, however, wanted something, and when she wanted a particular thing there was little anyone could do to stop her. This morning, she desired cod from the fishermen's market and sugar for the cake she intended to serve the men that night, for Murdoch was planning a private gathering at the manor house, for a few select men of influence.

The mist and rain swept fast across the cobblestone street. Raonaid leaned into it as she walked, uttering an oath of pain when a wooden pail rolled into her path, clattering noisily across the stones and hitting her in the anklebone.

Suddenly it became tangled in her skirts. The ground

flew up to meet her. Her front teeth went through her bottom lip and pain shot down to her toes.

Struggling to recover, she rose up on all fours and looked down at the cobblestones, glistening with wetness. The wind and rain pummeled her face. She touched a finger to her bloodied lip, then watched the blood drip onto the street.

Immediately the stones began to move like waves in the ocean, and a dizzying sensation swirled through her brain.

Familiar with the experience—though she had never had it with cobblestones before—she focused her eyes and blinked repeatedly, willing the vision to grow clearer, while she watched the movement of her blood mixing with the shiny water, trailing jaggedly through the grooves and deep spaces between the stones.

Shadows came to life, and the cobbles twisted and swirled. What she saw held her captive, fixed to the ground, while the vision played out in front of her eyes.

Then it was gone, as quickly as it appeared, vanishing into the street.

She glanced up. Murdoch was standing over her. He pulled her roughly to her feet. "You saw something, didn't you? What was it? Tell me. Will the Stuarts rule again? Will I be a part of it? How soon? *Tell me!*"

She staggered sideways, feeling nauseous and weak. "That's not what I saw."

Murdoch shook her hard, then paused a moment, his eyes flashing with impatience, before he pulled her into his arms. "Take your time, darling," he said. "Then tell me everything you remember."

Squeezing her eyes shut against the driving wind and rain, Raonaid rested her head on his shoulder.

A sense of calm came over her, and she stepped back. Murdoch regarded her peevishly.

"I saw Lachlan MacDonald," she told him at last, still astonished by the clarity of the vision.

He frowned. "Angus MacDonald's cousin? The Laird of War at Kinloch? The one you cursed at Kilmartin Glen?"

She nodded. "Aye, but I cannot tell you what I saw."

Turning away from him, she pulled the hood of her cloak tighter around her face, shielding her eyes from the storm.

"Why not?" he asked, following her across the street.

Wet and shivering, disturbed by the vision, she ran faster toward the coach. "It does not concern you, Murdoch! Leave me be, or I swear, by all that is holy, I will curse you, too!"

She reached the coach at last and pounded her fist on the door. Murdoch came up behind her and tore it open. It swung on its hinges and banged against the outside wall.

Raonaid tossed her empty basket into the coach, grabbed hold of the rail, and hoisted herself into the dry interior, sheltered at last from the wind. She sat down and wiped the water from her cheeks while Murdoch climbed in and sat across from her.

They stared at each other tensely. His dark eyes studied her with displeasure, but she would not tell him of her vision. He could never know the truth—that what she had seen was Lachlan MacDonald, his enemy as well as her own, making love to her while she cried out with boundless rapture.

Catherine woke to the sound of water dripping with heavy wet plops onto the roof of the tent. Drawing the woolen blanket over her shoulders, she rose and padded to the flap to look outside, hoping that the weather would not slow their journey, for she was impatient to reach Edinburgh and meet her sister.

She untied the ribbons of the tent flap and scrutinized the morning rain. A light mist rolled smoothly along the mossy floor of the glade. Everything was shiny and dripping wet, but at least it was not a torrential downpour. Not yet, at any rate. It was a soft, gentle rain—not nearly enough to deter Catherine from venturing onward.

Voices and footsteps interrupted the tranquility. It was Lachlan and the cook, Gawyn, their tartans pulled over their heads to keep dry.

"Ah, look," Gawyn said cheerfully. "Her Ladyship has awakened. Did you sleep well enough?"

She and Lachlan shared no more than a passing glance as he led her horse closer to the tent and tethered him to a nearby branch. In that brief moment, however, she saw in Lachlan's eyes a secret desire and her heart fluttered with anticipation.

"Will we travel regardless of the rain?" she asked, making a deliberate effort to speak with casual indifference while hiding her impetuous urge to pull Lachlan back into the tent and repeat every delicious intimacy they had shared the night before.

"Aye," Lachlan replied, without looking at her. "So you best get yourself up and ready, my lady, or you'll soon feel the poles of that tent coming down on your head."

Gawyn's eyebrows lifted with surprise. "He's just havin' you on, Lady Catherine. He wouldn't really do it, would you, Lachlan?"

He shrugged, as if to say, *Why not?*

Taking him quite seriously, Catherine retreated into her temporary abode and dressed for the day ahead.

Within the hour, they were trotting away from the beach and riding through the forest, where the tall evergreens provided at least some shelter from the rain. Lachlan and Roderick rode out front to lead the way while Gawyn, Rodney, and Alex followed behind Catherine in a single column.

They rode in silence for most of the morning, plodding along at a slow and easy pace, until the wind picked up and Catherine began to feel a wet chill seeping through the heavy wool of her cloak.

Soon Alex trotted up beside her. "Are you warm enough, Lady Catherine?" His expression was creased with concern.

The wind howled through the treetops and blew the bottom of her cloak across her lap. "I am well enough, Alex. Do not suggest we stop on my account, for I am eager to reach the village and enjoy a hot meal and warm bed tonight. It will be a welcome luxury, to be sure."

An awkward silence ensued while he glanced over his shoulder at the others.

"Is there something wrong?" she asked.

His cheeks flushed bright red, but not from the cold. "I fear it is not my place to speak of such things, my lady—but I hold you in the highest regard, and for that reason, I cannot hold my tongue."

"What is it you speak of, Alex?"

He hesitated, then cleared his throat. "I know that Lachlan was with you last night, Lady Catherine. I saw him leave your tent before dawn."

Catherine worked hard to control her anger. "You are correct in one regard, Alex. It is *not* your place to speak of such things."

His cheeks drained of all color. "I apologize, my lady. I did not mean to offend, but you asked me to speak freely."

She regarded him carefully for a moment, scrutinizing the purpose of his intentions. "I did," she admitted. "Was there anything else you saw? Or perhaps heard?"

Alex flushed anew. "I heard him say that he would visit you in your chamber again tonight, when we reach the inn. I heard him say he'd scale the walls."

Catherine fought to hold on to her composure while another part of her railed with indignation. "I must repeat myself, Alex. This is none of your business. It is a private matter between Lachlan and me."

"I understand that, my lady," he argued, "and I am deeply sorry, but I must speak my mind. I do not mean to intrude upon your private affairs, but I feel it is my duty to inform you that Lachlan MacDonald is not to be trusted with your heart. He has a reputation for seducing young lassies just like yourself. He makes them behave in irrational ways, and there's a curse upon him. I don't want to see you get hurt."

Catherine squeezed the leather reins in her gloved hands. "I am not one of those foolish young girls."

But did she truly believe that? What she felt for Lachlan was anything but rational. Whenever he touched her, she became blind to every sensible thought and precaution, and last night she would have done anything to make him stay with her. *Anything.*

"I appreciate your concern," she said nonetheless, "but I assure you I can take care of myself. Please do not speak of this again."

She kicked in her heels and galloped off to ride ahead.

Chapter Twenty-five

They reached the village of Killin sooner than antici-
pated, arriving at the inn not long after the storm gained
intensity, blowing bitter gusts of wind and rain across
the fields and through the muddy streets.

They rode into the stable yard, where Lachlan helped
Catherine down from her horse and through the driving
rain to the door. He secured the most expensive room
for her, on the third floor, and arranged lodgings for
himself and the others on the first.

"A hot bath would be most welcome," Catherine said
to the innkeeper, who snapped his fingers and sent a
young maid scurrying to the back room to make prepara-
tions; then Lachlan accompanied Catherine up the stairs.

The room was spacious and warm. A pile of logs
awaited lighting in the hearth, and a braided rug covered the wide plank floor.

Catherine strode all the way in and looked around.
"It will feel like heaven to sleep here tonight," she
said, swinging around to face him in the open doorway.
Slowly, she approached him. "You won't disappoint me,
will you? You will come?"

The double meaning in her words caused Lachlan's

blood to quicken in his veins, and he had to fight the urge to sweep her into his arms, carry her to the bed right then and there, and take her like a horny savage.

"Aye," he flatly said. "I'll make sure the others eat and drink plenty; then I'll let them know I'll be on watch until morning." A shiver ran through him—one of feverish impatience. "But once we are alone, lass," he added, "I'll need you to help keep the situation under control. You must not tempt me into doing certain things I cannot do."

"Of course," she replied, reaching out to straighten his tartan over his shoulder.

He wondered suddenly if he should not take this risk after all, for he was overwhelmed by the intensity of his desires. Each day they drew closer to Edinburgh—and closer to the end of his torment—the more eager he became. It disturbed him, to want her so badly.

She pursed her lush, cherry lips, and he was done for. He bent forward to kiss her but recognized something else in her eyes. Something apprehensive . . .

He drew back. "What's wrong?"

"Nothing," she answered, too quickly. "It was a long ride today, that's all, and I have been able to think of nothing but you."

"My feelings were no different," he confessed. "But are you certain there is nothing else you wish to tell me?"

She stood for a moment wetting her lips, then moved against him and slid her hands up and down his chest. "Only that I will not rest until you come back to me."

She tugged his shirt out from under his kilt and proceeded to kiss the sensitive flesh over his rib cage, then stimulated his nipples with her tongue.

Lachlan's blood pounded through his veins. His warrior's body ached with need. As he slid a hand around the back of her neck and toyed with the loose tendrils of hair at her nape, he said, "I thought you were going to help keep things under control, lass, but when you do things like this, I worry that we'll forget ourselves."

She lifted her heated gaze and grinned up at him. "It's much too late for *me*," she told him. "I've already forgotten everything."

With a small grin, he gently pushed her away. "You're a danger to my sanity, you know." He quickly tucked his shirt back in. "I must be raving mad, agreeing to come here tonight to frolic with such a lusty wench. How can I be sure you won't take advantage of me, when I'm most vulnerable?"

She followed him to the door. "You'll just have to trust me, I suppose."

He stopped and faced her. "I'm serious, lass."

Catherine's expression darkened. "I know. But it will be all right," she assured him. "I promise I will be good. Just please, do not change your mind."

He gazed down at her moist lips, the soft pale flesh of her bosom, then back up at her beguiling blue eyes, stormy as the winter sea. He wanted to lose himself in those eyes, and every other part of her, and give to her what she had given to him the night before.

"I won't," he gruffly replied before he finally tore himself away from her greedy hands and strove to quiet his heedless passions. At least until midnight.

Lachlan did not see Catherine again throughout the evening, for she bathed privately in her chamber, then ate a small supper alone, which was sent up on a tray, while Alex guarded her door.

Lachlan in turn kept himself busy and distracted by arranging for a coach and driver to take her the remaining distance to Edinburgh. A wheeled vehicle had been an impossible luxury before Killen, for in the north there were few roads adequate for such means of travel. But they were in the Lowlands now. Everything was different.

He ate supper with the clansmen in the tavern across the street from the inn while waiting for the clock to strike twelve. When at last it marked the critical hour, he took a careful look around and decided it was time to take over the night watch.

As he left the tavern and crossed the muddy street, a gentle breeze fluttered his kilt and the world seemed different somehow. He felt rejuvenated. Hopeful. Tonight he would share a bed with a woman he desired and cared for, and it was not so very frightening, for he knew she understood his limits—she understood his *heart*—and tomorrow they would travel to Edinburgh to meet Raonaid, her sister, who might finally put an end to his suffering.

There was some hope now, he supposed, and over the next few hours, he would allow himself to take some pleasure in that hope while doing everything he could to give generously to Catherine in return. Just the thought of it caused his blood to race, and his desire for her increased tenfold.

Climbing the stairs to her room, he focused on the internal workings of his body, determined this time to satisfy her before he satisfied himself, and by God, he would make it last much longer than before. Till dawn if she was keen.

Reaching the top of the stairs, however, he stopped at the sight of young Alex, who had volunteered to be on watch until Lachlan arrived. Alex was sitting on the floor outside her door, his legs stretched in a V across the corridor, his musket clutched tightly at his chest.

The top stair creaked under Lachlan's weight. Alex leaped to his feet and aimed the musket. The flame in the wall sconce danced alarmingly.

"I cannot allow you to go in there, sir," he said. "Angus the Lion sent me to protect Lady Catherine, and it's my duty on this night to protect her from *you*."

Lachlan felt his eyebrows pull together in dismay. "It's *my* job to protect her, Alex, not yours. You're my scout. I do not require anything else from you."

Alex shook his head. "*You* may not require it, sir, but Lady Catherine does. I saw you last night, you see. I know that you went to her tent, and I cannot allow you to take advantage of her like that again."

Slowly ascending beyond the top step, Lachlan held up a hand. He needed to keep the lad calm. "I'm not taking advantage of anyone, Alex. I am Lady Catherine's escort, and she wants me here. She invited me." Just to make the situation absolutely clear, he added, "She's *waiting* for me."

"But she's innocent and vulnerable," Alex shakily argued, "and has no memory of her life. Last night you seduced her. I have no doubt of it. I know all about your shady reputation. I've heard how you make the lassies swoon and do anything you ask of them. But Lady Catherine is different, and I won't allow such . . . *impropriety* to occur. Not with her."

Lachlan inclined his head curiously. "Did your cousin Gwendolen tell you to keep an eye on me?"

"Nay, sir. I have eyes and ears of my own, and as I said, I saw you last night. I know what's going on. I know what you plan to do here, and I cannot allow it to happen."

Alex tilted his head to the side and closed one eye, peering at Lachlan down the long length of the gun barrel.

Lachlan spoke in a calm, quiet voice. "I promise you, I'm here to keep her safe, Alex."

It was a lie, and Lachlan knew it. He was here for improprieties of the worst kind, and he was suddenly beginning to wonder if young Alex MacEwen might have been a better man for the job of her protector.

"I don't believe you," the lad said. "And I'll shoot you if you try to get past me. Go back downstairs." Alex cocked the hammer.

Lachlan was beginning to grow impatient. "Put the gun down, Alex. I don't want to hurt you."

The door to Catherine's room suddenly swung open on its hinges, and dressed in her shift with a woolen shawl wrapped around her shoulders, she stepped into the corridor.

Eyes blazing with fury, she glanced back and forth between the two of them. "What's going on here?"

Lachlan gestured with his hand toward Alex. "Go ahead. Answer the question."

The young clansman cleared his throat. "It's my duty

to protect you, Lady Catherine. I cannot, in good conscience, let this man cross your threshold. You know my reasons."

Lachlan regarded her with narrowed eyes in the dim candlelight. "You've already discussed this with him?"

"Yes," she confessed, her shoulders dropping in defeat. "Fine. If you must know, he told me today that he saw you leave my tent last night. I'm sorry I didn't tell you. I was afraid it would influence your decision, and you would stay away." She turned her ardent gaze to Alex. "But I assured Alex that I was capable of making my own decisions. Isn't that right?"

"Aye, Lady Catherine."

"And must I repeat myself again?" she asked.

"No, ma'am."

Every inch a noblewoman, she did not release him from her bold stare. "If you must know," she said, "I demanded that Lachlan guard my bed tonight, and I wish for him to stay. If you don't like it, you will have to point that musket at *me*, Alex, because my heels are quite firmly dug in on the matter."

In that strange, awkward moment Lachlan realized he was completely, irreversibly in love with her, and his mind clouded over with unease for the future.

"But Lady Catherine," Alex argued, "he's . . . I don't know how to say it without causing offense, but . . ."

"Speak freely, Alex," she impatiently responded.

The lad swallowed. "He's a debauched seducer."

"I beg your pardon?" she said.

It was true. Lachlan could hardly deny it, but he wasn't about to interrupt. He looked to the young man to explain himself.

"But there's more. He's *cursed*, my lady. It's not safe to be alone with him. You don't know the half of it."

Catherine turned her gaze to Lachlan and spoke with confidence. "I *do* know it, Alex. I know all of it, and I also know he would never do anything to jeopardize my safety. He is here, at my request, to protect me." She turned her eyes back to Alex again. "Have you told anyone else what you saw last night?"

Alex released the hammer and slowly lowered his weapon. "Nay. I would never say anything that would harm your reputation."

She gathered her shawl more tightly around her shoulders. "I am grateful for that, at least. And if you truly wish to protect me, you will continue to be discreet about what you have seen."

Lachlan decided it was a good time to shoulder his way past the young lad, simply to avoid a fight, because he would have flattened Alex if he stood in his way for another minute.

Lachlan entered Catherine's room and waited by the fire.

"I appreciate what you tried to do here," she quietly said to Alex, who remained in the corridor. "You were very brave."

"I suppose I must have been, my lady, because I seem to have lost all feeling in my legs. I'm feeling a bit dizzy, actually."

"Why don't you go across the street and join the others," she suggested. "And if you say a word about this to any of them, Alex, I promise I will not let you live long enough to regret it."

She firmly shut the door, turned the key in the lock, and faced Lachlan.

He took one look at her in her nightdress, and his body throbbed with desire. In that moment he knew that if he was not careful, the pleasure he was about to give—and take—could turn out to be the worst mistake of his life.

And hers. For he was completely out of control with wanting her.

Chapter
Twenty-six

"You look like you are about to change your mind," Catherine said, her voice falling to a hush.

"Aye. I'm thinking about it."

He was disturbed by the intensity of his feelings—not just his desire, but his adoration and affection—and the complete abandonment of his long-established caution when it came to intimacy of any kind.

What had she done to him?

She crossed toward him. "I won't let you. I've been waiting all day and night for you, and I want this."

"Do you always get what you want?" he asked. "Because I don't."

She dropped her shawl onto the back of a chair and reached up to unfasten the brooch at his shoulder. "Well, I promise that you can have it tonight. Some of it, at any rate."

She set the heavy brooch on the table, and with graceful hands, slid his tartan down over his arm while he kept his eyes fixed on hers and came up with a dozen and one reasons why he shouldn't allow this to continue.

In the end, however, he lifted his arms over his head so that she could remove his shirt, and when she tossed it to the chair on top of her shawl, he basked in the heat of her sultry gaze.

Slowly unbuckling his belt and scabbard, she regarded him with playful eyes, which aroused him further, then set everything on the table and unraveled his kilt.

"Now see?" she whispered with a sneaky smile. "I've removed all your weapons. You won't be able to fight me."

"It was never my intention to fight you, lass. All I want to do is love you."

Her eyes lifted, and neither of them spoke for a precarious moment. She idly dropped his tartan to the floor.

He stood very still, naked before the warmth of the fire, while the pounding of his blood through his veins provoked his emotions and crushed any previous impulse to leave. He wanted this woman with a fury that was too powerful to resist. There was no turning back now. Her beauty compelled him forward, and he swept her up into his arms.

Carrying her to the bed, he kissed her mouth with a passion that bordered on violence. He set her down on the soft mattress and stood over her while he stroked her body with hungry, joyful hands, relishing the fact that he could touch her so freely through the thin fabric of her nightdress.

He slid his palms across her luscious breasts, rubbing the pads of his thumbs over her pebbled nipples, then journeyed down her shapely hips to her thighs, where he gathered the white linen in a hand and began to tug it up over her knees.

"I am going to pleasure you tonight," he said, "and make you cry out in ecstasy."

"As long as it pleases *you*," she purred, squirming lavishly on the bed.

"Ah, it will."

She lifted her hips and sat up so he could pull her nightdress off over her head; then he crawled onto the bed to lie beside her sweet, voluptuous form.

His erection was bone hard and enormous, pulsing against her hip, but he would resist the urge to bury himself inside her tonight. He would enjoy her body in other ways. He would not lose control.

Leaning up on one elbow, he ran a finger slowly across the delicate line of her jaw, then down the side of her throat. With a featherlike touch, he drew tiny circles around her nipples, without ever touching the hardened peaks.

She sucked in a quivering gasp of desire. His gaze lifted, and he smiled at her, then spelled his name with a light, stroking flourish across her belly. "Tonight, you belong to me."

"*Every* night I belong to you," she whispered. "I've been yours since the first moment I met you."

Bending his head, he kissed her silky soft, porcelain skin and licked inside her navel. She melted into the bed, writhing pleasurably, letting out tiny whimpers of arousal. When her hand snaked out to rub his chest, he gently curled his fingers around hers, kissed the tip of each one, and shook his head. "No, lass," he said. "You're not to touch *me*. It's my turn to touch *you*."

Her arm fell limp onto the bed. "If that is your wish . . ."

He eyed her tenderly and rolled on top of her, with his elbows braced on either side of her hips, low down, so that his face was over her breasts and there was no chance of his manhood meeting accidentally with the sweet, soft, tempting dampness between her thighs.

Closing his eyes, he bent to take a lovely breast into his mouth and licked and suckled her delicious nipples. Catherine sighed and combed her fingers through his hair while he slid his tongue across to her other breast and pleasured her with great sensitivity and diligence.

Her legs spread wider, and he began to thrust his raging manhood into the bed, wishing he could rise up and slide into her now—she was certainly ready for him—but instead, he inched lower and dropped wet, openmouthed kisses down her belly to the glossy sweetness between her legs.

She took hold of his shoulders and arched her back, moaning against a flood of delight. "Please, Lachlan," she pleaded. "Do everything you can."

"Don't worry, lass. I intend to."

Kissing the inner planes of her knees, he made his way up her thighs, where he paused a moment to admire the succulent temptation before him. Irrepressible passion charged through his body. Riotous with a desire he had been suppressing for too long and starving for her in every way, he touched his lips lightly to her swollen sex, then plunged in with an avaricious indulgence that consumed him like a dream.

She held his head in her hands, pushing him deeper, moaning with pleasure while her legs trembled and fell open on the bed. "Don't stop, Lachlan," she sighed. "Please, don't ever stop. . . ."

Eager to fulfill all her desires, he slid a finger inside her throbbing wet passage while he continued to use his tongue on the glowing pearl at the heart of her folds. He stroked and tasted her for endless moments of rapture, losing himself in her inconceivable splendor, until at last she began to quiver. Her insides contracted around his finger while she thrust her hips toward the ceiling, pulling him closer, squeezing her thighs around his head.

"*Oh yes!*" she whispered as a deep, groaning climax overtook her.

When her body finally relaxed in complete surrender, he climbed over her on all fours and looked down at her lovely flushed face, damp with perspiration. She blinked up at him in a drunken haze of satisfaction.

"What I wouldn't give to make love to you now," he softly said, but he cared for her too much. Nothing would make him risk it.

"Let it be my turn now." She sat up and pressed her open palms to his chest. Pushing him onto his back, she began to stroke him below as she laid openmouthed kisses down the center of his abdomen. "I want to do what you just did."

He closed his eyes and groaned as her mouth slid over the thick head of his erection. Time stood still in the ensuing moments as he pondered the impossible, mind-numbing pleasure she gave him. The sensations swamping his body were staggering, penetrating, and wild. He drove into her mouth deeply and unbearably, imagining in his mind that he was making love to her on a moonlit beach, giving her everything, without limitation or restraint.

It went on and on; she was relentless and vigorous with her mouth and tongue. He never wanted to be without her.

The climax, when it came, bombarded his senses with a violent explosion of pleasure, and the whole world seemed to disappear for endless flashing moments. All he felt was an aching hunger to claim and possess Catherine in every way possible.

When he opened his eyes, he was on top of her, using his hand to coax his seed onto her stomach.

Panic struck him. He had lost himself for a moment. Thank God he had not given in to that dream.

As he shuddered and convulsed above her, he cursed Raonaid for this cruel torture. He wanted to choke the life out of her. All his violent warrior instincts rebelled and blasted out of him on that fierce, erratic orgasm. He couldn't take it anymore.

He collapsed onto the bed beside Catherine and wept.

A second later, he was up off the bed, running a hand over his wet face, fighting for composure. He hated that Catherine should see him like this. Hated it with every inch of his being.

He went to the basin and washed himself clean with a towel. He couldn't look at her. His mind was filled with shame.

The bed creaked, and he felt her careful approach across the room.

She laid a warm hand on his shoulder. "In two days' time," she said, "we will reach Edinburgh, and I will do whatever I can to help free you from this curse. Perhaps it is not even real. Perhaps it never was."

He tossed the towel into the basin and faced her. "It's real enough to keep me from loving you properly, Catherine. Real enough to make me weep in front of you like a broken man."

His temper flared. He wanted to pick up his sword and lash out at something.

"Come back to bed," she gently whispered, holding both his hands in hers. "I understand that you are upset. Let me help you. Stay with me tonight and hold me. All I want is to be close to you."

He felt very tired all of a sudden.

Catherine led him to the bed and drew back the covers. They climbed in together.

He gathered her close, spoon fashion, and they lay quietly in the dying firelight for a long time.

"What you did to me tonight . . . ," she softly said. "It was like floating up to heaven."

He ran his thumb across her shoulder, then kissed her tenderly between her shoulder blades. "I'm glad."

But it was not enough. He needed more. He wanted all of her, body and soul.

He was quite certain he had made a mistake, he thought, by letting down his guard. God help him, he had never wept in front of a woman before. He was out of his depth with her.

Hours later, just before dawn, he proved himself

right on that account when he woke to the tempting allure of her warm bottom pressed tightly against his pelvis, and he was overcome by an unstoppable wave of passion.

Chapter
Twenty-seven

Lachlan breathed in the lavender scent of Catherine's skin and laid soft, feathery kisses across the back of her neck and shoulders. She woke with a sigh and rolled to face him, meeting his heady desire with sweltering kisses of her own.

"Oh, Lachlan," she whispered, "I want you so much."

"I want you, too, lass."

He rolled on top of her but was careful, as always, not to position himself too close, though he wanted desperately to hold her against him, to worship her with his hands and adore her with his mouth.

He pressed his hot skin to hers, pushing, stroking, kissing . . . They were so close and tight to each other; her breasts were crushed against his chest. Her soft belly quivered against him, and she moaned and whimpered, digging her nails into his shoulders and wrapping her long, shapely legs around his clenching buttocks.

He couldn't seem to get enough of her. His hands stroked her back while he kissed the soft, warm tendons at her neck. A rush of sensation coursed through him. The extent of his yearning was incomprehensible.

His mouth covered hers, and she sucked at his tongue, thrusting her hips, stroking his hair away from his face. She gazed into his eyes with love, and his heart trembled achingly.

"I want to be closer to you," she cried, squeezing him between her legs, caressing his lower back.

He nodded and wrapped his whole body around her, groaning in the predawn light, so hungry for her, his feelings so raw. . . .

Then slowly, without ever meaning to, he slid inside the warm and welcoming haven between her legs. Her moist heat surrounded him in rapture, and he was overcome by emotion.

They both went absolutely still, for he was in deep, pressed firmly to the hilt.

"You're inside me," she whispered, her teeth colliding with his shoulder.

"I know. Please, don't move."

Neither of them spoke. He could barely breathe over the heavy pounding of his heart.

"It feels so good." She turned her head to the side on the pillow.

"Aye. But I need to pull out."

Yet he could not seem to do so.

His blood rushed wildly through his veins. Dangerous seconds ticked by on the clock. Her sweet, honeyed depths engulfed him in bliss, and he soon found himself pulling out, only to push right back in.

"Just for a few seconds," he huskily implored.

She nodded and pulled him in deeper, meeting his oncoming thrust with a firm push that placed the tip of his erection tight up against her womb.

His chest heaved with alarm. He could not continue this. He had to withdraw.

He promised that he would, but it was three strokes, then four, then five. Soon he was driving in and out of her with heedless abandon and vigorous haste, and she was squeezing his buttocks, pulling him deeper inside every time he tried to separate himself from her exquisite, glowing warmth.

Suddenly a scorching heat poured through all his bones and muscles. He recognized the signs of a climax, shuddered uncontrollably within, and a second too late pulled out and hauled himself up on his hands and knees above her. He finished his orgasm on her stomach.

When it was over, his eyes flew open.

She was staring up at him in shock.

"What have we done?" he asked.

Catherine's cheeks flushed with alarm. She sat up, but had no answer to give.

Chapter
Twenty-eight

Catherine gazed anxiously at the flurry of activity that surrounded her as she made her way down the front stairs of the inn, across the taproom, and toward the front door. A plump kitchen maid rushed forth to thrust a cloth-covered basket into her hands, and Alex appeared out of nowhere, taking hold of her elbow to escort her out.

"One would think there was a fire," Catherine mentioned, laboring to sound casual when she was, quite simply, paralyzed with fear. She had allowed herself to make love to Lachlan a short time ago, after dozens of promises and assurances that it would never happen, and now he was more agitated than ever. He would never trust her again. No matter what happened.

The rest of it—that she might fall victim to her sister's curse in nine months' time—did not bear thinking of. Surely it was absurd, she tried to tell herself as Alex opened the door in front of her. There could be no validity in such hexes and sorcery, and yet she could not seem to let go of the possibility that it was true. Lachlan certainly seemed to think so.

But neither could she let go of the memory of his

touch, and all the sensations she had experienced when he slid inside and made love to her at last. She was still light-headed and completely overwhelmed.

Alex led her outside, where the chilly morning air struck her cheeks. A shiny black coach was waiting for them on the opposite side of the narrow street.

The well-appointed vehicle, led by four handsome gray horses, sported bright yellow stripes along the side panels. Tassel-ornamented blinds covered the windows, which were cloaked in crusty frost. Sitting up front was a liveried driver with a curly brown wig under a tricorne hat, which he tipped at her as she approached.

"I don't know why Lachlan was in such a hurry this morning," Alex said as he led her across the street. "He was in a foul mood when he pounded on our doors to wake us. And he said we won't stop again until we reach Edinburgh, except to change horses. We'll be traveling until the wee hours of the morning, I expect."

Naturally, Alex was curious, and probably concerned about the sudden urgent need to reach their destination. But under no circumstances would Catherine reveal what had occurred in her bedchamber that morning. If news of their lovemaking got out, Alex and the others would likely put a pistol to Lachlan's head.

Alex opened the door of the coach and handed her inside while the horses grumbled and blew great puffs of steam out of their flaring nostrils. Catherine sat down on a deeply buttoned leather-upholstered seat and gazed around the cozy interior, taking note of two thick blankets folded and set upon the opposite seat, as well as a green-and-white-striped silk pillow with gold fringe, which looked as if it had just been snatched from someone's drawing room.

"Where did all this come from?" she asked Alex, who was leaning in the door, also looking around.

"Lachlan purchased it from the banker. He said he paid double what it was worth, but those were Angus's instructions."

"I see."

Alex pointed at the floor. "There are hot bricks there for your feet, my lady, and there should be enough food in that basket to last until nightfall."

"But we'll stop before then, will we not?"

"Aye, don't worry. We'll stop to change horses a few times. You'll be able to step out."

Scarcely reassured, Catherine tipped her head back and shut her eyes.

"They've already loaded all the bags on the roof," Alex told her, as if he sensed her unease and hoped to distract her with trivial conversation. "Gawyn, Roderick, and Rodney will be following close by, and I'll be riding ahead to scout the route."

"Where is Lachlan now?" she asked, needing to know if she would see him before they departed.

Alex looked up and down the street. "He's around here somewhere, but I don't recommend holding him up. As I said, he's in a foul mood this morning. He wants these wheels rolling. Can I get you anything else before I close the door?"

"No, Alex. That will be all."

He shut it, then shouted to the driver, who shouted to

the horses, and almost immediately the great vehicle heaved forward and began to rumble down the street—toward a very uncertain future.

The hours that followed brought Catherine no peace of mind, for she had not seen or spoken to Lachlan since he left her bedchamber that morning. He had dressed in a hurry and stormed out the door, saying only, "Get dressed. We need to get to Edinburgh."

Now, as the coach jostled and bumped over the frozen rutted roads of the Lowlands, through open lonely glens, into bleak forests with bare, skeleton trees, it was difficult not to feel completely catastrophic over the condition of her life.

She longed to tell Lachlan that she was sorry—that she had never meant to tempt him into doing what he did not wish to do. But she also wanted to tell him that she had loved every glorious minute of it and longed to do it again. That it was the most profound and beautiful experience of her life. At least what she remembered of it. She had not caught a single glimpse of him, however, not since they left the village.

It occurred to her that he might have ridden ahead to Edinburgh to face Raonaid alone. The thought made her feel sick to her stomach.

Later, Catherine ate the biscuits and cheese from the basket, finished the small amount of wine she had been given, and lifted her feet off the bricks. She wiggled uncomfortably on the seat, for she needed to use a convenience. Pray God, they would reach another village soon.

Putting away her lunch and peering out the window—immune now to the endless monotony of the passing forest—she tried to see what was ahead of them. There was still no sign of Lachlan, or Alex for that matter.

Growing impatient, she stood up in the swaying vehicle and pounded hard on the ceiling. *"Stop!"*

She was immediately tossed forward onto the opposite seat as the coach pulled to a sudden halt.

"Thank God," she groaned, flicking the door latch and spilling out of the coach onto the road, in a clumsy heap of skirts and petticoats. She looked up at the driver, who quickly hopped down from his elevated position out front. "May I be of some assistance, my lady?"

"No. I only require a bit of privacy." She turned toward the trees to examine her options.

In that moment, rapid hoofbeats disrupted the silence of the forest. Lachlan appeared from around a bend in the road, galloping at a brisk pace toward them.

He reined in his horse and spoke impatiently. "Why are we stopped?"

"The lady has to . . ." The driver gestured toward the woods with a discreet toss of his head.

Lachlan looked down at her from high up on Goliath's back. A wintry breeze lifted his dark hair while his enormous mount stomped restlessly in front of the team. "Do you need help?"

"No, I most certainly do not," she assured him. "I'll just be a moment."

She picked up her skirts and waded into the leafy green ferns along the side of the road and went behind a bush.

Greatly relieved to have that particular necessity taken care of, she dropped her skirts and returned to the coach. Lachlan dismounted and led his horse around to the page board at the back of the vehicle.

"What are you doing?" Catherine asked.

"I'm going to join you for a bit." He looked straight into her eyes while he tied his horse to the rear hand-rail.

Not knowing what to expect, Catherine returned to the side door and allowed the driver to hand her up.

Seconds later, Lachlan's broad, tartan-clad form filled the open doorway, blocking out the light. He took hold of the handle and swung inside, his long hair flying about as he shut the door behind him. His clean outdoorsy scent, mixed with leather and horse, permeated the interior. He settled himself on the opposite seat.

They faced each other in silence while the coach bounced under the driver's weight outside. Soon they were rolling again, less hurried now.

"I'm surprised you're sitting here with me," Catherine said. "I didn't think you'd ever want to look at me again after what happened, much less be alone with me."

He adjusted his sword belt and scabbard and took his time replying. When at last he spoke, his forehead was creased with concern.

"You were right," he said. "I did not want to see you. I've been avoiding it, because I cannot bear to think of what I did to you this morning. I will never forgive myself."

"It wasn't just you," she insisted. "It was my fault as well. I moved a certain way, and suddenly you were right there. . . . You slid in so easily, and I wanted you. I just couldn't bring myself to stop."

He wouldn't look at her. "I should have stopped it myself. Much sooner. I don't know why I couldn't."

"I couldn't, either, if it helps you to know that. I knew it was wrong, but I couldn't resist. I couldn't let you go."

Her racing heart compelled her to move across the coach and sit beside him. "I'm sorry, Lachlan. I didn't mean to cause all this."

"You're apologizing to *me*?" he practically shouted. "You're the one who stands to suffer the most. And besides, you didn't cause it." He frowned almost viciously. "Your sister did, and I swear, with every breath in my body, that I will make her pay for this. There is nothing I won't do to make her reverse it. I'll kill her if I have to."

Catherine shook her head. "Don't say such things. She is my sister."

A muscle clenched at his jaw, and he spoke in a dangerous snarl. "She is a witch, and her curse upon me came straight from the fires of hell. Do not forget that my wife died in childbirth. She cried and begged God not to take her from this world. Then she pleaded with Him to let the bairn survive. . . ." He paused a moment to steady his voice. "I loved my wife, but I had to bury her, and my child as well. I will not let that happen to *you*."

"But it's not up to you to control how, and when, people die," she argued. "You don't have that power. Even if there was no curse, there could be no guarantee that I would survive giving birth to your child. No woman can have that assurance. Life is a risk. Every day, for all of us."

Lachlan glared at her fiercely. "Raonaid shouldn't

have that power, either—to decide when someone will die."

He looked away from her, toward the window. The coach bounced over a rough patch of road, and Catherine's head pounded from the constant jostling and relentless strain of the situation.

He turned his searing, bloodshot eyes to her. "Marry me," he said.

Her heart turned over in her chest. "I beg your pardon?"

"You heard me, lass. We made love this morning. You could be carrying my child. I know I'm not good enough for a highborn lady such as you—I am a Highlander without title or property—but we've lain together. I must marry you."

She paused while all the blood in her veins slowly went cold. "You're only proposing to me because of the curse," she said. "You think I'm going to die, and you feel responsible. Isn't that it?"

He spoke with dangerous antagonism. "Don't say that. You're not going to die. We will reach Edinburgh tonight."

"But it's true," she continued nevertheless. "You would not be proposing otherwise, and I will not accept such an offer from you. I desire you, Lachlan, but how could I marry a man who only expects nine months of matrimony? What if I am not with child? What if we stopped in time? Have you even considered that?"

He dropped his head into his hands and refused to answer.

"I understand your concerns," she said, more calmly now, "but I think we should at least wait to see if I am with child. Perhaps I am not. Remember, you did not take all of your pleasure inside of me."

His gaze shot to hers. "*Pleasure?* You think I enjoyed that? It was torture!"

She frowned at him and sat back against the cushions. "How romantic of you. And here I thought you had a reputation for being *charming*."

"So your answer is 'no?' " he hotly replied.

"Of course it is 'no!' I have no memories! I don't even know who I am, much less if I am expecting because of your wretched curse. Besides all that, how can I agree to become your wife when I am about to meet a twin sister who was separated from me at birth—a sister you want to kill!"

"You are in danger because of her."

"She is still my sister, and she certainly didn't intend to curse *me*. She doesn't even know I exist."

Suddenly a grim shadow settled over his features, and he spoke in a growling voice. "Sometimes when I look at you," he said, "I see *her*, and I want to close my eyes."

Catherine glared at him with burning shock while a terrible knot of grief exploded in her stomach.

"Then you should be thankful I declined your offer of marriage just now, or you would have been quite miserable over the next nine months."

For a long moment they stared at each other; then he pounded on the roof. The coach pulled to a halt, and he did not wait for it to stop before he swung the door open and leaped out.

Chapter
Twenty-nine

Lachlan galloped ahead of the coach, determined to put some distance between him and Catherine.

Christ almighty. He had made love to her. Without ever intending to, he had slid into her depths and remained there for a perilous amount of time, unable to withdraw; then he had slid back in, again and again, until the pleasure had snuffed out all logic and self-control. He had taken her rashly and impetuously, and *still* he wanted to take her again.

Even in the coach just now, he had wanted to hold her, to kiss her sweet lips and run his hands through her hair. It was all he could think of—to lie with her again, to make love to her, every night, freely, without constraints, for the rest of his God-forsaken life.

Or *hers,* which might not be such a very long time.

It was an unpleasant reminder, and he had to shut his eyes against the image of her death.

Bloody hell, he had proposed to her!

And she had refused!

And yes, by God, he *had* considered the notion that it might be a brief marriage, but it would be better than no time at all.

He would give anything to know that the curse could be lifted, that she was not in any real danger. He would marry her either way, of course, which was why her refusal had pushed him over the edge.

Had she really thought so little of their lovemaking? Did she not understand? Did she not feel what he felt?

He was overcome suddenly by a terrible rush of grief. *Bloody hell!* He never asked for this. He didn't want this kind of pain.

And he meant what he had said. He would kill Raonaid if he had to. He would do anything to protect Catherine, even if it meant she would hate him forever.

He would protect her at any cost. Even that.

Because he loved her.

It was past midnight when the coach finally rolled to a stop outside the Edinburgh hotel. Catherine sat up groggily and rubbed her eyes. She had fallen asleep at some point and had no idea what time it was.

The latch on the door flicked open, and she squinted as light from a lantern spilled across the floor of the coach. It was Alex, holding the lantern aloft.

"I'm sorry to disturb you, Lady Catherine," he gently said, "but we've arrived. Lachlan has already secured a room for you. I just need to take you upstairs."

"Thank you," she replied.

She sidled across the upholstered seat and took his hand. A few minutes later, she was collapsing onto a soft feather bed with freshly laundered sheets and closing her weary eyes. It had been an exhausting day, crossing the Lowlands with few stops other than to change horses. Catherine could barely move.

Each endless mile of the journey from Drumloch Manor to Kinloch Castle—then south again to Edinburgh—seemed to merge together into one grueling blur of movement and scenery. Her body groaned in protest from all the jostling about in the coach that day. All she wanted to do now was sleep for an eternity.

When Catherine opened her eyes, it was pitch-dark in the room. She was still dressed in her day clothes, lying flat out on her back, on top of the covers. Every muscle in her body ached and throbbed.

Sitting up drowsily, she cupped her forehead in a hand. "Good Lord, what time is it?" She swung her legs off the edge of the bed to touch the floor.

"It's four o'clock in the morning," a voice said.

Lachlan.

Instantly awake, she noted his shadowed figure in a rocking chair by the window. He held a musket across his lap.

"Could you light a lamp?" she asked, squeezing the edge of the mattress with her hands. "I need to see where I am."

He rose from the chair and lit a candle. The room brightened to a warm golden glow.

"Are we in Edinburgh?" she asked.

"Aye. We arrived a few hours ago, but none of us are in any condition to meet Raonaid or Murdoch. It's been a long day. The others are sleeping. We'll ride out to Blue Waters first thing in the morning."

She ran her tongue across her dry lips. "I'm thirsty," she said. "Is there anything to drink?"

"I'll pour you some wine."

Catherine waited for her thoughts to stir into something tangible while she watched him uncork a bottle and fill a small glass. He strode forward and handed it to her.

"Thank you."

Still feeling groggy, she took it in both hands and sipped heartily. The dark flavor awakened her senses as she looked all around the large room. It was a luxurious space. The walls were paneled in oak, and the furniture was upholstered in a floral brocade.

"How long have you been sitting here?" she asked.

"Since we arrived."

"But you must be exhausted as well," she noted with concern.

"Aye," he admitted. "And I confess I might have dozed off for a minute or two in the past few hours."

She took another sip of wine. "I'm surprised it's *you* who is watching over me. You could have left Alex outside the door. I'm sure he would have been devoted enough to the task."

"He's a good lad," Lachlan said. "Now go back to sleep, Catherine. You need your rest. Tomorrow is an important day."

She set the glass down on the bedside table. "Indeed. I am going to meet the twin sister who was separated from me at birth. I hardly know what I will say to her."

"Don't get your hopes up for a tearful reunion. The last time I saw Raonaid, she was pouring a bucket of bones all over me, and hexing me straight to hell."

Catherine swallowed uneasily. "Perhaps she has changed."

He shook his head.

"How do you think she will react when she sees me?" Catherine asked.

"It's difficult to say. I've known her to be volatile, so I will go first and deliver the news. I will also make sure that Murdoch will not be a source of danger."

Catherine nodded. "That will be best, I suppose. She should be warned, for the news will come as a shock. No doubt she will need time to prepare herself."

Still half in a daze, Catherine pulled the covers back, kicked off her shoes, and slid between the sheets. She and Lachlan watched each other steadily through the flickering candlelight for a long while, and she wished things were different between them. She wanted to be close to him, but she dare not invite him back into her bed. She'd done enough damage and was not sure he would ever forgive her.

"Are you still angry about what happened today?" she asked, unable to avoid the subject of their argument in the coach.

"Just go to sleep, lass."

"But I want to talk about this. Please, Lachlan. You *proposed* to me today."

The rocking chair creaked slowly back and forth across the floorboards. "Do you mean to change your mind?"

There it was—the hint of seduction, the teasing quality in his voice that always excited her and drew her in.

She hesitated, then answered shakily, "No."

"Then what is there to talk about?"

She cleared her throat. "You *are* still angry with me. I only wish you could understand. . . ."

He stopped rocking. "What do you expect, lass? When a man makes love to a woman and proposes marriage, it's safe to assume his feelings have become engaged."

"You are *hurt* by my refusal?" she said, leaning up on an elbow.

"Nay, not hurt," he insisted. "*Angry.* Everything about this angers me, because you are in danger, and I cannot live with that."

She wet her lips and pondered how best to explain her true feelings.

"I wish to marry for *love,* Lachlan," she said at last. "Not for protection. Very soon, I will have a substantial fortune of my own, and I will be quite capable of taking care of myself. And under no circumstances will I allow any man to marry me out of *anger.* When I marry, it will be by choice—not force, or necessity. I want *love.* I want the passionate, all-consuming kind, where nothing is held back. I want babies and grandchildren, and I want to live a long and happy life with my husband, who will make love to me, regardless of the risk."

He sat very still, and all she wanted was for him to come to her, to drop to his knees and tell her that he felt the same way. To confess his undying love for her, to kiss her and hold her and convince her that she was wrong about him, that his proposal was not just about responsibility, or a need to protect. She wanted to hear him say that he could not live without her. Whether she died tomorrow or lived to be an old woman, she wanted him to be grateful for the passion that could be theirs, if only he could just *love* her.

But he said nothing. He started rocking in the chair again, and eventually he turned his eyes away.

Catherine inhaled deeply and let out a quiet sigh. "Well, now you understand my reasons for refusing you," she said, determined to keep a cool head. "We are hardly—either of us—in a position to make decisions about the rest of our lives. I have no memories, and you have just made love for the first time in three years. It's bound to make things seem more intense than they really are. I'm sure that when all of this is over, you will thank me for turning down your offer."

He rose quickly from the chair and walked to the door. "I'll keep watch from just outside," he gruffly said, "and tomorrow we'll see Raonaid. Everything will seem much clearer then. For both of us."

With that he left her to wonder if perhaps *she* was the one who needed to be reminded that this situation was not normal.

It's bound to make things seem more intense than they really are. . . .

Perhaps that's all it was, she thought, and all she needed to do was keep better control over her heart until life returned to normal.

Oh, she wished it could be so. But somehow she knew that was a wish not likely to be granted.

Chapter Thirty

How should one prepare to meet an identical twin for the first time? Catherine wondered anxiously as the coach rumbled up the long, steep hill to Blue Waters Manor and came to a halt at the bottom of the lane.

Lachlan and Gawyn had ridden ahead to announce her arrival and ensure that there was no danger while the others stayed behind to guard the coach. Catherine was to wait until there was some indication that she would be both safe and welcome.

While she waited, she tried not to think of Lachlan and the argument they'd had the day before, and how she could not bear the thought of losing him. It was quite likely, however, that she would. One way or another. Even if Raonaid agreed to lift the curse, he would soon escort Catherine home to her family.

Growing increasingly troubled, she thrust that thought from her mind and instead tried to focus on her first meeting with her twin sister. What questions would she ask? She would inquire about Raonaid's childhood, of course, her special gifts as an oracle, and her life in the Hebrides.

Catherine wondered curiously if Raonaid had an

aversion to onions, as she did, or if she could not fall asleep on her stomach. They were twins after all. Since they were identical, would they share the same tastes in everything? Would they have the same mannerisms? All these trivial questions and details seemed fascinating to Catherine, and each moment that passed seemed to stretch on forever while her heart beat faster and faster. Her life was about to change irreversibly. She was going to meet her twin, and nothing would ever be the same again.

Sitting forward, Catherine peered out the window, through the early-morning light. What was happening inside the manor house? Had Lachlan told Raonaid the news yet? Had he asked her about the curse?

With his targe hanging at his back, his hand gripped around the hilt of his sword, Lachlan strode slowly into Raonaid's parlor. A housekeeper had greeted him at the door and informed him that Murdoch was not at home and would not return until the evening. The lady of the house, however, would be downstairs shortly.

With a swell of dark, simmering impatience, Lachlan glanced around at all the seafaring portraits on the walls and other marine artifacts that decorated the mantel and tabletops.

Bloody hell, it was going to be a challenge to keep his temper under control.

The floorboards creaked at the top of the stairs, and someone began to descend.

His heart pounded like a heavy mallet as his thoughts rushed back to that night in the burial cist when

Raonaid had cut him with the knife and left him there, drugged and sick, tethered to the ground. Cursed for life.

How would he feel when he saw Catherine's identical twin? What if the sight of her made him think of the woman he had made love to? The woman who had cried out in ecstasy in his arms?

At last, the oracle stepped into the doorway, and he regarded her with careful scrutiny.

She looked different from how he remembered her. Today she wore an elegant morning dress and her red hair was shiny and clean, swept up at the sides.

"I knew you'd find me eventually," she said in that achingly familiar voice. It was so much like Catherine's, and indeed, he did find it alarming to see her image before him, in the body of a woman he despised.

As the seconds ticked by, however, he began to see how terribly wrong he had been when he first encountered Catherine in the stone circle. How could he not have seen the truth? For Raonaid was nothing like Catherine. *Nothing.* Raonaid flaunted a look in her eye that he remembered very well—a cruel, hateful fire that burned with spite and contempt.

No. There would be no more confusion. A lifetime apart had produced two very different women.

But did she know? he wondered, narrowing his eyes at her. With all her gifts and powers from beyond, had Raonaid ever suspected she had a sister?

"I never stopped searching for you," he replied, watching her stroll casually into the parlor. "For three years, I have been cursed to a life alone. I have not lain with a woman in all that time—not until yesterday—and that is why I am here. I have come on *her* behalf. I am asking you to lift the curse. Make it go away."

Raonaid's eyebrows lifted in surprise. "Are you jesting? For three years, you have been celibate? *You?* The great lover of the Highlands? I don't believe it."

The housekeeper walked in with a tray of tea and biscuits. She set it on the table by the sofa, glanced up at each of them, recognized the snapping sparks of antagonism in the air, then hastened from the room.

Taking a deep breath to settle his nerves, Lachlan responded in a controlled voice. "*Believe* it," he said. "I have been celibate since the day you laid the curse, and I hope that gives you the satisfaction and vengeance you desired when you concocted it. But enough time has passed. Lift it now, and let us both move forward with our lives."

She grinned teasingly, as if this were a game to her. "What if I say no? What*ever* will you do?"

He shut his eyes and squeezed the hilt of his sword. "Don't test me, Raonaid. Just let it go. I beg of you."

She frowned curiously at him, as if that was not the reply she was expecting, then moved to the tea table. "Would you like a biscuit?"

"I don't want anything, except for you to lift the curse."

Picking up the fine china teapot and placing the tip of her forefinger on the lid, she nevertheless poured two cups of tea, then sat down.

"Come and join me." She patted the seat cushion beside her. "Tell me about this lady friend of yours. Is she an innocent? Was she seduced by your charms, and did she fall madly in love with you? Or was she a common slut?"

Lachlan's blood began to boil in his veins, and he had to fight the urge to knock over that tea table and grab Catherine's sister by the throat.

"Be careful what you say," he growled. "You may regret it later."

"Why should I? Are you going to beat me to a pulp? Force me to surrender? That's not your usual style, Lachlan. I would expect it from Angus, but not you. You've always had such a talent for seduction. That's how you usually get what you want, isn't it? Why don't you try your skills on *me*? See how far you can get."

He stepped forward. "Lift the curse now, Raonaid, and then I'll tell you why I'm here."

She regarded him over the rim of her teacup as she brought it to her lips. "*That* is not the reason? I thought it was."

"There's more. A great deal more."

She set the cup down and paused uncertainly. "Are you here because of Murdoch?" she asked. "What have you heard?"

"I heard that he wants to stir up another rebellion— but no, lass. That's not why I'm here, either."

"Well, don't keep me in suspense."

"Lift the curse, and I'll explain."

For a long moment, she studied him in the morning light beaming in through the front windows; then her features seemed to relax. He had seen that expression before and knew she intended to toy with him a bit more, but his patience was wearing thin.

Leaning back, she stretched an arm across the sofa

cushions and shook her head. "Oh, Lachlan. Have you really been so very lonely all this time? Have you not enjoyed the love of a woman? Not at all?"

"I'm not a killer," he said.

Her brow furrowed with surprise. She seemed almost fascinated by his reply. "But you cannot be serious. Did you really think it was true? For three years? Even on that night . . . ?"

He stood motionless, his body tense, as he glowered down at her. "What are you saying?"

"What do you think I'm saying?"

A deep rage began to burn heavily through his body. "Are you telling me that it was a hoax? That it was never real?"

"Of course it was not real!" she blurted out with a laugh. "I have *visions,* Lachlan. That does not make me a witch, despite what people think and say. I was only having a bit of fun. I was getting even with you!"

His breath came raggedly in his throat. "Then she is not in danger?"

"Who? Your lovely lady friend? The one who spread her legs for you yesterday? Only God can answer that. I will have nothing to do with it, nine months from now. That will be *your* problem."

Lachlan couldn't look at her. He turned around and laid a hand on the wall to steady himself.

It was not real.

He was not cursed.

Catherine was not going to die.

"You are a depraved and soulless monster," he said over his shoulder. "What I wouldn't give to choke the life out of you right now. If it weren't for the fact that . . ."

He stopped and fought to control his wrath.

"What?" she asked, rising to her feet. "What is it that you have not told me?"

"You don't even deserve to know." He swung around to face her again, taking some pleasure in this small moment of revenge, however briefly it would last. "She's too good for you. If it were up to me, you would never get within a hundred miles of her. I would never let her near your vile, putrid soul."

A shadow of fear swept across Raonaid's face, and he relished it.

"What are you speaking of?"

"Your sister," he said at last. "You have an identical twin, Raonaid, and she is waiting outside to meet you. And when she does, I hope she sees what *I* see, and never wants to lay eyes on you again."

Catherine jumped when the coach began to move up the lane toward the house. Obviously they had been summoned.

Her heart thudded with nervous anticipation the entire distance, as they rolled up the tree-lined drive and finally stopped in front of the house. A ship's wheel adorned the front door, and flower boxes, bursting with evergreens, underscored each window.

Something about the layout of the outbuildings and vegetable garden was oddly familiar to her. Had she been here before?

The coach door opened, and Alex stepped up to greet her. "Allow me, Lady Catherine."

He, too, glanced all around, watching the fringes of the forest at the edge of the field, as if he half-expected an army of rebels to appear at any moment and whisk her away for ransom. He escorted her up the gravel walk to the flagstone steps, where Lachlan was waiting for her.

"Come in, Catherine," he said, sounding formal, unlike any other time.

Her voice wavered with apprehension. "Is she here?"

"Aye," Lachlan said.

"Did she know about me?"

"Nay, she did not know about you before," he explained. "She's waiting for you in the parlor, but there is something I must tell you, before you go in."

Catherine was vaguely aware of Alex handing her over to Lachlan, who took her aside and waited briefly for Alex to reach the bottom of the stairs before he spoke.

"Raonaid said the curse was never real," he told her.

Catherine shook her head in disbelief. "What do you mean, *never real*? Was it a trick, then? Some kind of joke?"

"I wouldn't call it that, for I can see no humor in it. It was her way of taking vengeance upon me. It was twisted and heartless." He took both Catherine's hands in his and looked down at them while he rubbed his thumbs over her palms. "But it's good news, nonetheless, that you are no longer in danger of that fiendish black magic. I would never have been able to live with myself if anything happened to you." He lifted his gaze to meet hers. "But I can never forgive her for it, lass, and I feel no better about what we did. I've been living with that curse for three years, and I still cannot let go of it. I know what can happen to a woman on the birthing bed, and I still fear for you." His eyes were dark with worry.

She reached up and touched his cheek and felt joyful inside. "You should be *happy,* Lachlan. This is what you have been wanting these past three years. You are free now. The curse is lifted."

His dark brows pulled together with uncertainty. "Is it?"

She did not know what to say. All her emotions were reeling. She had just learned she was not sentenced to die in nine months—which was wonderful news of course—but she could not escape the frantic apprehension of meeting her identical twin, who was waiting just inside. . . .

"You must be careful when you go in there," Lachlan said as if he could read her thoughts. "I know she is your sister by blood, but she is nothing like you. She has lived a very different life. She is not to be trusted, and I suspect she will try to poison your mind against me."

"I appreciate the warning," Catherine replied, "but I assure you I can think for myself. No one controls my opinions but me."

He nodded reluctantly, then led her through the entrance hall and into a room cluttered with articles depicting a seafaring theme, which was strangely fitting under the circumstances—for she felt as if the floor beneath her were pitching and rolling up the steep side of a great ocean swell.

Then all at once she was staring at her own mirror image—another version of herself, identical in every way—standing motionless before the hearth.

Chapter Thirty-one

"You are Raonaid," Catherine said, ignoring all proper rules of etiquette, but this was not a normal situation.

"Aye," her twin replied.

The cadence of her voice was eerily similar to Catherine's own.

They regarded each other warily. Though she knew it was wrong to stare, Catherine could not help but examine all the finer details of her sister's appearance—the indistinguishable shape of her upturned nose, the fullness of her lips, her vivid blue eyes, the size and shape of her breasts, and the particular curve of her waist. Even her hands were the same. How was it possible for such a miracle to occur? It was like some form of magic.

"Please . . . ," Raonaid said as she gestured toward the sofa with a hand.

Catherine let go of Lachlan's hand and sat down beside Raonaid. They faced each other in silence, though it was not uncomfortable. Catherine knew exactly what Raonaid was feeling: all the things *she* was feeling. Fascination. Disbelief. And strangely, despite everything that Lachlan had experienced because of this woman, a most unexpected joy was bubbling up inside Catherine.

"Lachlan said you did not know about me," Catherine mentioned. "I didn't know about you, either. At least, I do not think so. Did he also tell you that I have no memory of my life?"

"Aye, he told me. And though I never knew of you, I always felt your spirit hovering around me, even as a child. I did not know who you were, or *what* you were, but now I understand. The ghost over my shoulder . . . it was always you."

A lump rose up in Catherine's throat, and her eyes filled with tears. "I've been haunted, too," she said. "In both dreams and wakefulness, but I had no idea . . ."

Catherine glanced uneasily at Lachlan, who was standing in the doorway, watching them with some concern. She could see in his eyes that he was still wary of Raonaid, but Catherine would form her own conclusions about her sister, for there was so much she had yet to discover.

"Who raised you?" she asked.

"A woman named Matthea. She told me she was not my mother, but she never revealed how she came to be my guardian. She died when I was eleven."

"What did you do then?"

"I raised myself."

Catherine felt a deep and wrenching sadness for her sister as a young girl. "I am so sorry."

"Why? Matthea taught me all I needed to know in order to survive. I had a warm house to live in, and I knew how to care for the animals and feed myself. I don't need your pity."

Catherine's brow furrowed. "I meant no offense." She paused. "What kind of house was it? Will you describe it to me? I would like to imagine your life."

"It was a thatched cottage on the water," Raonaid flatly replied, "outside the village of Gearrannan. I also knew how to fish and make baskets. Some folks in the village were kind. Those who were not learned to stay away." She lifted her chin with a cool show of strength.

"They thought you were a witch."

"Aye, for I could predict the weather, and I foretold a few important deaths in the village, and abroad. No one bothered me much. I was feared mostly."

"Were you lonely?"

Her eyes turned instantly cold, and Catherine wondered if her own eyes had ever conveyed such an icy look of contempt.

For the first time, she understood what Lachlan had tried to warn her about. They were sisters, but they had been reared apart and they were not the same.

"Always," Raonaid replied.

Catherine inhaled deeply. "So you never knew you were the daughter of an earl?"

She scoffed. "If I knew that, dear sister, I would have traveled to Drumloch years ago, and claimed what was rightly mine. What was *taken* from me."

Catherine looked down at her hands in her lap and nodded, for she could not blame Raonaid for her anger. She felt it herself, for she may have been bequeathed a fortune, but she had been denied a sister, and for that she would always feel some resentment toward those responsible. But at least she had lived a comfortable life and had enjoyed many luxuries; she had known the identity of her parents. Raonaid, on the other hand, was given none of that, and Catherine could not even begin to imagine the extent of her sister's bitterness in that regard.

"What can you tell me," Raonaid said, sounding calmer now, "about our mother?"

Catherine lifted her gaze. "Very little, I'm afraid. She died giving birth to us, and I don't know why we were separated. My only hope is that once we return to Drumloch someone will know the answer to that question."

Lachlan stepped forward. *"Catherine . . ."*

She glanced across at him and saw the look of warning in his eyes. Clearly he did not think it would be wise to bring Raonaid to Drumloch. It was not his choice to make, however.

Catherine spoke to him in a polite tone but with a firm note of resolve. "If you would be so kind, Lachlan, I would like some time alone with my sister. Will you please wait outside?"

His dark eyes shifted to Raonaid again, and Catherine saw the look of triumph she gave him in return.

"If you wish," he gruffly said. "But I will wait outside the door, and I will send Gawyn around to the back, to make sure no one comes or goes."

The corner of Raonaid's mouth curled up in a subtle grin of self-satisfaction.

The instant he was gone, Catherine turned her eyes on Raonaid and spoke with reproach. "That was disrespectful."

Raonaid frowned. "Does it really matter to you?"

"Of course it matters. If it weren't for Lachlan, I would not be sitting here now. He has done nothing but try to help me recover the life that was lost to me."

"And how did he do that?" Raonaid asked, sitting forward and perching an elbow on her knee. "By making love to you? It's odd. You and I look exactly the same, but you lack a certain . . ." She bit her lip, as if she needed more time to ponder it.

"A certain *what*?" Catherine asked, challenging her sister to say exactly what she was thinking.

"A certain *worldliness*. How could you have given yourself to him, Catherine? He is the worst rogue in Scotland, and he took you to bed when he believed he was cursed. Did you know of it? Or did he tell you afterward, when it was too late to change it?"

Catherine clenched her teeth. "He told you about that?"

"Aye, it's the *first* thing he told me—that he had bedded some lassie the day before and that's why he needed me to lift the curse. Clearly he was using you to force my hand. Do you not see that?"

The chill in her sister's voice caused all the hairs on Catherine's neck to stand on end.

"He slept with you," Raonaid continued, "when he believed he was cursed. What does that tell you about him?"

"It was my fault, too," Catherine insisted.

Raonaid sat back and regarded her closely. "I doubt that very much. The man has a certain power over women, and he knows it. There is something about him that makes most women go completely mad with infatuation. I've seen it. He has the power to seduce, and that's why I cursed him—to save a few broken hearts once the word got out about his . . . *situation*. So do not look at me like that, as if I am some sort of villain."

Raonaid was not entirely wrong about Lachlan's sexual power over women. Catherine had experienced it herself and had seen it in Abigail, the young barmaid, on the first night of their escape. But that did not justify Raonaid's actions. She had cast a cruel spell on him—one that harkened back to his wife's death and made him relive it over and over.

"Do you feel it is your place to judge people?" Catherine asked. "To hand out punishment and control their lives, as if you were God?"

Raonaid's eyes darkened. "Are you in love with him?"

"That is none of your concern."

Her sister regarded her shrewdly. "You *are*. I can see it in your eyes. Does he know it?"

Catherine was not sure. She had never spoken the words aloud, and she had refused his offer of marriage and suggested that what they felt for each other was not real.

"No, he does not," she said at last.

Raonaid scoffed bitterly. "Then you'd best keep it that way, lass. He's not the sort of man you want to pin your hopes on."

Outside, Lachlan paced back and forth under the wide portico, wondering what poison Raonaid was feeding to Catherine now, when Alex approached and rested one booted foot on the bottom step.

"Don't worry, Lachlan," he said. "Lady Catherine will

be fine. I just took a look through the back window. They're only talking."

"Do I look worried?" Lachlan replied, glaring down at the young clansman with a pungent rancor he could not suppress.

"Aye, you look about ready to burst through that door swinging your claymore."

Lachlan inhaled sharply and looked toward the horizon. "That's about the best idea I've heard all day."

Alex sat down on the step. Lachlan decided he needed to relax, so he joined Alex, pulled the dirk out of his boot, and sat for a long time, turning it over in his hands, watching the sun reflect off the blade.

"It's obvious," Alex carefully said, "that you have feelings for Lady Catherine. I can hardly blame you, sir. She's a treasure, that one, and she cares for you, too. It's plain as day. Do you know what you're going to do about it?"

Lachlan turned his eyes toward the young Highlander, who continually surprised him. "I'm going to do nothing, Alex. We come from different worlds. She's a Lowlander under the guardianship of a cousin who detests Highlanders, and she's an heiress on top of it. And things have not gone . . . *smoothly* between us."

Besides that, he had already lost one wife. He could not bear to lose another.

"*Ach.* . . . " Alex waved a dismissive hand through the air. "What should any of that matter if you love each other? She's old enough to make her own choices, is she not?"

Lachlan considered that. "Aye, but she's not stupid, either. She knows I'm not the right sort, and she's made that abundantly clear. So have *you*. And now, with Raonaid in there, filling her head with all kinds of unflattering stories about me . . ."

Alex shrugged. "Maybe Lady Catherine will see the truth in it, and choose you over her sister."

Lachlan slipped the dirk back into his boot. "I doubt it. You know what they say about blood and water."

"Aye, one's thicker than the other, but does that apply when the sister is a witch?"

Lachlan inclined his head. "She's not a witch, Alex. She's an oracle."

"That's just splittin' hairs. Either way, she's evil. Isn't she?" He tipped his head back to let the sun warm his face, then opened one eye to squint at Lachlan. "Or am I wrong?"

The front door opened, and Catherine stepped outside. Lachlan and Alex quickly rose to their feet.

"I've made a decision," she said. "I have been discussing my memory loss with Raonaid, and she has explained to me that she always had her strongest visions at the stone circle at Callanais, not far from where she grew up. I told her about the standing stones at Drumloch, and how I, too, have been drawn to them since my return. We wish to go there together. It is my hope that she will experience a vision there, and perhaps see the missing years of my life."

Lachlan could not hide his misgivings. "You intend to introduce her to your family?" It would create a scandal like no other.

"Yes. I know that it will not be easy—especially with my grandmother—but we both deserve to know the truth."

Lachlan lowered his voice and moved closer to speak in her ear. "If that is your decision, lass, I will honor it. But are you certain you can trust her? What about your inheritance?"

"She is my sister, Lachlan," she whispered in return. "And a Montgomery. I am prepared to share my fortune with her, once it is transferred to me."

He shook his head when what he really wanted to do was shake some sense into her. "Are you sure that's wise? You only just met her. Have you told her this yet?"

"Not yet."

"Then, don't," he implored, keeping his voice to a hush. "Wait until we reach Drumloch. Take some time to think on it. That's all I ask."

A shadow of concern passed over her features as she looked up at him under the shaded portico. "Are you afraid she will give it to Murdoch, to support the Jacobite cause?"

"Among other things," he replied, for there were a dozen things that worried him. Just delivering them both to Drumloch without incident was enough to keep him on the alert.

Catherine glanced over her shoulder. "I must go back inside. Can we leave in the morning? She will need time to collect her belongings, and say good-bye to Murdoch."

"No," he replied. "She can say nothing to Murdoch. God only knows what they might plot together if he finds out the Drumloch heiress is his lover's twin. Tell her we are leaving now; otherwise she'll have to find her own way. I'll not risk your safety by spending another night here."

Catherine hesitated, but in the end she agreed. "Fine, but if you could allow her a few minutes to prepare."

She entered the house and was about to shut the door behind her when Lachlan stopped it with his boot.

"I'll need to make sure she doesn't leave some sort of letter behind. And tell her to summon the housekeeper. I want to speak to her, too, about what she saw here this morning."

Catherine nodded and stepped out of his way.

Chapter Thirty-two

Drumloch Manor
Nine hours later

Lachlan heard the shot before the coach made it half-way up the drive.

"What the devil?" He saw a flash of movement up at the house and spotted John Montgomery, Catherine's devoted cousin, clambering down the front steps, pointing his pistol at the sky.

Another shot rang out, and Goliath whinnied and reared up, clawing his hooves at the air. Lachlan fought hard to stay in the saddle.

"Whoa!"

The coach pulled abruptly to a halt. The door swung open and Catherine leaped out onto the lane, waving her arms and shouting, *"It's me, John! It's Catherine! Do not shoot!"*

Lachlan regained control of his mount and trotted closer to her. "Are you mad, lassie? Get back inside!"

"No! I will not let him shoot you again!"

She picked up her skirts and started marching up the

hill, on a wild mission to put her cousin in his proper place. She was like a pistol ball herself, Lachlan thought, and he quite loved that about her. God help him, he loved everything about her, and it was killing him.

"I have come home, John!" she shouted. "The Highlander has brought me back, and if you shoot him again I will knock your bloody head off!"

The earl lowered his gun and bellowed into the house to inform the servants of Catherine's return, then came running the rest of the way down the steps.

Catherine, too, began to run while Lachlan slowed his horse to a walk, convinced now that she was safe.

He watched her throw herself into her cousin's arms. The earl picked her up and swung her around.

Lachlan instructed the driver of the coach to wait there on the lane, then cantered forward to face the earl's impending displeasure.

Drumloch turned to face him. The earl's cheeks flushed instantly with antagonism. "I received Lady Catherine's letter three days ago. She insisted that you did not abduct her—that she went willingly—but after what you tried to do to her, I am hesitant to believe it. I still have half a mind to string you up by the heels!"

"I spoke the truth," Catherine insisted. "You must listen to me, John. This man has helped me solve many mysteries about my past, and he deserves our thanks. Allow me to properly introduce him to you. This is Lachlan MacDonald, Laird of War of Kinloch Castle." She gestured back to her cousin. "The Earl of Drumloch."

Lachlan nodded. "My lord."

John scowled up at him. "And what mysteries did

you help solve, sir, which required you to steal my cousin away in the dead of night, without permission from her family?"

"You ought to speak to Lady Catherine about that," he replied, "for it is a family matter, and not my place to say. I'm sure she will tell you all you need to know." Goliath grew restless and took a few steps backwards.

Catherine strode closer. "Wait," she said. "You're not leaving, are you? No, you cannot. You must stay until all this is settled—or at least long enough to replenish your supplies before you return to Kinloch."

And there it was. The assumption, spoken aloud, that he would not be a part of her life now that she was home again. But why should he be? He had fulfilled his duty by delivering her to Kinloch, where she was able to discover the truth about her identity—that she was indeed Lady Catherine Montgomery. He had also reunited her with her sister. It was time now to return to his home in the Highlands. To the life he knew before the curse. It was time to put all this behind him.

Perhaps one day he would be thankful that she had refused his offer of marriage, which had been proposed under extraordinary circumstances. *It's bound to make things seem more intense than they really are. . . .*

With a sudden knot of grief pulsing in his gut, Lachlan turned in the saddle to look back at the coach, which was still waiting halfway up the drive. He was surprised that Raonaid had not thrown a tantrum by now. He had never known her to be patient or docile.

Catherine turned to her cousin. "I have brought someone I wish you to meet."

The earl nodded, then waved a hand at the driver,

signaling for him to approach. "Is this the person you mentioned in your letter?" he asked with some unease.

"Yes."

The coach, led by four chestnut horses, rumbled up the drive and pulled to a slow, creaking halt in front of them. A footman hurried down the steps to open the door, and Lachlan watched it all unfold with a terrible ache in his heart.

Catherine kept her eyes fixed on her cousin's face, for she wished to measure his response. Had he known about this missing link in the family? Had he been keeping it secret from her all this time? Or would he be as shocked as she to learn of it?

John strode forward, curious and eager to view the woman inside the coach.

Raonaid's small foot emerged first; then her gloved hand reached out to accept the footman's assistance. At last, she showed herself. She stepped fully into the pink light from the setting sun and lifted her face.

Catherine glanced quickly at her cousin. His cheeks went pale. His eyes deepened with wonder.

"My word. . . ." He moved closer to take Raonaid's hand. "I am astounded. You are a perfect likeness."

Raonaid regarded him with suspicion. "Did you know about me?" she asked.

"I assure you, Lady Raonaid, I did not—at least not until recently."

It was the first time she had been properly addressed as a member of the aristocracy, and the importance of that moment was not lost on anyone. Especially Raonaid, whose head drew back in astonishment.

"When Catherine disappeared for the second time," John continued, "I took it upon myself to look into her past. Then her letter arrived only a few days ago and confirmed what I had been able to uncover on my own." He turned to address Catherine. "I have information for you both," he said, "regarding your birth. If you will join me in the drawing room."

Catherine felt an almost-dizzying rush of eagerness, for she was about to discover the truth at last.

She turned to Lachlan. "Will you come with us? I would like for you to be there."

In actual fact, she had never needed him more than she did in that moment.

He stared down at her, as if considering how best to reply, then simply dismounted and handed Goliath over to a groom.

"Where is Grandmother?" Catherine asked when Mrs. Silver, the housekeeper, appeared in the doorway to the drawing room, looking pale and distraught as she set eyes upon Raonaid.

"She will not be joining us," John explained. "I am afraid she has been keeping to her rooms lately."

"Why?"

Her cousin hesitated. "You will understand soon enough."

John waved Mrs. Silver into the drawing room, escorted her to a chair, and went to pour her a glass of brandy. It was hardly proper for an earl to wait on a servant in such a way, which left Catherine feeling shaken, for whatever information Mrs. Silver was about to divulge must indeed be most unsettling.

John poured drinks for everyone else, himself included, and sat down. "Mrs. Silver has proven herself to be an invaluable source of information," he said. "What she is about to tell you will, no doubt, be disturbing to you both, but it is time the truth was known. Please, Mrs. Silver, describe the events of twenty-five years ago to Lady Catherine and Lady Raonaid, as you remember them."

Catherine felt Raonaid tense beside her at the shock of hearing her name spoken for the second time with the proper form of address.

"When it was announced," the housekeeper timidly said, "that your mother was expecting a child, everyone of course hoped for a boy, to secure an heir for the earl, but shortly before she went into labor, a woman came to the door, bold as brass, and claimed she was a gifted midwife. She told me that the countess would deliver a babe with powers from beyond, and that she would need to put an enchantment on the child to cure it of this malady. She was mad, I believed, so I sent her away, but when I told the dowager of it, she ordered me to send a footman to fetch the woman and bring her back."

"Surely Grandmother would never believe such a tale," Catherine said with skepticism.

"Oh, but she did, my lady. And the very next day, your mother began her labor—two weeks early. She collapsed in the stone circle with terrible pains in her belly."

"Is that where we were born?" Catherine asked, feeling a cold shiver ripple up and down her spine at the memory of her own behavior on the night she walked in her sleep to the standing stone on the hill. "In the Drumloch Circle?"

"No, my lady. We managed to bring the countess back to the manor house, but the dowager insisted on using the midwife who had come to the door. Everyone else was kept out of the room—everyone but me—and it was many, many hours before you both were born. You came first, Lady Catherine, and then your sister. Your mother struggled hard. She gave you both everything she had, and I believe it's important for you both to know that she held you together in her arms for a full hour before she passed."

Catherine reached for Raonaid's hand and held on to it while a tear trembled down her cheek. She looked up at Lachlan. He was watching her intently, with concern, and she was grateful that he was here to learn all of this.

"What happened next?" Raonaid asked.

Mrs. Silver's hand quivered as she took another sip of brandy; then she lifted her eyes to meet Raonaid's and faced her squarely. "As soon as the countess passed, the dowager took you out of her arms, Lady Raonaid, handed you to the midwife, and told her to drown you in the river."

"Good Lord!" Catherine stood up.

"The woman did exactly as she was told, I thought," Mrs. Silver continued, "as that was the last I ever saw of you. I was instructed never to speak of it again, not to anyone, especially the earl. Your father never knew your mother had delivered twins."

An eerie silence ensued, and Catherine sank back onto the sofa cushions. No one spoke for a long moment.

"Why me?" Raonaid sharply asked. "Why not Catherine?"

"Because you had a birthmark on your neck," Mrs. Silver replied, "and the midwife told us that it was the sign of your unearthly power."

Raonaid drew her hand away from Catherine's and spoke in a contemptuous tone. "What was the midwife's name?"

"Her name was Matthea," the housekeeper replied. "Obviously, she did not end your life as the dowager believed. She took you away."

"Aye," Raonaid boldly replied. "She took me to the Hebrides and raised me as her own—and she was very kind to me, until the day she died." Raonaid shot Catherine a heated look. "I don't envy you, Sister, being raised by the dowager." She glanced quickly, poisonously, at John. "Where is she now? Why has she not shown her face? I suspect she fears me worse than she fears her own death. Does she expect me to cast some vengeful spell on her? Change her into a frog or a rat?"

Catherine glanced uneasily at Lachlan, whose expression stilled and grew very grim.

Raonaid scowled. "Well, tell her not to worry. I wouldn't waste my bones on her. She will simply have to live with what she did to her own flesh and blood. God will judge her soon enough." She stood up. "I want to leave here. Now. Lachlan, will you take me back to the Highlands? I don't want to see these people ever again. I want to go home. *Please.*"

When he did not respond straightaway, her voice grew beseeching. "I am sorry for what I did to you. I *beg* of you, Lachlan, *please,* just take me away from here."

"It's not up to me," he said, turning his eyes to Catherine, waiting for some signal from her.

She reached for Raonaid's hand and spoke with compassion. "You cannot leave, not like this. Please stay and give us another chance. Our cousin John is a good man. He had nothing to do with any of that. He didn't even know of it until recently."

"Indeed, Lady Raonaid." John rose to his feet. "I wish to make amends. You are very welcome here. It is your birthplace and your home."

"It is *not* my home!" she shouted. "It never was!"

Catherine stood up, too, and saw that her sister's face was flooding with color. She looked as if she might suddenly bolt.

"But it could be," Catherine implored, her heart filling with desperation. "I am your sister, and I want to be a part of your life. My inheritance—half of it is yours. No matter what you decide. I am sure my father would have bequeathed it to you if he had known of your existence. But please, do not go. You have a home here, and a family that wants to know you better."

Raonaid laid a hand on her stomach and spoke in a shaky voice. "Lachlan, please take me out of here. Away from these people. I cannot breathe."

Catherine watched in horror as he rose from his chair and held out a hand. Raonaid pulled away from Catherine and crossed toward him. Without uttering a word, he escorted her out of the room.

Catherine and John regarded each other in tense silence before Catherine ripped off her gloves and threw them onto the sofa cushions.

"Where is my grandmother?" she asked in a voice that seethed with fury. "I wish to speak to her. *Right now.* And God help her when she faces my wrath,

John. God help her!" She turned and strode out of the drawing room, calling over her shoulder at the last second, *"Make sure they do not leave! Lachlan and Raonaid must stay here tonight! I will not lose either of them! I have already lost enough!"*

Chapter Thirty-three

"Was I dreaming?" Raonaid asked as she paced back and forth in the garden outside the manor, her fists perched on her hips. "Did you hear all of that? Or have I lost my mind?"

"I heard it," Lachlan replied, watching her with some concern. He'd seen this woman tear an entire kitchen apart, and he didn't want to get in the way if she was so inclined this evening—for he rather thought this estate *deserved* a good tearing apart.

"My own grandmother handed me to a stranger with instructions to drown me like a dog! What kind of madness is that? I am *glad* I was not raised here. I pity Catherine. No wonder she disappeared without a word. She probably ran screaming from the place, and purged it from her mind intentionally!"

"Try to calm yourself," Lachlan said. "It's not all bad. You have a sister now, and a cousin who is a powerful nobleman. Neither of them had anything to do with what happened that day, and they both wish to make amends, so you cannot take your vengeance out on them."

She stopped in her tracks. "Did the earl not shoot you? Catherine told me about how you met in the stone circle, and how they sent you off with the magistrate to have you killed. I don't see why you are defending them."

"I cannot blame them for reacting the way they did," he replied. "I would have done the same. I came after Catherine like a ruthless savage, thinking she was *you*."

"Oh, and that excuses everything, does it?" she scoffed. "People can do whatever they bloody well please to *me*, because I am wicked and worthless. I don't deserve anyone's respect. According to a certain dowager countess, I don't even deserve to live!"

"What she did was wrong," Lachlan agreed, working hard to keep his voice steady and calm. "Everyone else knows it, so you cannot hold the whole world responsible. And surely the dowager feels some remorse in her old age. For that matter, the worst is yet to come now that Catherine knows of it. Your sister was just as horrified as you were, to learn what occurred. I *know* her. She will not let it rest."

Raonaid gave him an icy glare and began to pace again. "What am I going to do? I hate them. All of them."

"Not Catherine," he said. "You cannot hate *her*. I know that you don't."

She narrowed her eyes at him. "You are not going to take me away from here, are you?"

He shook his head. "Not yet. You need to resolve all of this and get a sense of who you really are. Otherwise you'll go on wreaking havoc on the world for the rest of your life. Besides that, Catherine needs your help. She needs her memories back, and there's a stone circle on the hill that's calling out to you, I can well imagine."

She gave him a mutinous look, as if she was angry with him for guessing the truth.

"And then what?" she asked. "If I help that chit get her memories back, what do I do then? I can hardly join their ranks, and start living like a bluidy princess."

He strode forward and regarded her steadily. "At the very least, you need to take the money. Catherine offered it to you, and by God, after what that wretched woman did to you on the day of your birth, you most certainly deserve to have it."

Her eyebrows drew together with disbelief. "Do you really think so?"

"Aye, but don't get too excited, Raonaid. It doesn't mean I like you." He turned to go back into the house.

She watched him for a moment, then quickened her step to follow, and gave him a small shove. "Nor I, you."

Immediately after speaking to her grandmother, Catherine went searching for Lachlan. She was so afraid he had left and taken Raonaid with him. What would she do if she lost them both? She would simply have to saddle a horse and go riding after them.

As it happened, she found Lachlan in the blue guest chamber, which had been prepared for him. He was sitting in front of the window, lounging back in a chair with his big booted legs resting on the sill, crossed at the ankles. Outside, the sun was setting in splashing streaks of light and color, and the dusky-rose radiance beamed in on his handsome face.

His targe, sword belt, and pistol were all tossed onto a pile on the bed, and he was relaxing with a plate of pink sugar cakes on his lap. He popped one into his mouth and licked the frosting off his fingers with a loud smack.

Fully entering the room, she closed the door behind her.

Lachlan casually dropped his booted feet to the floor and swiveled in the chair to face her.

"Jesus, lass. You look like you've been through a war."

"I *feel* as if I have."

He set the plate of sugar cakes on the windowsill. "If it helps you to know," he gently said, "I convinced Raonaid to stay."

Catherine swallowed hard over all the emotions that were mounting up inside her. She was terrified that her sister would not be able to forgive the family and would never wish to see any of them again. But Catherine was equally afraid that Lachlan would simply walk out of her life tomorrow and put all of this complicated madness behind him.

She must have revealed some of her thoughts, for he rose to his feet and crossed toward her. "You've had a rough day, lass." He slid a hand up the side of her neck and rubbed a thumb over her ear.

The sensation stirred a pleasant warmth inside her. Oh, how she longed to be held by him. She needed him now more than ever, and it was all she could think of—to lie with him again.

Closing her eyes, she turned her lips into his palm and kissed it. "I was so afraid you left me."

He shook his head. "No."

Catherine opened her eyes. "I don't want you to leave. Not ever. I won't survive if you do."

"I don't believe that for a minute," he said. "You're a survivor, Catherine, no two ways about it."

Fighting to stay strong, she nodded and backed away from him.

"I just spoke to my grandmother," she explained, working hard to regain her composure. "I told her that she was no longer welcome in this house. John agrees, and he is making arrangements for her to live elsewhere, on one of his other properties. He will provide her with servants and a small allowance, but that is all. Outside of that, we will say good-bye to her and her wretched little dogs. I don't ever want to see her again."

"How did she take the news?" Lachlan asked.

"Surprisingly well, as a matter of fact. She didn't utter a word of disagreement. In fact, she barely looked at me. She kept her back to me the entire time, and simply gazed out the window."

"Do you think she might regret what she did?"

Catherine considered it, then shook her head. "She did not indicate that to me. She offered no apology, so as far as I am concerned, this is the end of our association. I will wash my hands of her. I don't ever want to see her again, and Raonaid should not have to see her, either."

Catherine looked up at Lachlan's beautiful, arresting face and was again tempted to draw him close, to lead him to the bed and lie with him for a while.

He turned his gaze away, however, and she had the distinct impression that he would not welcome her advances.

Spotting the plate of sugar cakes on the windowsill, she moved past him and reached for one, but took one look at it and felt her stomach turn. So much had happened. She had no appetite, so she set it back down.

"What do you want, Catherine?" Lachlan asked, striding forward across the carpet. "Why are you here?"

Her heart throbbed painfully in her chest. She was so desperate for him, she could have dropped to her knees and wept. "Isn't it obvious?"

"Not to me," he said. "The last time we spoke, I told you that the curse was lifted. Then you were reunited with your sister. We finished what we set out to do—we each got what we wanted—so I believe we are done with each other now."

Catherine shook her head. "Please don't say that."

"But you know it's true. Ours was a strange situation. You were lost, and I was cursed. We needed each other in ways I still do not understand, and probably never will, but it's over now. And you were right about the proposal. I'm sure that one day, I will thank you for turning me down, and you will be very glad that you did."

"You don't mean that," she said.

He pinched the bridge of his nose and shook his head, as if this was just as difficult for him as it was for her.

She took a few steps closer. "It's not that I didn't *want* to marry you. . . ."

His eyes lifted, and she saw pain and confusion in their depths. "What are you saying now, lass?"

"I'm saying that I didn't think you were proposing to me for the right reasons. You thought I was going to carry your child for nine months, and then die. Surely you understand why I said no."

He nodded. "I do."

But everything was so different now, she thought. There was no curse. There had *never* been one. Couldn't they start over? Perhaps he could court her properly. She would have her own money soon, and she was of age. She didn't care that he was not a suitable husband for her. She would soon be a woman of independent means, and she could do whatever she pleased.

But did he still want her? That was the question, and there was only one way to find out.

She took a few careful steps forward and laid her hands on his chest.

Raonaid ran her hand up and down one of the ornately carved bedposts in her private guest chamber and was positively awestruck by the superb workmanship. She'd never seen anything like it before.

The room was paneled in dark cherry oak, with arched windows that overlooked a small courtyard below. Elegant depictions of swans and peacocks were woven into the drapes and upholstery, and there were at least two dozen candles in gold-plated holders, waiting to be lit.

How odd it felt, to be surrounded by such opulence. It hardly seemed real to her. She felt like an interloper, and yet she had been born into this world. She had the blood of an aristocrat running through her veins; her father was a famous Jacobite war hero—a nobleman who died on the battlefield at Sherrifmuir.

Angus, her former lover, had fought in that same battle, and she wondered suddenly if he and her father had had the opportunity to meet. Perhaps they had ridden beside each other into battle.

It was a strange thought—how they were all connected in the most mysterious ways.

Tomorrow she would go with Catherine to the stone circle where their mother had begun her labor. There, in that sacred place, Raonaid would try to evoke a vision that might help Catherine regain her memories.

Raonaid feared what she would see, however. What if she envisioned her mother's death or a thousand other painful moments from the past? Was it not possible? Now that she knew where she came from, a whole new world of visions might open up to her.

A knock sounded at the door just then and she realized it was getting dark in the chamber, so she quickly lit a candle.

"Just a moment," she answered. When the wick absorbed the flame and a warm, golden light infused the room, she called out to the visitor, "Come in."

The door opened, creaking on its hinges, and a stout older woman stepped across the threshold. She was dressed in black, her hair pulled into a tight knot at the back of her head. She regarded Raonaid in the ghostly light of nightfall, then covered her face with a trembling hand.

"God in heaven," the woman murmured. "It cannot be. . . ."

A sudden chill hung in the air as a stark and bitter realization washed over Raonaid.

"You are Eleanor," she said flatly. "My grandmother."

The woman's face sagged with a tomblike expression of contempt. Her jaw went slack, and she reached out a hand, moving forward.

"Do not come any closer," Raonaid warned.

Eleanor shivered, as if she was holding back a violent urge to spit out a mouthful of poison, then stopped mere inches away. "I knew it was you," she said. "For years, I heard tales of the Witch of the Western Isles, with the mark of the devil on her neck, and I knew it could be no other."

"And you were correct," Raonaid said with an unexpected surge of pride as she lifted her chin. "I am that notorious witch, but only because you made me so. I know what happened on the night of my birth. I know you tried to have me drowned in the river. But I survived, Grandmother, and here I am—home at last— about to claim half of your only son's fortune. What say you to that?"

Eleanor's mouth twisted with loathing. "I should never have trusted that midwife. I should have drowned you myself, or put you in the fire to burn."

Raonaid felt strongly inclined to grab the woman by the throat and toss her out the window, but she fought to keep her anger in check. Perhaps it was something about this room. Or the fact that someone had addressed her as Lady Raonaid earlier in the day. She did not think throwing the dowager countess out the window would be the appropriate response.

"Get out," Raonaid said simply. "Or I will drop *you* into the fire." It was the best she could do.

Eleanor backed up a few steps. "No need. I only wanted to see your face. That is all. I wanted to see if you were truly diabolical, or if it was all just a lot of nonsense."

Raonaid frowned. "You weren't *sure*?" She strode forward aggressively, forcing her grandmother to quicken her pace as she backed into the doorjamb. "You sent a baby to be drowned when you weren't even certain it was true?"

"It was not worth the risk," Eleanor replied, "and I see now that I did the right thing. You are most certainly diabolical."

Raonaid stopped and glared sternly at the vile woman. "No. *You* are the diabolical one, and one day, you will discover I was right—when you are screaming through the gates of hell. Now get . . . *out*."

Eleanor bristled with indignation. "No need to ask twice. In fact, I am being forced to leave this house because of you."

"I'm so sorry to hear that. Now get out of my sight this instant, you wretched woman, or I will turn you into a garden snake."

Eleanor's eyes grew wide as saucers just before Raonaid shoved her out and slammed the door in her face.

Chapter
Thirty-four

As Catherine slid her hands up over Lachlan's broad shoulders and touched her lips tentatively to his, she realized he was the one and only person who made her feel like herself. Her life had been turned upside down and she had lost her identity in every sense of the word, but whenever she was with him, she knew what she wanted and understood her feelings. Everything made sense.

It made even more sense now that she was kissing him—for the instant their mouths touched, his passions exploded. He swept her into his arms and returned the kiss with wild abandon. His hands roved over her body, and he groaned with urgent need.

"I need you, Catherine," he said, his lips parted, his breath hot against her neck. "I cannot bear to be away from you. I've been in hell since we made love, knowing I could not have you again, and regretting how I made such a mess of it. I did not love you properly. You deserve so much more. I could give you everything. . . ."

"Make it up to me now," she pleaded, cupping his face in her hands. "There's no curse. We can have each other tonight. We can do whatever we want."

His mouth covered hers again, fiercely and hungrily, as he carried her across the room to the bed. He laid her down, then went to lock the door. There was a firm *click* as the key turned, and then he was standing over her again—her beautiful Highlander—crawling onto the bed, and lowering his heavy body onto hers.

A breathless sigh escaped her. She was in heaven, holding him close, knowing that he still wanted her—and she wanted him with an unstoppable fury that overwhelmed her. She needed to open herself to him, to let him inside without fear, to hold nothing back. It was all she'd ever wanted, and now, at last, she would have it.

Wrapping her legs around his hips, she wiggled to lift her skirts while he fumbled with his kilt, pushing it out of the way. Everything was a heart-pounding, blinding blur of movement and desperation. She reached down and took hold of his manhood, guided him to her throbbing, greedy entrance. He looked her steadily in the eye and was inside her a second later, pushing very deep, as far as he could go, stretching her wide until everything went quiet and still.

"I can't get deep enough," he whispered, burying his face in her neck. "I don't want to ever lose you."

She wrapped her arms around his shoulders and held him close. "I don't want to lose you, either. Please, Lachlan, say that you care for me."

His head drew back, and he slid out and pushed back in. "Of course I care for you, lass. I *love* you, but I cannot lose you."

Again he thrust deeply and without restraint. She experienced a rush of scorching hot delight. Had he really spoken the words? Did he say he loved her?

He drove into her again and again, and she welcomed his invasion with a series of sighs and moans. Their bodies moved in a smooth, even harmony. He rose up on both arms so that he could look down at her face in the soft evening light. Tirelessly and devotedly, they made love, later rolling over so that she was on top, controlling the tempo and intensity of the sensations.

Sometime during their coupling, she pulled his shirt off over his head and he unhooked her bodice at the back. Piece by piece, their clothing was tossed to the floor while the lovemaking never ceased.

Catherine rolled onto her back again, and he pushed inside with a meticulous skill that began a flood of tingling sensations from her toes up to her shoulders. She clutched at his back and thrust her hips forward in a wild, shuddering release of passion, crying out at the last moment, while her body exploded with hot sparks of ecstasy.

He quickened his pace, grunting with exertion, for they had been making love fast and hard for quite some time. She could feel the heat of his pleasure, ready for release, poised for an orgasm of significant proportions. He leaned up on an elbow and looked down at her face.

"Come inside me," she said. "I want you to. I don't care if you put a child in my womb. I *want* you to."

He shook his head. "No. I cannot. I won't lose you."

"But there is no curse."

His body convulsed and he squeezed his eyes shut, shuddering feverishly and withdrawing at the last to ejaculate his seed onto her stomach.

She waited a moment for him to recover his senses; then he rolled to the side. They both lay exhausted and spent, gazing up at the canopy in the near darkness. Catherine struggled to gather her thoughts and regain her composure. It had been an exquisite sexual experience. He had made love to her, and he had told her, with tenderness, that he *loved* her. She hadn't imagined it was possible to feel so close to another person, and when he spoke those words her heart had ached with joy.

But at the last moment he had withdrawn and refused to take his pleasure inside her. She needed to understand why.

"Do you no longer wish to marry me?" she asked.

He turned his head on the pillow to gaze at her in the flickering light. "I care for you, lass. Do not think otherwise. That is why I cannot put a child in your womb. It's not something I can take lightly."

"But what if I *want* a child with you? What if I don't want to ever live without you?"

He tossed an arm up over his face. "I've done that before. It did not end well. I told you I don't want to lose you."

"But what does that mean?" Her anger was aroused, and she sat up. "Are you saying that you don't want children? Or now that you are *not* cursed by black magic, you don't want to risk the possibility of cursing me the old-fashioned, natural way?"

"No, lass. It's not that." He sat up, too. "Just please understand that I cannot be cavalier about such a thing. I must be careful. I just learned, only yesterday, that you were not going to die. Let me enjoy you for a while. Let me believe that we can have some time."

"But no one can live like that," she replied, "always expecting the worst to occur. I told you before, there are no guarantees. *You* could die tomorrow from a knife wound in a tavern, and then where would we be?"

"It's not that simple, Catherine."

"Yes, it is." She slid off the bed and pulled on her petticoats. "If you truly love me, then offer me a real life. Propose to me again, and promise to give me babies. Lots of them. That's what I want. I want to build a family with the man I love—and you are that man, Lachlan. There, I have said it. I have changed my mind. I would marry you in a heartbeat if you were willing to live fearlessly with me. But *this* . . ." She pulled on her skirt and gestured toward the bed. "This cannot be enough."

She picked up her bodice and slipped it on and hurried to the door.

He leaped off the bed. "Catherine!"

"We will talk again tomorrow," she said, holding him back with a hand, "after Raonaid and I come back from the stone circle. We are going there at sunrise, and everything may seem very different after I return. Thank you for this," she added as she turned to unlock the door. "It was lovely, and I do care for you, Lachlan. But I must get my life back. And you need to think about what you want from yours."

It took every ounce of mettle she possessed to leave the chamber and shut the door behind her, when all she wanted to do was go back inside and lie with him all night.

Chapter
Thirty-five

The Drumloch Circle dominated the summit of the grassy ridge, one mile north of the manor house and half a mile east of the dense hemlock forest. Catherine and Raonaid reached it just as the sun appeared over the horizon and cast long black shadows across the grass. The ground was crusty and hard beneath their feet, cloaked with a layer of frost, and the air was crisp with a wintry chill that Catherine could feel inside her lungs as she breathed.

Cheeks flushed with exertion, they reached the top of the steep hill and walked into the center of the circle. Neither spoke a word, for there was a melancholy silence about the place that demanded a moment's reflection.

Catherine looked down at the grass and thought of their mother, who had begun her labor here. What emotions had she experienced when the pain began and she collapsed? Had she felt joyful anticipation? Or had she known that something was wrong, and she would not live to see her children grow?

Raonaid turned slowly around, her blue-eyed gaze

sweeping over each individual standing stone. Catherine watched her sister curiously, not sure what to expect.

"How will it happen?" Catherine quietly asked. "And when?"

Raonaid lifted a finger. "Hush. I have no control over it. All I can do is wait for one of the stones to speak to me."

"How will it speak?"

"I will see the surface begin to shift and move, like water," she replied. "I usually feel something in my belly before it occurs, and I know that I must keep my eyes focused on the stone."

Hoofbeats thundered up the hill just then, and Raonaid spun around. "Who is that? They'll spoil it."

Both women walked to the edge of the circle and spotted John and Lachlan galloping up the hill.

"You shouldn't have come here alone," Lachlan said, his eyes dark with agitation. "It's not safe."

Catherine slanted a look at him. "I'm not alone. I walked with Raonaid. We are here to reclaim my memories, so you must leave us."

"No," he firmly replied.

Raonaid laid a hand on one of the stones. "I cannot do this if you are watching. The visions will not come. You must go back to the house."

John's horse grew skittish. "We'll be quiet," John promised. "You won't even know we are here."

"Turn around and go back," Raonaid demanded. "At least to the bottom of the hill. We will call out to you when it's over, but it may take all day."

Lachlan fixed his eyes on Catherine. "Are you all right with this?"

She saw the concern in his expression and was immediately whisked back to the pleasure they had shared in bed the night before.

"I am fine," she assured him. "I will come to you afterward. I promise."

As she stood in the place where they first met, she knew without a doubt that she loved him—and desperately so—but she needed to remember the past, to understand the dreams and nightmares. How could she ever give her whole heart to him—or to anyone— without knowing who she really was?

"Will you wait?" she asked.

"Of course I will wait. I'll keep watch from below. I will not leave."

She felt almost dizzy with love for him and prayed that a vision would soon come and free her from this empty cage.

"Go away now." Raonaid scooted them off with a flick of her hand. "I need the world to stay quiet."

Lachlan wheeled his horse around but gave Catherine a quick nod before he and John galloped away.

With a hopeful rush of anticipation, she turned to follow Raonaid back to the center of the circle.

Shortly before noon, a low cloud cover moved across the sky and the wind picked up. Raonaid's gaze shot instantly to the tallest standing stone. She stared at it for a long moment while the wind whipped at her long flowing hair and heavy skirts.

She held out a hand and said to Catherine, "Come with me."

They walked together to the stone and knelt down before it.

"Look there." Raonaid pointed at the tiny grooves and ridges in the rock. "Do you see it moving?"

Catherine squinted and pushed a lock of hair behind her ear. "No, I do not see anything."

"Keep looking. Let your eyes lose their focus. Breathe slowly and try to relax. Hold my hand."

They sat side by side, staring at the stone.

Flashes of images began to appear, impossible to identify at first, but then Catherine began to recognize elements from her dreams—the baby and the blue pillow, the dirt flying through the air, landing on her face and body. She saw a man—a handsome man standing over her grave—shoveling the dirt. Light flashed in her brain.

There was a house in the woods.

A carriage.

The man again.

He was so handsome. He shouted as he drove the carriage through narrow streets, past buildings of white stone. He was agitated. He slapped the reins on the horses' backs.

Catherine ran out the front door of the house in the woods. She threw her ring at him.

Oh . . . Her head throbbed in agony as she watched the visions in the stone. Unable to bear it, she pressed her fingers to her temples and squeezed her eyes shut.

The images disappeared.

She opened her eyes.

They reappeared.

The man ... he was very handsome, with golden hair. They were on a sailing ship together, standing at the rail. . . .

Suddenly everything vanished. Catherine felt as if her soul had been sucked out of her body.

The face of the standing stone was now vacant and still.

"No!" She rose up on her knees and slapped her open palm against it. She pounded with her fists. "Come back! I didn't see everything! I don't remember!"

She stood up and hurried around to the back of it, rubbing her hands over the rough surface. She ran to the next stone, and the next, searching for something more, but they were all silent and ancient, looming over her, staring down at her like grim, solemn judges from beyond.

Still, she could remember nothing. None of the images made any sense to her, and she wanted to cry.

Catherine moved into the center of the circle and knelt down. She sat back on her heels.

Where was her sister? She was alone here now, and the wind had grown cold. It was gusting all around her.

Then at last she saw her twin entering the circle, holding her skirts in her hands, running. There was fear in her eyes.

Raonaid reached her and hooked a wrist under her arm. She pulled Catherine to her feet. "We have to leave," Raonaid said with alarm.

"Why?"

"Murdoch is here. *Lachlan!*" Raonaid shrieked.

But Catherine's mind was still in a fog from the visions. She barely managed to stagger to her feet before

Raonaid began dragging her to the edge of the circle. Dizziness overwhelmed her. She feared she might be sick. "What does he want?"

"To kill you."

"I beg your pardon?" The dizziness subsided, replaced by a shot of adrenaline through her veins.

"He's the leader of the new rebellion," Raonaid explained as they ran, "and if you are dead, your father's fortune is bequeathed to the cause."

"He was your father, too," Catherine argued, just as a pistol shot cracked through the air.

A spasm of pain exploded in her back, and the breath sailed out of her lungs. She tripped over her feet and fell forward onto the ground, rolling uncontrollably down the hill outside the circle.

Her body tumbled and plummeted at great speed. Her wrist snapped like a twig. All she knew was sharp, piercing pain as the world spun around and around.

Then everything stopped, and the sky turned white. She slowly blinked up at it, as her heart opened to a blinding and beautiful radiance.

Chapter Thirty-six

Lachlan heard the gunshot and urged Goliath into a fast gallop up the hill. *"Yah! Yah!"*

He saw Catherine fall forward, then tumble down the grassy slope in a jumble of flying skirts and petticoats. If not for the raised knoll halfway down, she would have kept rolling straight to the bottom.

His heart exploded in a burning fireball of terror. What in God's name had happened? Who fired the shot?

He was acutely aware of the earl galloping at a breakneck speed behind him. They both rode hard toward Catherine, now lying motionless on the hillside.

Lachlan reached her and leaped off his horse. He knelt down and laid his hands on her shoulders. "Catherine!"

Her eyes fluttered open, and she grimaced with pain. "My arm . . ."

He glanced down at it. It was mangled and twisted. Unquestionably broken.

Blood was seeping through her bodice, just below her rib cage. He pressed a hand to the wound. "What happened?"

"It was Murdoch. . . ."

He turned on his heel to look up at the stone circle, cursing Raonaid for her treachery! Had she brought her lover here? Was this her plan all along? To kill Catherine and take the money for the Jacobites?

John galloped past him, riding up the hill just as Murdoch appeared from behind one of the stones. He was reloading his pistol.

Lachlan rose to his feet, drew his sword, and whipped his targe around to shield Catherine.

John drew his own pistol and fired a shot while still galloping. The ball missed its target, and John reined in his mount to reload.

Murdoch continued to advance upon them, his arm outstretched, his pistol aimed squarely, as if he fully intended to plow straight through Lachlan's wall of defense and shoot another ball into Catherine's heart.

Lachlan roared with fury and bolted forward in a full charge—with his shield in one hand, his claymore in the other. He would strike Murdoch down before he could reach Catherine.

I will not lose her.

But something from above caught Lachlan's eye.

Raonaid moved out from behind a stone. She knelt down on one knee and threw her dirk. It spun through the air, end-over-end, and lodged itself deep in Murdoch's back. His eyes glazed over with shock. His pistol dropped loosely from his grasp, and he fell forward onto the ground at Lachlan's feet, twitched and moaned, then went still.

Lachlan glanced with surprise at Raonaid, then hurried back to Catherine. He dropped his sword and shield.

She was unconscious now, bleeding from the stomach. He rolled her over and saw the blood-soaked puncture wound at her back.

John came galloping toward them and skidded to a halt. "I shall send for the surgeon! May I leave her in your capable hands, sir?"

"Aye," Lachlan replied as he gathered her limp form into his arms and whistled to Goliath. "I will bring her to the house. Fetch the surgeon, *quickly*. There is no time to spare. Tell him she has been shot in the back."

John kicked in his heels and galloped furiously down the hill while Lachlan shifted Catherine in his arms. Carefully, he mounted Goliath. Once in the saddle, Lachlan cradled Catherine across his lap and clicked his tongue.

"Wait!" Raonaid came dashing down the hill. "Is she alive?"

"Aye," he said. "Are you hurt, lass?"

"No, I'm fine. Murdoch is dead."

Lachlan took note of the fact that she had a bloody lip and a cut eye. She must have fought Murdoch before he fired the shot.

"You did well with your dirk," Lachlan said. "Your aim was true. Meet us back at the manor?"

"I will. Please get her home safely, Lachlan. I will bring your weapons back to you."

He urged Goliath into a gentle canter and held Catherine close to his heart as they descended the hill.

Three hours after the shooting, Catherine still had not regained consciousness. The doctor arrived not long after Lachlan laid her in her bed, and later informed them that the pistol ball had passed through her abdomen without puncturing any organs, and he had been able to successfully stop the bleeding, but it was difficult to say whether or not she would survive. There was a dangerous risk of infection, and these things were impossible to predict.

"What about her arm?" Lachlan asked.

The doctor explained that he had set the bone in place and that it was fortunate that Lady Catherine had not been conscious during the procedure, or they would have heard her screams in the farthest reaches of the house.

Lachlan thought of his wife suddenly. How clearly he could recall the sound of her cries, the horror and the pain. He almost doubled over in agony at the thought of Catherine enduring such an ordeal.

There was nothing to do now but wait, the doctor told him, so Lachlan went to her bedside, got down on his knees, and cupped his hands together. Bowing his head, he prayed that she would wake up and that the fever would never take hold.

For the next hour, he held her uninjured hand in his. He wept quietly, his tears dripping onto her arm, and told her that he loved her. He pleaded with her, in shuddering, painful sobs, to wake up, but she offered no response.

Day turned to night, and he was devastated. Would he have to see her buried in the ground? He could not bear to think of it.

Darkness enveloped the room. A maid crept in to light candles and change the water in the basin, but Lachlan was barely conscious of her presence, for he was weary with grief and a terrible, harrowing anguish.

Why had he not loved Catherine the way he should have? he asked himself, over and over. Last night he had let her go. He had let her leave his bed because he could not love her the way she deserved and wanted to be loved.

It was all a sad, pointless waste. He had spent every day trying to protect her from a curse that was never real—and even when he learned it was a hoax, he *still* could not love her. He could not commit to her. Why? Because he feared he would lose her in childbirth? That she might die?

What was *this* then?

Had he spared himself this pain? No, he had not. She was dying, regardless of all his careful measures and precautions.

What had he been thinking? He was not God. He was just a man, and he could not control when, and how, someone he loved would be taken from this world. All he could do was treasure each day, spend each precious moment with her, and worship her in every possible way.

He bowed his head and kissed her hand. "Please wake up, Catherine. *Please . . .*"

A knock sounded at the door, and it quietly opened before he had a chance to wipe the tears from his face.

Raonaid walked in and moved to the other side of the bed. "How is she?"

"No change," he replied in a husky, shaky voice. "I cannot bear it, Raonaid. I cannot lose her." He met the oracle's deep blue gaze. "I *love* her."

She regarded him intently for a long moment. "I suppose we have something in common, then."

He paused. "Who would ever have imagined it?"

She nodded with a profound measure of understanding, then pushed Catherine's hair away from her forehead and laid two tender kisses upon her eyelids. "I always knew you were with me," she whispered to her sister, "and now that I've met you, I feel very different. Nothing is the same as it was. Please come back to us."

There was still no sign of recovery, however, so Raonaid sat down in the chair on the opposite side of the bed.

"Where have you been?" Lachlan asked, for it was hours since Catherine was shot, and Raonaid had not returned until now.

"I remained there, in the circle," she told him. "I wanted to see more."

"What happened this morning?" he asked. "Did Catherine have a vision? Did she see her life? Did she remember anything?"

Raonaid shook her head. "We shared a vision, and we saw pieces of things, but nothing as a whole. When it was over she still did not remember. She was frustrated."

Lachlan looked down at Catherine's face, so peaceful now, and wished he could have helped her, but her lost memory was something mysterious, something beyond his control.

"What did you see?" he asked.

"There was a man," Raonaid replied. "He was handsome, with flaxen-colored hair, and they were on a ship together, traveling abroad. They were together for quite some time. I could see it in her face, in the way she aged and matured. I would guess she was barely twenty on the ship, but later, they were in a carriage together, riding through city streets of stone. It might have been Rome."

"She was found in Italy," he told Raonaid.

"I know. I am also aware that King James has been living in exile in Rome, and that is where his son Charles was born, last Christmas."

Lachlan watched Raonaid carefully in the candlelight, studying her expression, wondering if she had seen anything in her visions about the infant in the cradle. Did she know Catherine had dreamed of killing a child?

Raonaid gave no indication, however, of any such suspicion. She merely regarded him with challenge, as if to suggest it was *her* job now, too, to protect Catherine. Not his alone.

He supposed, if she survived, he and Raonaid would have to share that responsibility in the future, because he was not about to give it up.

"Put your worries to rest," she said at last. "She did not try to kill the prince."

His eyes lifted as a welcome wave of relief washed over him. "How can you be sure?"

"I saw it in a vision," she explained. "A full year ago, though I believed I was seeing myself. I was often confused by my visions, and believed they were false. I did not always trust them, for I saw myself walking in her shoes, wealthy beyond my imaginings. But now I realize it was always Catherine I saw. She *saved* the prince, Lachlan. It was the flaxen-haired man who wanted to kill him. Catherine tried to stop him, and when she fought him, he tried to kill her, too."

The deepest realm of Lachlan's gut heaved with rage and aggression. He spoke in a low, quiet voice laced with a dark undertone of fury. "Who is this man? I will find him."

Raonaid shook her head. "You cannot."

"Don't tell me what I cannot do," he warned.

Her eyes flashed with confidence and satisfaction. "He is dead."

The news came as a surprise, and Lachlan had to work hard to calm his temper and his breathing. "How? Who was he? I must know."

Raonaid leaned forward and laid a hand on Catherine's forehead, gazing down at her with sorrow and compassion. "He was her husband, Lachlan. That is all I know. And I am glad he is dead, for he was not kind to her."

Am I dead? Catherine wondered, struggling relentlessly to lift her heavy eyelids.

No, I cannot be dead, for in heaven there could not exist this pain.

Her entire left side was throbbing. She felt like she'd been stabbed, yet all she could think of was the blinding light that had warmed her soul when the world stopped spinning.

But *oh*, there was also an excruciating pain in her left arm. She couldn't move it. It was wrapped in some sort of splint.

At last, she opened her eyes and lifted her arm, curious to look at it. Confused and groggy, she gazed up at a frescoed ceiling. There were gods, angels, and clouds. . . . The sky was a lovely shade of gray blue. . . .

"Sweet God in heaven."

His mouth covered hers, and Catherine lifted her good hand off the bed. She slid her fingers through his hair to hold him close, to kiss him lovingly in return.

Lachlan. Her beautiful Highlander. The man who had come from far away to rescue her from the strange empty black oblivion of her existence.

"I remember," she said as he drew back and sobbed over her shoulder, weeping endless tears of joy. "I remember everything." She ran her hand over his hair and stroked the long dark locks away from his tearstained face. "Am I going to live?"

"Aye," he replied, laughing and kissing her on the mouth again. "You're going to live, lass. You're awake now, and the doctor says you are strong."

"Well, I would have to be, wouldn't I?"

He laughed joyously, and his dark eyes gleamed with gorgeous flecks of gold. "I always said you were a survivor, and here you are, so lovely. So alive. Do you remember what happened to you?"

Yes, she remembered running with her sister, away from the circle of standing stones. There was a gunshot, and an explosion of pain in her back.

"Murdoch shot me."

"Aye, but your sister stopped him before he could finish what he started. He came after you again, but she saved your life."

"How?"

"She dirked him, from a very great distance, and hit her mark. It was an impressive strike. She's quite a woman, that sister of yours."

Catherine touched his cheek. "But you hate her."

"Aye, I did. Maybe I still do, for many things, but I think I may be able to forgive. After what she did for you . . . For both of us."

Catherine closed her eyes for a moment as all the

events of her life over the past five years shifted the foundation of her existence. There was so much she had not known, but she could see it now. She understood. She remembered.

"Can there ever be an *us*?" she tentatively asked. "I am not sure you will think so, after I tell you everything." She regarded him in the dancing light from all the candles in the room. "I know where I was before. I know what happened to me, where I went, and what I did. I am afraid to tell you."

He kissed her hand. "Nothing will ever change what I feel for you, lass. You can tell me anything."

"Are you certain? Because there are things . . . I was very young, Lachlan. Very foolish." She paused and swallowed hard. Her throat was painfully dry.

He seemed to read every thought that materialized in her head and crossed to the washstand to pour a glass of water.

"Drink this." He returned to the bed and helped her sit up. He held the glass to her lips.

Catherine devoured it greedily, then lay back down on the soft feather pillows.

"The doctor has prescribed laudanum for the pain," Lachlan said. "You must tell me if you need it."

"Later perhaps, but not now."

He climbed onto the bed beside her and gathered her close in his arms. His warmth was like a blanket from heaven, and she did not want to let go.

"Tell me everything," he said. "I'm listening."

She buried her face in the soft wool of his tartan. "You know that my father died six years ago?"

"Aye."

"Well, nothing was the same after that. He hadn't even been dead a year when my grandmother pushed me to marry someone. Someone I did not love. He was too old."

"Love is important," Lachlan said.

She nodded wearily. "I always thought so. So I ran off. I ran away with a handsome young English officer I met at a political assembly, hosted here at Drumloch. All the guests were Hanoverians, because of John's political opinions, which differed from mine. But there was one young man who had Jacobite sympathies. His name was Jack. We snuck off and talked all night, and I believed him to be a great hero for the cause."

"Was he not what you believed?"

Catherine shook her head. "No, but I didn't know that until it was too late. He was good to me at first, you see. We ran away together to France and were married in secret."

She glanced up at Lachlan carefully, not sure what he was thinking, but he gave almost no reaction, so she continued.

"I didn't tell anyone where I was going," she explained. "I hated my grandmother, and I barely knew John. All I knew was that he had taken my father's title and possession of this house, which was my home. I felt he had no right to be here."

"He was your father's heir," Lachlan gently said.

"I understand that now," she confessed. "I knew it then, I suppose, but I was so grief stricken over the loss of my father. I resented John. I wanted my old life back."

"What happened after that?" Lachlan asked. "After you married this Englishman?"

She lifted her gaze. "He used me and my father's friendship with King James to gain entry to the Stuart court in Rome. That was his intention all along, I believe. He made the acquaintance of many powerful people, but he was a spy for the Hanoverians, and when the prince was born he tried to convince me to . . ."

Lachlan's face became a glowering mask of fury. "He wanted you to do his heinous work for him? To kill the prince?"

"Yes," she replied. "But I refused. I told him I would expose his plot, and that's when he tried to kill me. He wrapped his hands around my neck and he choked me." Tears spilled from her eyes, and she took a moment to gather her composure. "I lost consciousness, and when I woke, he was burying me in the yard."

Catherine couldn't describe any more of the hellish nightmare. She turned her face into Lachlan's tartan and wept openly.

"Don't cry, lass," he whispered, stroking her hair away from her face and kissing her forehead. "I'm here now, and you're safe. It's all in the past. No one will ever hurt you again."

"He was my husband, and he tried to bury me alive."

"I know."

She wiped the tears from her eyes and needed to tell Lachlan everything. To describe exactly what happened. "When I woke up, I remember sucking dirt into my mouth. It was cold and damp, but thank God, it was a shallow grave. I was able to crawl out of it. I found the shovel and I struck Jack over the head. I killed him, Lachlan, and then I ran."

"You did the right thing."

She nodded, though it was not an easy thing to accept. Jack was her husband, and she had loved him once. Or at least she had thought she did.

"That's when I lost my memories," she said. "I was found shortly after that, huddled in the farmer's stable, and taken to the convent."

For a long time she and Lachlan lay together on the soft feather bed, holding each other close, stroking each other with gentle hands, kissing each other tenderly.

"What will be done about Murdoch?" she carefully asked.

"Your cousin is taking care of that. He called for the magistrate. There will be a report sent to the King about Murdoch's attempts to raise another rebellion. He tried once before, you know. He was arrested, but later released. Raonaid has agreed to provide any information that will help to keep the peace in our country. I believe the King will reward her for her efforts on his behalf, for she brought down the leader of a new rebellion."

Catherine snuggled into the corded muscles of Lachlan's chest and breathed in the intoxicating scent of his clothes and hair and skin. All she wanted was to lie with him forever.

"But Raonaid and Murdoch were lovers," she said after a time. "She must be grieving, in some ways."

"Aye, but she's a survivor, like you are."

Catherine pondered that. "I suppose we have more in common now than ever before. We will have much to talk about."

Lachlan nodded and rubbed a hand over her shoulder. She was grateful for the warmth of his arms as he cradled her.

"I am sorry for everything," he said. "For all the pain I caused you. I never meant to hurt you."

She tried to rise up on her arm to look into his eyes, but the pain in her side would not permit it. She had no choice but to lie very still against the softness of his tartan. "I can forgive you for anything, Lachlan. All I need to know is that you care for me."

"*Ah, lassie.* If you only knew the half of it."

"Well, I *don't* know," she told him, sounding more irate than she intended. But she loved him. She needed to know what he felt. "Please Lachlan, you must tell me."

He cupped her face in his hand and kissed the top of her head, then sighed heavily. "You have no idea how I suffered when I saw you tumbling down that hill. I knew you were hurt, and when I saw the blood on your gown, a part of me didn't think I could do this again. But the alternative—to deny my love for you—was worse than anything. In that moment, I knew that a single day spent loving you was worth any price—even the future loss of you. What is the point in living, if I cannot enjoy the passion that exists between us?"

She held back a cry of relief. "What are you saying, Lachlan?"

"That I want to be with you forever. I want to make love to you, make babies with you, give you everything that you could ever desire. I never want to leave your side again. I want all the things you said *you* wanted, when you walked out on me yesterday. You were right to do it. I needed a good kick in the arse."

He leaned up on an arm and pressed his mouth to

hers. It was a warm and tender kiss, filled with affection and desire.

"I'm not doing this right," he whispered, drawing back. Slipping out of the bed, he dropped down to one knee. "I love you, Catherine Montgomery, and I want you as my wife. I will live anywhere with you, be anything you want me to be. I will give up my sword if you ask me to. I've had enough of this wandering warrior's life. I want to be your lover now. Just yours. No one else's. You are my angel and my love. Will you have me?"

Tears pooled in her eyes, and she laughed out loud with joy. "Of course I will have you."

He was beside her again in a heartbeat, holding her close, but gently, so as not to hurt her. His mouth covered hers in a sweet, heady kiss that made her forget all the pain in her heart and body. He belonged to her now, and she would never have to say good-bye to him. He had pulled her from the bleak abyss of her life and shown her who she truly was.

She had a sister now, too.

"Where will we live?" Catherine asked as his soft lips grazed her earlobe and his hand cupped the side of her face.

"Anywhere you want, lass. I'll go anywhere to be with you."

"What about John? Do you think he will object?"

Lachlan looked at her. "Will it matter?"

"No," she replied with a chuckle, ignoring the pain in her arm and her side, so that she could touch him all over. "I am of age. I can do what I want."

"So you always said."

He was smiling when his lips met hers, and she felt their shared joy within the magic of the kiss; then at last he took her mouth with a savage intensity that sent her reeling.

It was divine ecstasy, every moment in his arms, and she clung to all of it, embracing the promise of a new life.

"I hope you will heal quickly, lass," he said, "because I owe you a proper shagging. I'll want to do everything for you next time we make love. I'll not hold anything back from you, not ever again."

"Well then," she replied with a playful grin of seductive allure. "Your words have given me great reason to recover as quickly as possible."

He brushed the hair away from her face, and when she expected him to say something seductive in return—because he was a man of astounding sexual prowess—his expression grew serious and he spoke the only words that really mattered.

"I love you, Catherine Montgomery," he whispered. And a tear fell across his cheek.

Epilogue

FROM THE PRIVATE JOURNAL OF
CATHERINE MACDONALD

I have decided that today, since the weather is fine, I shall write in my new journal from the stone circle at Drumloch—the place where my life truly began ten years ago.

I can scarcely believe it has been a full decade since Lachlan found me here. So much has happened since then—marriage, children. More children . . .

Since our wedding day, we have been living in the West Tower of Kinloch Castle. Lachlan continues to hold the title Laird of War. He and Angus are as close as ever. I have also grown close to Angus's wife Gwendolen, who is like a true sister to me. Our children play together every day. (We have seven children. Angus and Gwendolen have six, but Gwen is expecting another in the spring.) Sometimes I want to pinch myself when I think of how happy we all are.

Twice a year we travel to Moncrieffe Castle to visit Angus's good friend, Duncan MacLean, who was recently awarded a dukedom for his tireless efforts to fight for Scottish rights, while still supporting the Union of Great Britain. He is a brilliant diplomat and a great favorite of the King.

Duncan's wife Amelia, the duchess, is an Englishwoman and she, too, is well loved by the King. Just last month she sent me a beautiful diamond brooch as a gift to commemorate my tenth wedding anniversary. I was deeply touched by the gesture, and Lachlan—not to be outdone—gave me this leather-bound journal to write in, and promised to take me home to Drumloch for Christmas to visit my twin. It is the one thing he knew meant more to me than any priceless jewel.

Raonaid is transformed. She is no longer an outcast, but is instead mistress of this great house, Drumloch Manor. She and Cousin John have become good friends and his kindness and loyalty have softened her heart in the most remarkable way. She now believes in happiness and the blessings of a close family, and she is the most tender person.

We write letters to each other often and sometimes in our dreams we reach out to each other. I have difficulty explaining it in words, but we are somehow connected on a spiritual level that defies reason.

But isn't it the same with love? It is simply not

possible to see it or define it, but it exists just the same with more strength and power than any sword or musket.

My husband and my children are the core of my life. I would die for any one of them and I know they would do the same for me.

Oh, look, here comes Lachlan now. He is walking up the hill to fetch me for dinner. Raonaid and John have promised a great feast, and I am famished.

If only you could see how handsome he is in the winter light. How is it possible that I have married such a beautiful man? Sometimes I still wonder if it's all a dream, for he always makes my heart soar, and I love him more with every passing day.

Here he is now. I must go. I shall write again tomorrow, I promise.

Catherine

Don't miss the first two novels in this sensational series!

CAPTURED BY THE HIGHLANDER

ISBN: 978-0-312-36531-8

CLAIMED BY THE HIGHLANDER

ISBN: 978-0-312-36532-5

From St. Martin's Paperbacks

Coming soon . . .

BE MY PRINCE
ISBN: 978-0-312-55277-0

First in a brand-new series from

Julianne MacLean

Available in May 2012 from St. Martin's Paperbacks